POWER

POWER

A NOVEL
Sky Curtis

INANNA poetry & fiction
Toronto, Ontario, Canada
www.inanna.ca

We gratefully acknowledge the support of the Canada Council for the Arts and the Ontario Arts Council for our publishing program. We also acknowledge the financial support of the Government of Canada.

Cover design: Val Fullard

Power is a work of fiction. All names, characters, businesses, places, events and incidents in this book are either the product of the author's imagination or used in a fictitious manner.

All trademarks and copyrights mentioned within the work are included for literary effect only and are the property of their respective owners.

Library and Archives Canada Cataloguing in Publication
Title: Power : a novel / Sky Curtis.
Names: Curtis, Sky, author.
Description: Series statement: A Robin MacFarland mystery ; 5
Identifiers: Canadiana (print) 20240353617 | Canadiana (ebook) 20240353625 | ISBN 9781771339650 (softcover) | ISBN 9781771339667 (EPUB) | ISBN 9781771339674 (PDF)
Subjects: LCGFT: Detective and mystery fiction. | LCGFT: Novels.
Classification: LCC PS8605.U787 P69 2024 | DDC C813/.6—dc23

Printed and bound in Canada

Inanna Publications and Education Inc.
210 Founders College, York University
4700 Keele Street, Toronto, Ontario, Canada M3J 1P3
Telephone: (416) 736-5356 Fax: (416) 736-5765
Email: inanna.publications@inanna.ca Website: www.inanna.ca

To my lovely family

CHAPTER 1

I'M IN SUCH A BAD mood.

March has to be the worst time of year. Thank God this is the last week of the month. It's supposed to be spring and of course it isn't. Forlorn robins huddle under bushes, trying to keep warm, their feathers puffed up and their heads hanging low, glassy eyes peering out into the cold and grey. I know how they feel because they are just like me, Robin MacFarland. Here I am, yet again, huddled over my steering wheel, trying to keep warm with the heater on high, puffy from eating all winter long, and peering out into the dirty dark abyss of March. My eyes are as glassy as the birds' and my head is also hanging low, only in my case, it's because I'm hungover. I got sloshed last night and now my car is sloshing through cappuccino coloured snow on my way to the office.

Notice I say, "the office" and not, "my office," nope, because Toronto Express Newspaper Inc., my employer, only has offices with actual walls for their senior editors. They get a dental plan too. Not to mention acupuncture and osteopathy. I don't. In fact, now that I think about it, it's preferential treatment and it pisses me off, just like everything else this morning. So much for equality in the workplace. Those seminars last month about respect and dignity were a farce. The honchos get way more money too. I ponder that for a minute. Does that piss me off? Well, I guess I don't mind *that* so much, they earn it—besides, who wants to be an Oxford comma cop?

I am only a lowly Home and Garden journalist. I use the word "journalist" very loosely because I certainly don't write about life-altering world events. No, I write on intriguing topics like the stuffing in pillows, you know, polyester versus feathers. And floor cleaners. Dish drainers. Potato peelers. Last week it was soap dishes. The week before that, thermometers. Today I'm motoring down the toad-coloured snow on Jarvis Street to reveal to my waiting readers, whom I'm sure have bated breath, the hidden and very interesting facts about light bulbs.

Geezus. What a stupid job.

But it pays the bills. Especially the winter power bills because my house is heated with electricity. I've finally switched my current-sucking baseboards to an energy efficient heat pump. I refuse to burn fossil fuels to heat my home. This country is frozen five months of the year, and that adds up to a lot of pollution from the oil and gas used to keep houses warm. Ontario's electricity, on the other hand, is mostly created by hydraulic power; in other words, non-polluting, fast-flowing water that spins generators. The rest of it is generated by nuclear power plants and I won't get into that can of slippery worms.

I sigh. Because of my job, I have accumulated a lot of useless data. I hunch over in my seat even more. My short brown hair—yes, it's dyed—is almost touching the dashboard as I outmanoeuvre the lingering patches of ice that are still out to get me. I'm so sick of winter.

The wheel tugs in my hands as my car wallows through three-inch clumps of slush the consistency of brown sugar. A big fat Mercedes that's been close on my tail since it turned off Carlton pulls over to pass me on my right. My right! Doesn't he know about driving etiquette? You don't pass on the right. Even I, a Schumacher wannabe, a person who loves to zoom, but not on my computer, abides by this main rule in the Young Drivers handbook. He grins to himself as he cruises past, his white teeth sparkling against his southern vacation tan. I don't like this guy. There he is with his multi-million-dollar salary, his Rosedale mansion, his capped teeth, his fancy schmancy car, and driving as if he owns the road.

I watch the rich guy, now up ahead, and see that he's up to something. He seems to be sliding to the side of the road in front of me. What on earth is he doing? Just shit. He's heading for a massive puddle of slush in the gutter by the sidewalk. Oh God, he's going to splash the pedestrians. A professional young woman leaps back from the curb as his wheels fling gobs of gritty brown granules at her bright red, goose down parka. I know what that costs. More than a monthly mortgage. She probably saved up all summer for that coat. And now it's wrecked.

Well, maybe not wrecked. I know, from my riveting job, that goose down coats are washable, despite the instructions of the label that read dry clean only. I know a lot of dumb crap, although I have to admit, it comes in handy sometimes.

I give the woman a sympathetic look as I whiz past her in my rusted old Nissan Sentra. We are comrades. The shithead driving the Merc snuffles his car through the slush back into the passing lane. When I get to the next stoplight, I pull up beside his phallic symbol and show him my middle finger. Arrogant, conceited asshole. He's pretending not to look at me, but I can see his black pupils darting to the corner of his eyes, sneaking glances. I jerk my finger up and down, miming it probing where the sun never shines.

Oh, I'm in such a bad mood.

He's just screwed with the wrong person. I am a well-known writer! My name appears in the largest national paper every day! I am Robin MacFarland! I buzz down my window and shout to his probably bullet-proof glass, "You're screwing with the wrong woman. Do you know who I am?" I ask this as if I'm the Queen of England.

And then, bizarrely, God knows why, I yell, "Neither do I."
Oops.

Ya, whatever. I am pissed off today. Actually most days, but perhaps more so today. Hard to tell in this long gloomy month of depressing days.

Then, perhaps sensing some capitulation from me, the asshole turns his head and deliberately stares at me and then at my car, at me, at my car, as if he were appraising it for a cattle auction. I replay the scene of what just transpired with the goose down coat. I know exactly the kind of guy he is. He'd splashed that woman on purpose. He'd *aimed* at that puddle. Getting his jollies from harming women. Using his car as a symbol of power, probably because he can't get it up.

Well, fuck him. I put my foot on the brake, toss the gearshift into neutral, and rev my motor. I'm going to burn some rubber. The car obediently growls ominously. I act as if I have a refurbished, four-hundred thousand horsepower turbo-powered twin engine and look the dickhead straight in the eye, inclining my head, just a bit, and raising my eyebrows. Bring it on. Only I know my jalopy is making this spectacular noise because there's a hole in the muffler, the thrumming coming from duct tape flapping.

I set my mouth in a "take that, asshole" look, nodding with authority that my car's been souped up and his is a piece of shit. In my mind, I see a bull pawing at the ground, snorting, clouds of hot breath billowing from its nostrils. As the light turns green, I stomp on the gas and throw the car into drive. I am going to squeal away from the light.

Hahahahaha—

Big mistake.

Robin, I shriek to myself, *that only works on dry pavement.* My wheels spin in the snow, the car's rear end slides to the side, the steering wheel jerks out of my hands, and I narrowly miss dinging the shiny black door of the Mercedes sedan with a fabulous sideswipe. The man gives me a condescending look down his thin, patrician nose and slowly, daintily, pulls into the intersection, not a waxed black hair out of place, a sneer curving his thin lips.

Now I really hate him.

We drive along, side by each, him on the right and me of course in the fast lane, pretending we are civilized, or at least I am, and I spot my weapon of revenge up ahead—a small mountain of soggy brown snow missed by the plow. I aim my right tires at the left side of the lump. My wheels hit it perfectly. I fix my eyes straight ahead, acting all innocent. I feel a satisfying squelch under the car and hear wet plops of gobs splattering metal as I cruise along. Take that, you misogynistic fuckwad. His shiny black Mercedes baby now has a strange skin disease.

I gleefully watch the gobs slide down his front door. I do my best not to laugh and take a deep breath. That felt divine. I am the Queen of Power. I am strong. I *win*. I drive past the dickface, my hands on the wheel, eyes straight ahead. I can feel a hurricane of hatred escaping through his windshield.

But then guilt floods through me and drowns the wave of road rage. *Robin, Robin, Robin, what are you doing?* You are a *nice* girl. You like to please. You mind your mouth. You smile at strangers. You like children and dogs. You're fifty-eight years old for heaven's sake. A senior citizen in some stores. Way too old for these kinds of games. And most of all, you know revenge is a bad thing, it contributes to violence in the universe. I do a Buddhist chant and sit up straight, patting my hair. *Smarten up*, I say to myself. Do no harm. What on earth had gotten into me? As the Mercedes pulls up beside me at the next light, I mouth at the driver, "sorry."

He tilts his head in a condescending nod and gives his upper body a little shake. Perhaps it's an acknowledgement of my apology, or perhaps his bum itches because he has hemorrhoids from being such a tight ass. His Rolex flashes from under his French cuff as he reaches his left arm forward to flick on his turn signal. He's making a right turn onto Queen Street. Whoever he is, whatever he does, he makes way too much money. What business is along there? Oh, right. Ontario Hydro, the administrative office of the province's electric power. I can smell the stench of white entitlement belching from his shiny exhaust as he rounds the corner. This jerk is so white he looks like one of those bleached slimy creatures from five hundred fathoms under the sea.

And off he goes to his slice of pie in the sky with his dandy car, in his dandy clothes, his dandy teeth chomping away at the money pouring in from people who can barely afford to heat their homes, from people who live in basement apartments. My chest tightens. A heart attack? No, frustration probably. I hate inequality. The Red Sea gap between the rich and poor in the country has widened so far that not even a Moses look-alike could get across.

I drive off, feeling impotent. What can I do to address these terrible insults to humanity? Nothing. Nothing at all. I have about as much power as a bandit wielding a crochet hook in Toronto's high crime Jane and Finch corridor. I do my best to shake off the feeling of helplessness while I continue down Jarvis. I remember who I am. I write about turkey basters. I am a mother of four children. I am a widow who lost her husband to a drunk driver eight years ago. I have a nice boyfriend. I drink like a fish and eat too much. I love cheese. These facts do nothing to alleviate my mood. I want to have the power to change the world. I want to be Superman. No, Spider-Woman! And meanwhile, I'm the Michelin Man. Righto.

I wait for that extra-long light under the Gardiner Expressway to change, thinking what's with those computer programmers anyway, can't they coordinate the flow of traffic better? As I sit trapped in my car, I am approached by three youths, all wielding squeegees and grins, sporting ragged, brown teeth, the sign of a drug habit. The last thing I would ever do is criticize anyone with an addiction, and we know why. I think about how much I love my wine as I listen to the roar of traffic on the elevated highway above me. I really should get some counselling for that little habit. I have a naturopath, Sally Josper, who is fantastic. Kind, gentle, smart. I just love her and I know she would help me. I should see her once a week. I never do.

Greasy streaks of crystalized frost smear my windows as they get sort-of cleaned by scrawny fingers with dirty nails at the end of long skinny arms with frayed cuffs on coats that don't fit. It's the same every morning, but today I rummage in my purse so I can pay each person a loonie for the service. It's not much, I know, and I also know I am enabling a drug addiction, but we all do the best we can. Far be it from me to judge.

I see the disconnect, the ridiculousness, the hypocrisy, of a Home and Garden reporter giving a donation to a person with no home or garden. But I am overwhelmed with the need to help these kids. Why are they on the street? Why have they turned to drugs? My fingers scrabble in my bag and I pull out three toonies. Somehow a loonie seemed too little for their suffering.

This really hasn't been a good day so far. My anger shifts into sadness. The very wealthy and the very poor chase each other in the movie playing across my inner retina. A knot of pain sits heavily in my chest as the encounter with the smarmy, rich white guy bumps up against the pathetic efforts of the three homeless people, kids really, trying to conjure up some dignity by working for a handout. Today, not even the sight ahead of Lake Ontario's moving water loosens the knot. All I see is worn-out sunlight shivering on black waves.

I turn right at Queen's Quay and immediately open my window. I do this here every morning on my way to work, winter and summer. It's an automatic reflex. I pause in the snorting traffic congestion to listen for the sound of seagulls as they soar over Toronto's harbour. I search around in my heart for a smile and dig one up. It makes me feel a bit better. To my left is Sugar Beach, the city council's idea of beautification, with its jaunty umbrellas already erected, despite snow in the forecast. Talk about optimism. I laugh just a little at that.

I crawl in the rush hour traffic past a rusting hulk of a tanker moored beside the Redpath Sugar Plant. Plastic water bottles and Styrofoam containers float in oily water amongst belly-up fish. Curiously, the front of the building next to the ship is painted with an underwater scene of cavorting whales. I've never understood this. There are no whales in Lake Ontario. Who ever thought a painting of whales at Toronto's waterfront was an appropriate idea?

Today, they remind me of the holiday I had in Nova Scotia last summer with my family, my partner Ralph, and of course, my best friend and colleague, Cindy. What a roller coaster that was. Murders, environmental racism, systemic racism, the travesty of fish farms, my daughter and her partner announcing their inter-racial marriage and pregnancy, not to mention Cindy almost being killed. On top of all that, I got another great story on the front page.

The whales also remind me of how I look in a bathing suit. I shake that delightful image from my brain and try to turn my focus to work. I should try harder to have a more positive and accepting view of myself. But no, I continue to beat myself up. I have terrible habits. My wine drinking is usually accompanied with hunks of cheese and bowls of chips. I have what's called an addictive personality. No guff. I like sex way too much as well. I dwell on Ralph, my newish boyfriend (well, not that new, we've been together for two years now) and think about his various body parts and one in particular. *Robin! You are driving to work! Think about work, work, work.*

For the past three years my career has been a series of staccato-like bursts of success onto the front page. Every now and then I'm secretly proud of these articles and my role in solving suspicious deaths, but this flight of satisfaction always lands with a crash as I remind myself that fundamentally, I'm just a hack. But last summer, I figured out that the owner of a fish farm had been murdered by a lobster. I loved the irony. Fish farms harm the lobster industry and wham, down goes the fat cat owner guy in a puddle of vomit after eating one. Poisoned. I cheer up a bit at the memory but then chastise myself for gloating over a death. *Not nice, Robin.* I do a short Buddhist chant.

And then there was that awful story about a poor young woman who was mauled to death by a bear who had been, I personally discovered, incited to kill with bear pheromones. Bear bait. That guy, the famous actor guy who manoeuvred the murder, was another pompous asshole who thought he was being so damn clever. Ha. Before that, there was the story about the nice bisexual guy who'd been felled by a bee which had been conveniently placed in his pocket by a homophobic

8

woman so it would sting him. She knew he was allergic to bee stings. She then tried to kill me by forcing me to eat a handful of almonds, to which I am severely allergic. Ralph, my saviour, was a saviour. Front page stories felt good, and maybe there'd be more in the future. In the meantime, I now had a reputation around the newsroom: I solved mysteries about Mother Nature killing people. I think of it as Gaia exercising her power. It was just three front page articles in a sea of House and Garden drivel, but still, people on the editorial floor remembered.

And because of the very power of nature, my career seemed to be on an upswing. Climate change was a force to be reckoned with and, as of last week when stories were assigned, the lowly Home and Garden reporter, namely me, had an elevated importance. Climate change is Mother Nature at her bitchiest. She is really angry about humans wrecking her planet and shows it in the weather. Daily videos on the Weather Network highlight her handiwork in floods, tempests, and locusts of biblical proportions. I know what products deflect rain, wind, snow, hail, you name it. I am used to writing about homes. I know the suppliers. I understand the physics and the chemistry and the durability of products on the market, including roofing metals and fireproof insulation. After the lightbulb story this week, I had been told by Shirley Payne, my editor who was nicknamed Hay Hair for obvious reasons, that my next article was to compare the survival of shingles versus metal roofs in high winds. And now that spring is here, winds are going to be an issue, because sometimes March comes in, as they say, roaring like a lion.

Up ahead, the grey hulk of the 1970s *Express* building looms over the cars grumbling along Queens Quay. The edifice stands like an erected middle finger against the surrounding condominiums. I've been working at the *Toronto Express* for several decades, we won't count how many, as that would indicate my pathetic aversion to change, and have watched the waterfront vistas shrink every year behind tall condominium buildings. And every morning, the same thought crosses my mind: what were the city planners thinking, destroying something so beautiful by pouring cement all over it? But far be it from me to think I had the power to stop such a travesty. No, sadly my power only went as far as splashing cars.

I turn right onto Yonge Street and then right again to creep down a cement driveway to the entrance of the *Express's* underground parking lot. As I go under the surface of the earth, my problem with being underground flares up—sweats, panting, dizziness, the usual side effects of claustrophobia. Nonetheless, I flash my ID at the gate with a nonchalant flourish for the benefit of the hidden camera and the handsome guy monitoring it. I feel guilty, just for a second, as thoughts of Ralph, who has recently become my sort of live-in partner, trample over my admiration for the security guard's biceps, barely concealed when he logs me in.

I drive slowly down a level, trying not to get the heebie-jeebies as I dive deeper into the bowels of the earth, go down another level, and finally stash my car in the spot allocated to me. C38. It's easy to remember because it's also my bra size. I don't tell anyone this. I gather my lunch and briefcase, do my best to walk slowly and not race with my tongue hanging out to the elevator. I push the up button with my knuckle, being a bit of a germophobe since the pandemic, and control my breathing. In, out. In, out. The clock beside the shiny elevator doors says nine-fifteen. Not too late then. In fact, I have time to get a coffee and a snack.

Momentarily diverted from my fear of being under the earth, my mouth gets all tasted up for a nice gooey bran muffin. With raisins. And butter. I repeatedly punch the elevator button. I tap my foot. I fiddle with my purse strap. I check out my teeth in the reflective elevator door. Why the hell is it taking so long? Finally, there's a melodic ding and the doors swoosh open. I stand in the car, looking at my image in the brushed metal doors. My neck is elongated and my torso is a beach ball. My workplace is such a fun house. I don't care what I look like and stab the floor for the cafeteria. Again, repeatedly. The car grinds upwards and the doors open to the smell of coffee, bacon, and something unidentifiable, perhaps soggy napkins mingled with bleach, or perhaps my turtle bowl when I was eight.

I make a beeline for the source of the distinctive cafeteria aroma, my mouth watering.

CHAPTER 2

I GROAN ALOUD WHEN I SEE the cafeteria line stretching almost to the hallway. Everyone wants coffee. Except me. I want a muffin. Well, I pretend I want coffee too, but that's a disguise I employ to give the muffin some respectability. Having the two together makes it look as if I am buying breakfast. I'm not. I had breakfast. Low fat yogurt with blueberries. Coffee with skim milk. Ralph calls this breakfast. And of course, Ralph is muscular and thin. I'm not. I'm short and round. These days I'm trying not to say the word "fat."

Despite his bony bum and my...let's call them pillows, Ralph and I are good together. My mind wanders over his body as I stand in line. I am fantasizing about standing on tiptoe to kiss him when my eyes snag on the red curls of my friend Cindy flaming above the morning crowd. At close to six feet, she is easy to spot. Fantasy ditched, and seeing an opportunity to bypass the line, I elbow my way forward, apologizing all the way, and poke her in the ribs from behind. She doesn't flinch or turn around.

"Hi, Robin."

"How'd you know it was me?" I'm talking to her back.

She tilts her head to the left and I see our blurry reflections in the buffed metal shelf under the lemon meringue pies. Ah.

"Aren't you the smarty pants." I poke her again.

She still hasn't turned around. "Stop that."

Cindy doesn't sound quite right.

I sidestep around her and look at her face. She has a swollen lip. "How did that happen?" I ask, pointing at it.

"It's nothing." Her lips contract. Maybe it was a smile.

Then I see how she's standing: a little hunched forward and listing to the right. She's definitely hurt. "What happened, Cindy?" I am a trifle alarmed.

Cindy has a dangerous job. She is a crime reporter, which she tells me is a little different than an investigative reporter, although I think that's bullshit. One just has a fancier name. But the *Express* makes the distinction. Karen Marumbo and Stanley Wong are designated Investigative Reporters, whereas Cindy's title is Crime Reporter. Because of her job, she and my cop partner Ralph do not get along. If she tries to pump him for info, he puts his hand on his gun.

"It's nothing."

She speaks while tightening her fat lip over her front teeth, hiding it. Has she lost a tooth as well?

I say, "No, it's definitely something, Cindy. You're injured. Did someone attack you? Did you get a tooth knocked out? You going to see Max?"

Cindy's ex-husband Max is a dentist. About five years ago, maybe more, I'm not good with time, she'd asked him to leave their North Toronto home that was resplendent with cherry wood flooring, stainless steel everything, and three teenagers. She'd discovered he'd taken a deep probing interest with his tool in his hygienist's mouth. Several years later, but more importantly, after the hygienist ditched him, she'd forgiven him enough that she used him as her dentist. Her kids hadn't forgiven her though, probably because she'd slid over to what she called the Dark Side, or the gay world. I hoped that would change, not that she should change her orientation, but that her children would accept it.

It was complicated.

I grab a muffin and three pats of butter. Cindy snags a plastic cup of butterscotch pudding. We shuffle towards the cash, Cindy with her easy-to-slurp pudding and me with my muffin. Yes, I held back from the lemon meringue pie, although that's what I really wanted. Both of us have scored coffees. Cindy says out the side of her mouth, "I'll tell you in a minute."

I take that to mean when we are alone and no one can hear. Sometimes she works on top secret crimes involving mafia or gangs and can't reveal anything until the story comes out. She tells me, of course, because my lips are sealed, even from Ralph. That works in reverse with him as well. Anything he tells me, I don't repeat, even to Cindy. Me? I don't care if he leaks to all and sundry that I've told him that silk is warmer than wool, but acrylic beats them all. This is an astonishing fact that I unearthed and broadcast to my readers, sparking nasty letters to my editor from people living in New Zealand, where sheep outnumber people seven to one.

"Okay," I say.

We walk in companionable silence to the elevator and head up to our floor. Both of us make funny faces in the brushed metal walls as the elevator zooms upwards. We walk past Derrick Johnston, the dimwit sports reporter with an IQ of dog kibble. He points a gun hand at us. "You guys are late. Again."

"Oh, fuck off, Derrick," says Cindy.

She pulls no punches, that one. I smile at him sweetly as I pass by, being the nice girl that I am, although he inwardly makes me shudder.

I watch her lower herself carefully into her chair. Definitely injured. I sit next to her at my desk. "Out with it, Cindy. What exactly happened?"

"It's a little embarrassing."

"Who cares. Certainly not me. My whole life is embarrassing."

Cindy sighs. "Okay, so I've been assigned by Doug to write about the homeless and drugs. Crime."

Doug Ascot is her editor who has a hot/cold affair with my editor, Shirley Payne. I could see his office door was closed, so Shirley was probably in there, cooing about something or other. What exactly went on in that office was the subject of much speculation.

"Okay-y-y."

"So, I hear there's an encampment down under the bridge in the Rosedale ravine. I think that's a perfect place to start my research."

"Right." I think I might sound a little impatient but I'm trying to encourage her to hurry it along. Everyone knew about that encampment. It was persistent—no matter how many times the police tried to move the people away, they always set up their boxes and tents again. The city people cheered their determination to protect their homes. The mayor backtracked every time and opened up more shelters. The encampment people didn't go into shelters except when it was minus ten. It was an interesting Ping-Pong match.

"So, I'm climbing down the embankment and I slip."

"Oh. Was it muddy? Did this happen yesterday in the sleet?"

Given that Cindy is as sure-footed as a mountain goat, albeit a very tall one, and could easily scale chain-link fences in freezing rain, which she's done, and can climb huge pine trees as if it were nothing, which she's also done, there must have been a good reason for her to slip.

"Actually, the day before."

"Oh right," I say, thinking back, "There was a thaw. So, lots of mud. Anyway..." She sure is drawing this out.

"So, I fall sideways, flipping a bit, and do a face plant as I slide right into the tents. I whacked my mouth on a rock while I was slipping down the hill on my belly. Wrecked my coat."

I try not to laugh at this vision of flailing arms and legs, it must have looked hilarious, but despite my efforts, a squeaky hiss sneaks out the side of my mouth. She frowns at me so I clamp a steel trap on my reaction. God, that must have been so funny.

When I trust myself to talk, I say, "You were wearing that goose down, right? Don't worry about it. It's washable. Spray the mud with some extra strength stain remover and throw it in the wash. It'll come out."

Cindy looks at me sideways as if she knows she's going to push one of my buttons and proceeds to do just that. "You know all sorts of useless stuff."

I don't take the bait and keep my face slack, although I am bristling a bit. It's fine for me to say that about myself, but not others. I guess that makes me a hypocrite. Oh well. Could be worse. We can't all be perfect. I'm tempted to be defensive and tell her I just saved her a coat, but I let it go. I back up in the conversation.

"That explains why I didn't see you the day before yesterday. I was wondering about that." In truth, I wasn't at all. Cindy is often out of the office, tracking down the criminal element, and impossible to keep track of. "And where were you yesterday?"

"Working from home."

"I see." So, in bed. "What exactly did you hurt?"

She leans in over her desk and smiles, grimaces really, to show me what happened to her tooth. I would have guffawed—the chip is miniscule—except Cindy's green eyes are watering and the last thing I want is to see her cry. She's meant to be the strong one and I don't want to rob her of that role.

"It's not too bad," I say. "Max can fix that in a flash."

"But then I'll have to tell him how it happened," she wails. "I don't want to admit I was a klutz."

I am a little shocked by her being a baby. So unlike her.

"First of all, you're not a klutz. And secondly, just tell him you chipped it on an olive pit in a Greek salad."

She looks at me for a minute and nods, dignity restored. "You're good."

I shrug. Not only was I a hypocrite, I was also getting good at lying. Was that something to be proud of? I used to be so honest, up until I wanted to get stories on the front page. Cindy had warned me that if I had ambition to move upward in the journo world, I would have to learn how to lie. I found it remarkably easy. Well, that's not completely true, the lying was the easy part. Living with myself for lying? Not so much.

"Did you get some background for your story? Drugs and the homeless? Or is it more general? Crime and the homeless?" I change the topic to get her away from feeling sorry for herself. I know she got good research. Cindy always gets good research.

She sits up straight, tucks her chin in, throws her shoulders back, and then tries to disguise a squint as a smile when she is overcome with pain from all the movement. "Of course I did. And more."

"What do you mean, 'and more'?"

"Did you know that many of the people living down in that ravine in tents are immigrants, or Indigenous?"

"Oh?" I pretend I don't know this.

"Yes, they've come to Toronto looking for a better life but can't find work. So they end up on the street. Homeless. And then they eventually find their way to a shelter."

Cindy spat out the word "shelter" as if she were saying "hell."

"But that's good, right? At least there are shelters with enough beds."

She screeches, "Are you kidding me?"

Wow. Did I ever I touch a nerve. "What? There aren't enough beds?" I mentally flipped through recent newspaper coverage of the bed situation in Toronto. If I recalled correctly, I thought it looked adequate after the mayor finally opened up some more spaces.

"Oh, there are enough beds. *Now*." She stretched out the word into two syllables to make a point. "But the drugs circulating in shelters is unbelievable. That's where these poor people, these people from all over, so full of hopes and dreams, end up becoming addicts."

I repeat the word. "Addicts." I want her to know I'm listening. The image of the kids cleaning my car this morning zips through my brain. I clearly saw their rotten teeth, eroded into dull points. Crack. "So, that's how it happens? They get drugs in the shelters?"

"Of course. Where else? The Rosedale Golf Club? And who wants to be homeless? When a teacher asks a five-year-old, 'What do you want to be when you grow up?' nobody puts up their hand and says 'Homeless.'"

I think of my children with their plans for the future. None of those plans included being homeless. "You're right."

"Of course, I'm right." Cindy taps her desk with her forefinger. "We are all just a heartbeat away from being homeless." *Tap, tap.* "From being a drug addict so we can forget that we have no home." *Tap, tap, thump.* "And then, from. being with other drug addicts so we have a family." *Thump.* "From being part of that family. In the ravine." She is now thumping her desk so hard that it vibrates. She drives the point home. "And no one is lazy. No one. People want to work. Who wants to be homeless?" She's hiss-yelling. "And I'm supposed to write about these poor people stealing? Just fuck it." Suddenly, she stops banging her desk and rubs her lower back. She's really hurt herself.

I wait a beat so she can catch her breath and then try to deflect her. "Looks like you hurt your back as well. Should you see a doctor? Or your chiro?"

Cindy was always seeing her chiropractor. Being as tall as she is, she often has body issues. She'd told me it was a height thing. She stretches to the right and then left, "Naw, I just got poked in the kidneys with a flashlight."

"A flashlight?" I was puzzled. "Why do they have a flashlight?"

Cindy looks at me as if I were living in an alternate universe.

"Oh right," I say, the truth dawning slowly. "There's no electricity down there. They have no power."

Cindy takes a long gulp of her cooling coffee and sucks back a spoonful of her butterscotch pudding while looking away. "You can say that again."

She is clearly upset by what she found out about the homeless people living in the ravine, not to mention her physical pain. I watch her as she fidgets with her computer mouse, as she blows on her keys to get rid of the dust, as she listlessly rocks her foot up and down.

I say, "Oh Cindy, I'm so sorry you're upset."

She looks away. "Goddamn crime beat."

I roll my chair closer to her so I can hold her in one of those awkward sitting-down hugs. The casters on our office chairs squeal when they collide and we laugh. Cindy isn't great with talking about her feelings. Despite her harsh and sometimes brittle demeanour, her feelings can rise up explosively and overwhelm her. Like today. Sometimes working with Cindy is like being with one of those wind-up dogs that turn somersaults but don't quite land on their feet. This is why I don't call her a baby for snivelling about going to see Max for her tooth.

Just then, Doug Ascot's office door is hurled open and Shirley Hay Hair prances out, her hips wiggling while she straightens out her pencil skirt, today a shiny-blue, fake silk item. It has creases along the crotch and a wet spot. I'm hoping it's not what I think it is.

"Nice to see you two having a tête-à-tête, or should I say a 'tit-a-tit,'" she blatters like a moped, looking at Cindy's chest pressed against my arm. It's an old joke that has circulated around the newsroom, pushed like a puck to an uncertain goal, although probably to denigrate our close friendship, and probably started by Derrick. Cindy and I didn't care what people thought—we were comfortable with our relationship. "Robin," she continues, smoothing a thinly plucked eyebrow with a pointy nail, "if you can pull yourself away, come to my office." She struts off on her navy blue stilettos, leaving a perfume of eau du smoke in her wake, the back of her head looking like a rabid badger has been nesting in her hair.

I roll my eyes at Cindy and lurch out of my chair, using the desk to help me up. I really need to lose ten pounds. Or thirty. I grab the rest of my muffin and gallop through it like a misbehaving pony. As I follow Shirley into her office, I see out of the corner of my eye that Derrick Johnston is primly smirking. He makes that stupid gun hand at me again and mimes hitting the trigger with his thumb. What's with sports guys? Why do they do this? He's probably hoping I'm getting a scolding because I was late. And maybe I will. I brush crumbs off my 38Cs as I go and inwardly brace myself.

CHAPTER 3

I SCURRY BEHIND MY GIRLIE-GIRL BOSS to her office, feeling more than a little frumpish in my Birkenstocks, woolen socks, and peasant skirt. She sidles around her desk to face me. I look at her for just a few seconds and notice that she's wearing enough makeup to make the cosmetic technician at Shoppercs Drug Mart proud. She coughs twice and says in a voice that has been sandblasted with too many cigarettes, "Close the door, Robin."

This doesn't sound good.

My brain is fizzing. It does that when I'm anxious. A warning prelude to it hissing, like a snake when it senses danger. I suffer from anxiety. Like everyone else in the world.

"And sit down," she commands, her voice now bubbling like peroxide on an open cut. Maybe she thinks it's alluring.

I scatter a tipping mountain of files off a chair onto the floor and perch, wondering what is going on. I feel like a recalcitrant child, my feet swinging in the air. And lo and behold, whammo kazam, there's my old friend, the hissing snake. It's come out from under the rocks in my head and slithers around my brain. My feet tingle as I swing them.

Shirley lights a cigarette. Smoking has been banned indoors for decades, and yet, here we are. I tuck my chin into my turtleneck, using it as a filter. I have asthma and protect my lungs the best I can. Once her cigarette is going, she reaches into her desk and sprays the air with Febreze. She likes the papaya scent. I hope she doesn't spray too close to me or the cigarette. I'm not sure how flammable Febreze is, but I know hairspray can be used as a blowtorch if it's sprayed over a flame. It's one of those maybe-useless details I've picked up from my work. I pull the cowl neck higher over my mouth and nose, trying to keep the scent from scraping the inside of my nostrils.

"Oh Robin, don't do the turtle act. Here, I'll put it out." Her cough is juicy and her voice sounds like it's been pressure-washed with too much scotch. She takes a long drag and then stubs out her butt on the inside of the metal garbage can under her desk. I bend over and look into it, making sure the paper recycling isn't bursting into flames. My throat is getting itchy and I'm thinking she'd better hurry up and yell at me before I need to dash out and find my inhaler.

Shirley tilts her head and looks at me from under her false eyelashes. They're somehow a little messed up today and look like the tassels on a geisha's skirt that have wound themselves together. This probably happened from the calisthenics in Doug's office. "I want you to quit the lightbulb story and go straight to writing about the homeless."

What? Really? Me? "But Cindy's writing about the homeless. I thought my next story was roofs. Metal versus shingles. Because of climate change."

"I know all that. Time is of the essence. Forget the lightbulbs and the roofs for now. Spring is coming and being homeless as a story loses its punch in April, when it's nicer to be outside. And Cindy's writing about the homeless and drug addiction. Roofies." She chortles. "Maybe the criminal element. No, probably." Shirley's crumpled cigarette butt is still between her fingers and she waves it in the air. The funeral home smell of dead ash floats over to me. I'm relieved I'm not in trouble, but I'm not happy about being in this office. Shirley seems mesmerized by a sight outside her window.

"She was in the Rosedale ravine, doing background research." I say, bringing her back to the topic.

"Right. I want you to go there too, and elsewhere of course, maybe the Don Valley, under some bridges, shelters, and find the human stories. Where the people come from, why they're on the street."

"But I'm a Home and Garden reporter. Shouldn't this be in the Life section? Or the Health section?"

I really don't want to do this story. The homeless situation upsets me so much. I would much rather deal with lightbulbs. LED versus fluorescent is not so emotionally charged. Shingles and metal are exactly my speed. Not the kind of roofies she's talking about. I feel so badly for the people on the street. Besides, Shirley is the editor for all the soft news sections at the *Express*. She could easily assign this story to someone in a different section.

"No, I've decided it's a story for the Home and Garden section."

"But that makes no sense. These people don't have homes or gardens."

Shirley puts both hands on her desk, her blue-shellacked nails facing me. She raises herself a little out of her chair. Oh God. This is Shirley at her fiercest. Her hair is standing on end, like her head has been chewed on by a beaver. Somehow, I've made her angry. I sit up, paying attention, fortifying myself against what is no doubt going to be an onslaught. "And that, my dear girl, is the *point*." She repeatedly points at me. "The street *is* their home. I'm fed up with the disparity, the gap between rich and poor. They live in ravines next to multi-million-dollar homes. Some of them go off to work or school from their *tents*. Their *boxes*. Their *tarpaulins*. Did you know that?"

I shake my head. No. Although I did.

"Some of them are suffering from such terrible depression they can't stand up. Did you know that?"

I shake my head again, no, although I knew that as well.

"And almost all of them have suffered a head injury. A concussion. From being beat up. Usually by a family member. Did you know that?"

That I didn't know. What a terrible fact. Was it true? Probably. Shirley's blue eyes were blazing. She knew her facts. But if she knew so much, why didn't she write the damn story? I would be so churned up writing about all this and I wanted to avoid that. I already suffer from anxiety. My heart is cringing. My ears are hissing. Am I going to faint?

"These people need help. They need support. They need understanding. They need to be written about by a compassionate person in a dignified section of the newspaper. They need exposure. They need to be *seen*."

Me? Compassionate? I wasn't so sure about that. And frankly, I was tired of that phrase, "I see you." It was all over my Facebook. Too cool by half and why can't people just say the big word, *acknowledge*?

I make one last stab at getting out of the upsetting story. I formulate my sentence carefully, to make sure I'm *seen*. Given that her passion was satisfying the readers and keeping them interested, I have a small wedge of a weapon into her enthusiasm. "But the readers," I pause here, making my emphasis clear, "they might get *over-saturated*, you know, what with Cindy's story appearing around the same time." I was proud of myself for scavenging through my alcohol-sodden brain for the word "saturated." That was a word that Shirley used often, in speeches about keeping readers interested. Don't want to saturate the readers, she'd say, if I suggested a story similar to one that had been done recently.

"I was checking with Doug about that this morning. Cindy's hook is on the drug angle, crime, et cetera, et cetera. I want your hook to be the human story. Why are these people without homes? How on earth has the city ended up with over eight thousand homeless people?"

That seemed like an exaggeration to me. "Eight thousand?" I raise my eyebrows in doubt, although I should know better than to question Shirley.

Shirley takes up the challenge and leans forward. "You heard me. Eight thousand. Documented by social services. Probably more. Some hide really well. That's a lot of homeless people and we should do better."

I'm not going to fight her on the statistic. She seems

determined to have little ol' compassionate me write this story. I'm dreading it, knowing it will keep me awake at night.

"There's been quite a bit written on the homeless the last little while," I say in a last-ditch effort to get out of the article.

"That's because it's winter and some are dying in the deep freeze. And now that spring is coming, I don't want people to forget that there's a serious issue here."

I wonder why Shirley cares so much.

As if she's reading my mind, she says, "Look," her tone softening, "I have a personal interest in this." She looks out the window again. Off in thought. Watching the clouds sauntering by.

I try not to look overly interested. A personal interest? I don't know much about Shirley, despite seeing her almost every day for decades. I am very curious.

Shirley looks away from the window and peers at me from under her tangled tassels. I think she's deciding on whether or not to confide in me. Now I try to look trustworthy. Apparently, I pass the grade.

"I was homeless once."

I'm not sure I heard that correctly. Shirley, my capable boss, who is sitting in front of me perfectly coiffed, fancily dressed, and self-confident to boot, had been *homeless*?

Shirley continues, "I ran away from home when I was fifteen and lived on the streets until I was nineteen. Four years."

That makes absolutely no sense to me at all. How could that be? I fumble for words. The first thing that comes to mind is that she couldn't possibly have a high school diploma given those circumstances, and I know that to be a senior editor you had to have at least a university degree. "But you must have a university degree, a BA."

She explains, "Yes, I do. My first two years on the street were near an alternative school. I would drop in every now and then. They were cool with that. So, I got my grade eleven and some of my twelve. I futzed around for two more years and then heard about a program at the University of Toronto. U of T has an academic bridging program for mature students who don't have a high school diploma or don't meet admission requirements."

"I've heard of that," I say. I'd looked into it because Evelyn, my middle child, was goofing around and veering off the path leading to a high school diploma. I wanted to know what options would be available to her in the future. But she surprised everyone by hunkering down and pulling off an over-eighty average in her final year. "Isn't it at Woodsworth Campus?"

"Woodsworth *College*."

Shirley likes to be accurate.

With that, she throws back her shoulders. I try not to stare at the formidable result. "What I'm saying is that being homeless can happen to anyone, even someone like me," she taps her large chest with a long navy blue talon, "and once you're homeless, all sorts of bad things can happen. Addictions to drugs and alcohol, disease, jail. Death. So, Robin, I want you to write an article about why people become homeless and why they end up where they do. Maybe throw in a success story."

I look at Shirley with new-found respect. She was certainly a success story. The boss I often ridiculed, the woman who I mentally chided for being too girly, too dressed up, too highly-sexed, had had a very difficult adolescence. "I'm sorry this happened to you Shirley, you've had a hard row to hoe."

She suddenly laughs delightedly and crosses her legs, the thin gold chain around her ankle flashing in the overhead fluorescent light. She looks at me dead on, her dark blue eyes sparkling, "You calling me a ho'?"

I smile at her joke and add it all up. I was boxed into a corner. There was no getting out of it. I might as well be gracious. "I'd be happy to write an article about the homeless."

Shirley scrutinizes me and I watch as her mind pings over my credentials. "I think you'll do a good job with this, Robin. Thanks for being flexible."

Oh, right. If only she knew. Flexible? I could hardly bend over to pick up my dog's toys. "As I say, I'd be happy to write a story about the homeless."

Shirley relights her bent-out-of-shape cigarette and puffs deeply. "Watch your vocabulary. At all times I want you to remember that these are people first. They are *people* who don't have homes or gardens. They are vulnerable, frightened, cold, and hungry people. They will not trust you. Call them *people*, not *the homeless*. They are people with insecure housing. Do you understand me? They are experiencing homelessness."

What? She'd been calling them *the homeless* for the past ten minutes. It was as if she'd suddenly been infected by a random politically correct virus. I wasn't going to poke at that wasp's nest with a ten-foot pole.

"Yes, Shirley."

"And you're to treat these people with care, respect, and dignity at all times. Do you hear me?"

I have never seen Shirley so earnest and serious. But of course she would take this subject personally. She'd lived it. I want to find out more about her. Why did she end up on the street? What caused her to run away from home? Why was the street safer than her family? I fast forward through all the possible scenarios and am mortified by all the times I've made fun of her.

"Yes, Shirley."

"Don't look so pensive, Robin. You can do it. I have cleared with Doug that you and Cindy can chase down your different articles but work together. It's safer to be in pairs. Just don't let Cindy get in your way. And don't get in hers. Work with her by your side, but don't collaborate. You are on different stories. Doug should be telling her the same thing. Do you understand me?"

I wonder if the two articles won't overlap heavily, the subjects are so intertwined, but I say, "Yes, Shirley, I understand."

Shirley walks over to her door and peers through the glass. "Harrumph. Cindy isn't in with Doug." She raps sharply on the glass and gestures with her hand for Cindy to come into her office. She shoots a glance at me. "Oh, that silly Doug. He has a mind like a sieve." She giggles.

My resolve to not make fun of her slips a notch.

Cindy opens Shirley's door and swings it back and forth. She's making a statement about the cigarette smoke. She stands tall, chin up. "You wanted to see me."

"Sit, sit." Shirley commands. "Nice fat lip."

Shirley walks back behind her desk and puts her butt out again on the edge of the garbage can. Cindy sits as ordered, hand hiding her mouth, and glances into the can. We both know there have been many fires there. Shirley says, "I know you're doing an article on the people living on the street and their problems with drugs."

Cindy nods and picks a fight, as she is wont to do. "In parks. Down in ravines. Under bridges. In shelters. Not just on the street."

Shirley's lips tighten into a smile so sharp it cuts the air. "You know what I mean." She glares at Cindy and we both suddenly remember that Shirley, not that long ago, could have had Cindy fired for plagiarism. We owe her big.

Cindy quickly dodges to be on the smart side of this skirmish. "Yes, Shirley. Sorry."

Shirley relaxes and tilts back her chair. "I've asked Robin to do a story on people who have no homes as well, only her slant is going to be *why* they are homeless. I want her to find out why we have so many people living rough. You, I understand from Doug, are doing the drug/crime angle. I want the two of you to be together while doing research, you know, for safety, but please keep in mind that you are both working on two very different stories."

Cindy looks at me with raised eyebrows. Questions swirl in the pool of her wide-open green eyes. We both know that the two angles are threaded together and that teasing them apart would be impossible. We also both know that it would be very unwise to challenge Shirley on this. Shirley may have fluffed up hair, but it was sprayed into an immovable helmet over an immovable brain. I shake my head imperceptibly at Cindy. She should not fight Shirley on this. We will work it out.

Managing to keep all doubt and sarcasm out of her voice,

Cindy says, "I totally understand, Shirley. We work together, but apart."

I let out a sigh of relief. Everything was hunky dory.

Shirley stands up and smooths down her skirt. An odd noise burbles out of her nose which I thought might be a laugh. She's pleased. Her hand brushes over the wet spot I noticed earlier and she winks at me, knowing that I know. "Okay, you can go." As we stand up to leave, she says, "Lots of coming and going around here."

Oh God. That's disgusting.

I decide that I can continue to mock her. Respectfully.

CHAPTER 4

CINDY AND I STAGGER BACK to our desks, sucking deeply at the fresh air.

My friend says, "God, how can you tolerate that woman?"

"Listen, one shouldn't judge. One never knows where one comes from."

"What? You're on her side now?"

"No, I didn't say that. I'm just saying, one never knows why people are the way they are."

Cindy looks at me, her head tilted, probably wondering what got into me. "You've been reading schmaltzy quotes on Facebook again?"

"Cindy."

"Okay, okay. But there's no way your article and mine are two separate articles. That's ridiculous. Why is she being so dumb?"

"Who knows." Although I was thinking that it might have something to do with her own personal path. She didn't end up in trouble with the law or as an addict, so maybe she thinks her journey through that homeless phase of her life is typical. "She probably has her reasons."

"You *are* taking her side."

"No, I'm not."

She looks at me out of the corner of her eye. Her finger is on her fat lip. She's thinking. "You're holding out on me. I can tell. The two of you were talking. In there." She thrusts her thumb at Shirley's office. Then she leans forward and gets in my face.

"I told you about my face plant, you can at least tell me what Shirley told you in her office. You were in there a long time. She told you something." She taps her watch, signifying that I had better come clean, and soon. "What's going on?"

Cindy's in the right career, that's for sure. She can smell a rat a mile away. She has good instincts and figured out that something was revealed in Hay Hair's office. I am now faced with a moral dilemma. What do I do? Should I tell Cindy what Shirley said, or keep my trap shut? Had Shirley told me about her history in confidence? Maybe. Even if she didn't, it doesn't matter. I shouldn't say anything. It isn't my story to tell. On the other hand, Cindy knows that something is up and my not telling her could create a split in our relationship. She could accuse me of not trusting her. Cindy is my best friend, and Shirley's insistence that our stories were separate is close to bizarre. I do trust Cindy. Actually with my life. That decides it.

"I'll tell you, but it goes no further. You can't use it." Telling this to a newspaper journalist is like telling a sponge not to absorb water.

Cindy rolls her eyes.

"I mean it."

"Okay. Off the record." She focuses her green eyes on me and wiggles her fingers. *Give me more.*

"Shirley was homeless as a teenager."

Cindy's eyes widen and she gestures with her head at Shirley's office. "Her? Homeless? Our Shirley? Naw, I don't believe it. She's lying to you. I wonder why."

"It's true."

"But she has a degree. And a pencil skirt."

"I know! I don't know the story of how it happened or why she picked the street over her family, I don't even know if she had a family. Not everyone does."

"Those are the lucky ones."

Cindy's family is often in shambles.

"She went to an alternative school for a bit and then did that bridging program at U of T."

Cindy leans back and rubs her chin. Checking for a whisker? Loosening up a jaw muscle? Thinking?

Then she spouts off my exact same theory about why Shirley thinks the two stories are separate. "I think that because she transcended all the difficulties of living on the street without being thrown in jail or ending up addicted to crack cocaine, she thinks that's the way it is for most people with insecure housing."

"Those were my thoughts exactly."

"Well, she's wrong. She's an anomaly."

"You're using awfully big words today, Cynthia."

"What? No, I'm not." She shakes her red frizz.

"Transcended. Insecure housing. Anomaly."

"Oh, come on."

"Okay, so 'transcended' and 'anomaly' aren't that big. People say them. But 'insecure housing'? Who says that?"

"Are you kidding me? 'Insecure housing' is a perfect phrase to describe the situation. Those are the new words. And for good reason. The word 'homeless' doesn't really convey the anxiety, the upset, the struggle, of having no home. 'Insecure,' on the other hand, speaks volumes."

She's right. I let it go and say, "So what are we going to do?"

"About what?"

I sigh. Sometimes Cindy doesn't follow the plot very well. Right now, she's jiggling her foot. Her leg is bobbing up and down. Her fingers are wiggling like an octopus's tentacles, perpetually gesturing for me to give her more. She is wound up tighter than a yo-yo.

"Drink less coffee, Cindy. Look at you, vibrating all over the place."

Her fingers take up speed. "About what?"

"About Hay Hair's directive. Two separate stories. Obviously they are one story."

Cindy says, "Maybe Doug will straighten her out."

"Ya, like that'll happen. Maybe when pigs fly." I wasn't going to say that Doug was useless. He is Cindy's editor and she has to work with him.

"So how are we going to do this then? It's not as if I can just write a whole article about drugs and insecure housing. That would be about one sentence." She wags her head back and forth and places a fake smile on her face. She's pretending to talk to a kindergarten class and raises her voice to a squeaky octave. She twitters, "Homeless people use drugs because they can get them easily and they make them happier."

"Cindy, you know there's more to it than that."

She obliges and sings, "They sell stuff they've stolen so they can buy the drugs." She lowers her voice to her normal range. "That about covers it. Homelessness, drugs, and crime."

"It's not funny, Cindy. Let's do a little research, find out what the issues are, and then divide them up between us. We can follow up different issues. You and I will prove that her situation was an...*anomaly*...We can write one article and deal with Hay Hair when we hand it in."

Cindy spreads her arms as if welcoming manna from heaven. "Now you're talking."

"Okay, let's start googling."

"There'll be overlap. We will find out the same stuff."

"So?"

Cindy shrugs. "Just saying. We'll be wasting time if we don't set some parameters before we start."

"Again, so? Let's see where our searches take us. It doesn't matter if we overlap. Each of us might miss something the other catches. We can edit everything later. Decide who takes what issues." I repeat what I'd just said because sometimes Cindy doesn't pay attention, especially if she disagrees.

"Okay, boss. But you focus on causes and I'll focus on crime."

I give up.

As I turn my chair to face my computer, I sing-song whisper, "'Parameters.'"

She's on me like a hawk. "What? What did you say?"

"Nothing, Miss Big Words."

She laughs, the balance between us is restored. I Google 'causes of homelessness' and see pages and pages of reasons, a veritable litany of explanations. I quickly glance down the sites and know

I'll be here a while if I want to do it right, which I do. I click on the first site, an old article about the James Bay Project, whatever that was, in the early 1970s. But the article was written not that long ago, really only a few years, so whatever the James Bay Project was, I assume it was responsible for some homelessness today. I start to read the article when Derrick Johnston, the asshole sports reporter, saunters up the aisle.

I smell his cheap aftershave long before his shadow darkens my monitor. I automatically straighten my back in anticipation of a confrontation. As he gets closer, I gag. He smells like insect repellant. Cindy is much better at handling him, but she's hunched over her keyboard like an old lady over a jigsaw puzzle. This guy creeps me out. He stops at my station and rocks back and forth on his heels. He thinks he's being casual.

He probably wants to know if we got blasted for coming in late. Without raising my eyes from my work, I see in my peripheral vision that his personal man junk is exactly at eye level. I can't help myself from looking. No, I don't turn my head from my monitor, I have more couth than that. Not much more, but some. I cast a furtive glance sideways at his crotch. Ha!

"So," he says, hands clasped over his belly, taming his various rodents, "what did Shirley have to say?"

Cindy rockets out of her chair and bellows, "Fuck off, Derrick. And get your shrivelled limp cannelloni out of my friend's face."

Her legs whack her chair as she jumps up and it careens across the carpet tiles, finally clanging into the metal desk behind her. It belongs to Karen Marumbo, the senior investigative reporter for *The Express*. She jumps out of her mocha skin, her brown eyes flashing in anger, and shouts, "Derrick, get out of here. I'm trying to work."

He scuffles away, shrugging, "Just getting some coffee. Geez."

"Ya, right." I shout, knowing he has other motives. "Don't be ridickulous." I emphasize "dick."

Derrick turns and looks at me. His smarmy smile has slipped off his face and is replaced by a sneer. I've gone too far. There'll be revenge. His voice slides across the floor like molten mercury.

"As I said, I'm just getting a coffee."

Most people at *The Express* go to the cafeteria for the better coffee, but there is an elevated platform with a kitchen of sorts, at the far north side of the building, which has an electric coffee pot. Derrick is too lazy or perhaps too cheap to take the elevator down and stand in line and then, horror of horrors, pay for a cup. A few times every day he scuttles past my desk.

Cindy says to his back, "Don't drink too much of that, it'll rot your brain. Oh, wait. Too late." She wheels her chair back across the tiles and tucks herself under her desk.

Cindy is good at interruptions. I'm not. I'm still hearing the echoes of the clang of her chair against Karen's desk. I look back at Karen who is also already focused on her keyboard, typing away. She's investigating the government spending during COVID-19. Billions of dollars. Karen has no trouble getting back to being a great reporter, tenacious and talented. Me? I'm still a bit of a mess, jangled. I don't know why that dickhead Derrick sets me off so much, but he does. Despite his fake bonhomie, he makes my nerves twitch. There is something dangerous about him that I can't pinpoint. I lick the wax paper my muffin was wrapped in, wishing there were more crumbs and maybe a glass of wine.

Good food and the thought of wine always seems to be able to turn me around. The curse of Derrick's visit is broken and I turn back to my computer. I excavate the information about the James Bay Project and get more and more upset as I unearth the bare facts. Without consulting the people who held the land claims to the area, the Cree and Inuit, Hydro-Québec and the Quebec government diverted the waters of three massive rivers on the eastern side of James Bay to create a giant reservoir on La Grande Rivière. This flooded almost 11,500 square kilometres of Inuit and Cree land on the eastern shore of the bay. An area about the size of a small country, like Belgium. All to create hydroelectric power. They built a tiered spillway three times the height of Niagara Falls and manufactured North America's largest generating station.

At the time many praised the resulting hydroelectric power because it was virtually pollution-free. However, the harm caused to the environment and the Indigenous peoples was catastrophic. Ten thousand caribou were drowned. The flooding stirred up the vegetation and released mercury into the water, poisoning the fish, which swam in it. Thousands of people lost their homes.

There was an outcry.

The Quebec government did a pathetic little polka dance to right the wrongs. First Nations land claims were surrendered for money and hunting rights. The Cree and Inuit ended up getting chump change. In my opinion, not nearly enough to compensate them for their losses, especially given the millions and millions of dollars made by selling the power. Their people were relocated upstream. And then the project, powered by a wave of white greed, moved forward to its second phase.

The second phase involved a mega-deal to sell electricity to the New England states. When it was finalized, all hell broke loose. Indigenous protests garnered support everywhere. Opposition to the environmental and social impact of more flooding grew by leaps and bounds. The fierce national and international disapproval caused this phase of the project to be cancelled. Well, I thought, at least that showed the power of protests and took heart.

What I didn't understand was the connection of the James Bay Project to homelessness in Toronto. How could a situation in the northern Quebec wilderness have any ramifications in an urban centre like Toronto? It just didn't make any sense to me. Why did this article show up in a Google search for causes of homelessness? I tapped Cindy on the shoulder.

"Did you come across an article on the James Bay Project causing homelessness in Toronto?"

"No, why?" She wasn't looking at me. Her wiry fingers were flying over her keyboard. "And don't bug me. I'm focusing on crime. Like I said I would. Statistics. Although I'm not finding much. It all seems pretty petty, in comparison to truckloads of guns."

I didn't stop. "Well, I just don't get why a hydroelectric project in the far north contributes to homelessness in Toronto."

She says one word. "Flooding."

As if that explained it.

"I still don't get it."

She says the word louder. "Flooding."

"Cindy." I match her volume.

Then she draws out the word. "Flooding."

"Cindy. I hear you, but I don't see the connection."

Her fingers finally still and she turns to me. "The *flooding* poisoned the fish, their main source of food. The *flooding* poisoned their drinking water. The *flooding* drowned herds and herds of caribou. The *flooding* covered the land they lived on."

"Yes, the article I was reading mentioned all that. But the people were rehomed. And how do you know all this?"

She ignores my question. "I can't believe you don't see the connection. The land they were moved to was crappy. It was poisoned as well. If you have nothing to eat or drink, what are you going to do?"

"Oh," I say, feeling stupid. "You're going to pack up and move. But why Toronto?"

"Ya think you'd go to Montreal if you could help it when it was the Quebec government that ruined your life?"

"Oh," I say again. "So, you land in Toronto, but your skills aren't needed, so you can't get a job, and you end up homeless."

"Bingo. That's the connection. But that's just one small cause of homelessness. Think about it. That project was fifty years ago, in the seventies. At first it might have been a fairly major cause, not so much now. But even still, the effects are ongoing today. I mean, how long can you wait for clean drinking water? Eventually you give up and move."

"So people are still leaving from that flooding half a century ago. They've finally given up hope."

"Did you notice that hopelessness and homelessness are only off by one letter?" Cindy raises her eyebrows at me, grimly nods, and turns back to her computer to continue on her research.

I can tell that this story is really going to upset me.

CHAPTER 5

MY ATTENTION WANDERS MILES AWAY from my research. It does that when I'm trying to face upsetting things. There are still a dozen sites on the causes of homelessness for me to look at. What an enormous challenge. Plus, I was getting hungry. I do that as well when I'm faced with upsetting things. That lemon meringue pie in the cafeteria is bouncing around in my head, tantalizing me. After all, it is coming up to ten-thirty and a good hour since my muffin. I can probably justify going to the cafeteria if anyone looked at me funny. I push my chair away from my desk and Cindy's head boings up.

"Where are you going?"

"Nowhere."

"Can I come?" She knows where.

Cindy had only had a small cup of pudding. "Sure."

We strut past Derrick's desk, heads held high. He growls, "Where are you going?"

Cindy diddles a wave in the air as we pass. "We won't be long," she sings while measuring an inch between her thumb and forefinger.

Oh God, she's so funny.

On our way back, I wipe my mouth so there's no evidence of the pastry and fold myself into my chair. It creaks. I really have to lose some weight. I'd read that lemon meringue pie was the pie to eat if you want less calories. I wasn't that worried. I have a rapid metabolic rate. Or that's what I tell myself, although truth be told, I may simply be a glutton. I wonder if I'll ever get my addictive personality under control. Probably not. I don't seem to have the time to go see my naturopath, Sally Josper. Maybe I should contact her right now. On the other hand, I really shouldn't make personal calls at work. We aren't allowed to use our phones except for business calls and research. But everyone keeps their phone on their desk. Just in case. Should I call? Shouldn't I? Back and forth, back and forth. I look up and see no one is paying any attention to me. Well, duh. Maybe I'll text her. Yes. I covertly send off a text asking for an appointment and then quickly refocus on my computer.

I'm such a goody two-shoes.

The second Google site about causes of homelessness mentions "aging out." I don't know what "aging out" means so I click on the headline and wait for the information to appear. Oh. Aging out happens when a child who's in foster care turns eighteen, meaning they no longer qualify for care. They age out of the system. Great. Just what an eighteen-year-old needs, to be pitched out of a house with no more follow-up into the unforgiving city.

I think about where my kids were when they were eighteen. They were all so young. And in university residences. That was the extent of their aging out of my house. They came home for holidays. I sent them money and care packages. I made their dentist appointments. But foster kids are likely not in university, unless they have incredible ambition and drive. And if they do manage to get there, where do they go on holidays? Who sends them money when they need it? Who reminds them of their healthcare appointments? They have no solid homes, no community. I read that the government gives them a little money until they're twenty-one after aging out. I read the amount and am disgusted. It surely isn't enough to pay for rent. Even if they share a house with several others, bringing the rent down, they simply don't have enough money. Period. I wish I'd given those kids under the Gardiner more than a toonie each.

On top of that, the article says, many of the kids are

traumatized by a lifetime of abuse at the hands of the system, not to mention their foster parents. Sure, most foster parents are well-vetted, or one likes to think so, and there seems to be less horror stories about kids being locked in a basement and not provided with the necessities of life. But even if the kids are lucky enough to be placed with kind adults, they are constantly moved about by the system. They might stay a year, possibly even two, in one place, but then they are uprooted. Because of this, they have no sense of home, no foundation. Nothing solid in their souls. And then, when they turn eighteen, they are put out like garbage. With a pittance.

I lean back in my chair and speculate if this is what had happened to Shirley Hay Hair. No, wait. She was on the street before she would have aged out. She said she was on the street from fifteen to nineteen. I wonder briefly what happened in her life before she turned fifteen to make her leave home. I wonder if she even had a home. Would I be like Shirley if I had her background? All things considered, I couldn't help but admire her. She has struggled and come out on top. She's a managing editor of the largest newspaper in the country! What a trajectory. What perseverance and determination.

And then there's me. I haven't moved upward in my career for decades. And why am I so addicted to things. What happened to me? I had no excuse. Did I? I grew up in a mediocre house in a mediocre part of Toronto with mediocre parents who gave me a mediocre childhood. They did nothing really awful to me. I wasn't hit. I can still hear my mother's voice. "I don't believe in spanking. That's not right, Robin." Although I sort of remember wishing I'd been spanked rather than getting an hour-long lecture on the evilness of my behaviour. But I was fed. I went to a nice school and had nice friends. Everything was *nice*. Wasn't it? A dark mysterious shadow plows through these thoughts like a small dinghy bobbing in the ocean trying to race away from an ocean liner coming straight at it. What on earth have I forgotten?

I surreptitiously check my phone for a text message from Sally Josper. Nope. Not a word.

Cindy taps me on the shoulder. I leap out of my skin. "What?" I shout.

She tosses her purse over her shoulder. "Come on. Let's go."

I stand up and grab my bag. I'd say purse but my bag is the size of a roll-on suitcase without the wheels. My shoulder sags with the weight of it. Perhaps I should take out the curling iron, dog biscuits, emergency beef jerky, manicure set, hairbrush, and whatever else I don't use very often. "Where to?"

"I just want to investigate a few of the things I read about. In particular, some safe injection sites."

We hustle to the elevator doors, past Derrick's desk. Luckily he isn't there. Probably in the can, he's so full of shit. I wheeze, trying to keep up with her long legs. "Safe injection sites? What about them?"

"Just to see, Robin. I need to actually visualize what I'm writing about. I find it very helpful. And I'd like to look at a few food banks."

"So, you think looking at these places will help you know about crime and for me to know about causes?"

She doesn't have time to answer before the elevator doors slide open. Lo and behold, Derrick is standing sideways, sucking in his belly and admiring his body in the distorting brushed metal, likely daydreaming about his youth when he was a football player at an obscure high school somewhere. He sees us, jerks forward, makes a fish sound with his mouth, and then quickly scoots past us, fast-walking to his desk, head held high. I do my best not to laugh.

The doors sweep closed after us and Cindy punches 'G' for the garage. I ask, "Your car or mine?"

I know she'll want to take her car as she won't be seen dead in mine. She drives a fancy Honda Accord, the newest year, in a light silvery grey with aluminum wheels and Bluetooth. She doesn't have to stick a key in the ignition to turn the car on. I personally think we should be in mine so we don't look quite so entitled, given where we were going.

"Yours," she says, surprising me. "Better to look like we fit in."

40

I doubt that but say nothing as I think about how much gas I have. I try to stick to my budget and only fill up once every two weeks. It's been an expensive winter. Even with my new heat pump, my power bills are higher than they were in the summer. It's only Monday and payday is a full week away. I juggle a few items in my head. I need more wine. It's a toss-up. Gas for the car or gas for me? Maybe Ralph will pick up a bottle for tonight. He's good about that. Maybe too good. Do we enable each other in our drinking habits? I check my phone. Still no text from Sally Josper. Left to my own devices, I make a decision. "I have to get gas." I feel very adult.

"No problemo." She's on her phone and looks up. "Kids."

I check my phone again as well. By way of an explanation I say, "I'm going to have a grandchild sometime this month."

"You excited?"

The elevator doors open and we walk to my car. I feel better about being underground when I'm with someone. I gush, "I can't wait. I love babies."

"How'd your parents take the news?" Cindy is so incisive. Right to the crux of the matter.

I know exactly what she's talking about. Winchester and my oldest daughter, Maggie, got married without letting anyone know right before last summer and were now expecting their first child. Not having a wedding colossally disappointed my parents, my mother mostly and me too, to be honest, but that isn't the main problem. The main problem for them is the colour of Winchester's skin. Black. My father, in particular, is a racist. If you ask him, he'd say no, of course he's not. He might go as far to say that he even has Black friends, but everyone would know that was a lie. Everything he does around Winnie screams racist. He was shocked that Win went to university, that he drove a car, that he had a good job, that he was a responsible young man.

I reply, "Not well. It'll take a little time."

"Maybe," Cindy says, letting the word echo in the cement parking lot. Her kids still haven't accepted her sexual orientation, even after five years.

"There's so much hatred in the world. I'm tired of it." I stand up taller.

"It doesn't help when political leaders spout hatred. That gives everyone permission to hate. Nonetheless, I hate your car."

She tugs at the door handle and grimaces a fake smile at me. "Oh look, you fixed it." She's being sarcastic.

My car doors don't lock unless I actually wiggle the locks down with my fingers, and they don't really open either. Well, they do eventually, if one perseveres. "You were the one who wanted to fit into the neighbourhood. Pull hard."

Speaking of fitting in, I struggle to fit in behind the wheel. I nudge my recalcitrant muffin top with the palm of my hand to the left, hoping Cindy isn't watching. Not that it really matters, she knows the score. "Where too, Tonto?" I ask.

"Not to Moss Park, that's for sure."

I try to suppress a shudder. "Well, that's good. Queen and Sherbourne isn't the best neighbourhood. So much violence."

"Get over yourself, Robin. That's not why. That safe injection site is closed on Mondays."

I look at her sideways as I pull out of the parking spot. "It's not open? After a weekend? In that area? That doesn't make any sense."

"Talk to your premier, not me. He's the one who cut out hours. Money. Now he wants that site, plus a few others, to be funded by public donations. Like that would ever happen. The mayor is beside himself."

"Sometimes the mayor does the right thing." I personally like the mayor.

"Ya right," says Cindy. She hates all politicians. "But most of the time he doesn't. And because of the funding cuts, most of the sites are shut in the evening. You know, like when people need them the most."

Cindy was ramping up to one of her rants, her anger sizzling from her chest up to her mouth.

I quickly ask, "But what's open now?"

She's deflected and calms down. "Let's check out the site at

Queen and Sherbourne."

"I thought you said the site there was shut on Mondays."

"There's another site there. I should have clarified. It's not just a safe injection site, it's a shelter and community centre as well."

"Let me write that down on my calendar, the day you admitted you'd made a mistake."

"Fuck off."

"Maybe I won't need gas after all. That's pretty close. Onward, ho."

Despite not wanting to head over to that neighbourhood, I pump the gas pedal and do my best to zoom up the concrete driveway to the street. I smile at Cindy when she looks at me. But she is not impressed and rolls her eyes.

"What's with the yawnathon?" she says.

I ignore her. "Maybe we should get some lunch. There's probably a Subway nearby."

"And you're the one watching your budget. Didn't you bring lunch?" She nods at my bag that's been tossed onto the back seat.

"Of course I did, but I'd much rather eat a Subway sandwich." At least she didn't mention the lemon meringue pie from twenty minutes ago. "Eating out is more fun. And speaking of eating salads that contains olives, did you book online to get your tooth fixed?"

"I have walk-in privileges. I'll pop in after work."

"He'll still be there?"

"Oh God, yes, that guy never stops. It's his clinic, so he feels responsible for the other dentists there. He's the main rainmaker. I remember there were some nights he didn't get home until eight or nine."

I don't say that was because he was probably screwing around with the hygienists.

"Wow, must be nice to get immediate treatment. I waited over two weeks to get a cracked tooth pulled out. The pain was unbelievable."

"I can't believe we are talking about our teeth. We're getting old, Robin. Next thing you know we'll be comparing implant costs. At least we haven't begun that constant chatter about our health."

Just then my phone pinged. I toss it to Cindy. "Read me the text."

Cindy pokes around at my phone. "What is this, an iPhone 6?"

"Leave me alone. I had to pay off my mortgage." Cindy's mortgage was paid off by her guilt-ridden but fun-loving ex. "What's the text say?"

"It's from a Dr. Sally Josper. It says that you have an appointment today at six-thirty." She looks at me. "I take back that not talking about our health. Is something wrong, Robin?"

"Oh no," I reassure her, "it's just a check-up. More an anxiety thing," I finish lamely. But it's true. I get anxious if I can't get a glass of wine.

"Ya, you should get that under control."

"What? It shows?"

"Just a tad, Robin, just a tad."

"Well, at least I'm doing something about it."

"Are you accusing me of something?"

"No, why? Are you anxious?"

"What do you think?"

"I'm guessing not." Defensive maybe. Paranoid, a little. Hyper, yes. Cranky? Most of the time. But anxious, no.

"You'd be guessing right." She says this way too firmly. Then: "There it is." Cindy points up ahead to a tall, imposing edifice. It looks like a prison that has metastasized into several square blocks. "See it? On the left? And look, there's a parking spot."

"Friendly looking joint," I say, my eyes fixated on a drunk with slippery eyes leaning against the corner, his hand in his pocket, fiddling. I'm hoping not with his thingy.

"Pull in here, Robin. Let's go."

I wrench the steering wheel and sigh. I knew I wasn't going to like doing this story.

CHAPTER 6

THE DRUNK'S EYES SWIVEL IN our direction when my car door grinds shut. Our gazes meet and I am slapped in the face by his angry judgment. What did I ever do to him? Who does he think I am? I feel his rheumy eyes dig into my back as Cindy and I skitter up the concrete steps to the main door of the community centre. I am looking forward to inspecting the safe injection site housed here. Not. I pull my jacket sleeve over my hand before I touch the door handle. My pandemic habits really have a hold on me. That's my excuse, but the truth is that I've always been a bit of a germophobe and opening doors this way all my life. Cindy marches around me and palms the inner door open. She turns around and looks at me, lifts the same hand to her mouth and pretends to lick it. Something in my stomach curdles. The meringue on the pie, I'm thinking.

"Stop it," I hiss.

A woman with glowing mocha skin and beautiful brown almond shaped eyes bustles out of a corner office into the foyer. She's been alerted somehow that people have arrived. Maybe a security camera? I look around for one. Right. There's a fisheye lens mounted high in a corner.

"Can I help you?" She is well-trained; her eyes barely flickering downwards as she scrutinizes our clothing. She knows we don't belong.

"Oh hi," says Cindy. "We're journalists from *The Express* and are doing an article on homelessness in Toronto. I'm Cynthia Dale

45

and this is Robin MacFarland."

"Nice to meet you, Cynthia. Robin." She nods at each of us in turn and smiles, revealing a row of perfectly white teeth. I wonder if she has a good dental plan. Probably, she works for the city. "I'm Lydia. That's kind of a big topic."

So, no last name. I check out my surroundings. The decor is Salvation Army Thrift Store meets Toronto General Hospital. The lights are flickering fluorescent and the glass doors are smudged. There are black scuff marks on the grey linoleum and the chairs lining the walls have greasy looking seats. The baseboards are a shiny grey rubber slicked with yellowing floor wax embedded with years of grime.

I step forward, having had enough of Cindy dominating the conversation. And everything in general. "It certainly is, Lydia." I'm practising my interview technique. I learned it on YouTube. I speak her name clearly and look right into her eyes. I'm not sure what I see there, maybe compassion tamped down with despair with a side order of too much coffee. "We've broken it up into topics to make it a bit easier to get a handle on it. Cindy is taking care of the crime and drugs angle, while I'm focusing on causes." I point at Cindy and then tap my chest while I say this to indicate who's doing what.

She looks at Cindy. "I thought you said your name was Cynthia." She's not accusing, just clarifying.

"It is, but people call me Cindy. It's a nickname for Cynthia."

"Well, come into my office and we can have a little chat." Her office is a tiny hole in the wall with no windows and is lined with derelict grey metal filing cabinets, chipped along the sides, clearly rejects from another government building. Her desk is sagging under paper and there's an odd smell. I try to identify it by covertly sniffing the air. It's a mixture of body odour, tuna casserole, and cat litter. I understand the source of the body odour and tuna casserole, but the cat litter leaves me flummoxed.

Cindy sweeps her arm over the room. "I guess it takes a while to get digitized."

Lydia's look at Cindy borders on sympathy. "Our clients are

very suspicious of their private information being logged into computers, stored there for anyone to look at. Paper records give them a sense of privacy and security."

To Cindy's credit, she doesn't look embarrassed at not knowing more about disenfranchised people. "Right. Tell us more about this centre."

Lydia begins her spiel. It sounds rehearsed and it probably is. "There's a main eligibility criterion. Our clients must be homeless or very marginally housed. Usually, they're coping with some sort of mental illness or an addiction, often both. We aim to offer a social setting where they can gain social skills in a non-judgmental atmosphere. We offer breakfast and lunch, showers, and laundry. Our recreation program includes yoga, mindfulness, games, music, movies, and every now and then, an outing." She ticks off her list of activities with her unpolished but buffed fingernails and then continues. "We offer support with housing acquisition, counselling, and advocacy." She crosses her arms over her chest. The litany has been proudly completed.

I say, "So, basically, your clients are homeless."

Lydia nods, "Yes, as I just said." I was being admonished for not listening closely. "That is a requirement for using our services. Our criterion."

Right. My ears had snagged on her use of the word "criterion," smack at the beginning of her spiel. Most people would say "criteria." I'd been so busy thinking about her government lexicon that I hadn't heard the next sentence. "Your criteria," I say.

Lydia looks at me as if I were trying to pick a fight but rises above her urges to engage.

I did notice that she had left out any mention of the main reason why we had picked this centre. "And you have a safe injection site here on the premises." I'm not asking a question.

She shifts in her metal chair self-consciously. Her polyester black pants make a farting noise as she adjusts her posture. I do my best not to laugh. Lydia coughs, as if trying to disguise her own laughter, but of course, her camouflage is too late. The damage has been done.

"That was my chair," she says, "not me."

Cindy acts as if nothing out of the ordinary has happened. As a mother of four, she's heard worse.

Lydia continues. "We do have a safe injection site, but it's not open right now. That's why I didn't mention it."

I think that not being open is a pretty feeble excuse for not mentioning it and wonder about the real reason.

Lydia continues, "It opens later this afternoon and then shuts down after dinner."

So, not in the evening, when people are actually injecting. "What are the statistics of the common times people shoot up?"

Lydia doesn't like the insinuation of my question and shifts in her chair again. No fart this time.

Cindy interjects, smoothing this over. So unlike her. "I was wondering if we could look at it."

Lydia's arms are still crossed over her chest. "Nope." She smiles with her pearly whites, perhaps trying to take the edge off her denial.

"Oh?"

"The room is locked when it isn't in use. We have a lot of equipment in there that we have to keep under lock and key."

"Oh?" I ask. "What sort of equipment?" And didn't she have a key?

"Needles, syringes, tourniquet bands."

Cindy is pretending to take notes and looks up from her phone. "Any drugs?"

"Sure. Methadone, in case someone needs it." She nods her head earnestly. "We support rehabilitation."

"Any other drugs?" Cindy is trying to ferret out the truth behind the locked doors. Are there illegal drugs stashed in the room?

Lydia rubs her chin. She wants us to think she's thinking. "Naloxone for overdoses."

Cindy abandons this line of questioning, although I know her antennae are up, and abruptly switches topics. "I've noticed there are other security features here. You have problems with theft?"

"Of course we do. Our clients are homeless. They carry their few possessions, everything they own, with them. If they need something they don't have, chances are good they'll steal it from either us or another homeless person. So, yes, we have a lot of security."

"Cameras?"

"Sure. Outside the building on all four corners, over the doors, and quite a few inside. There are at least three on both floors. This floor has three, upstairs has four. I have one in my office." She points to a lens in the corner, mounted behind a plant hanging in a string macrame planter. "There's one in the foyer aimed at the front doors, and another one aimed at the elevator doors. We like to keep track of clients coming and going."

I would hate to have this kind of surveillance on my activities. It would make me feel like a child. "That's a lot," I say.

Lydia shrugs. "Some of our clients complain about being infantilized, but we have to have some accountability."

Infantilized. I'm learning a whole new homeless-speak.

Cindy asks, "Is someone monitoring the cameras?"

"I always have them on my computer." She turns her computer so it faces us and I see about twenty little squares all jerkily vibrating. Her screen looks like a Zoom meeting that's been through a woodchipper. "I monitor the building until about noon when there are more people around. They show up for lunch, which is in," she consults her watch, "about twenty minutes. Then there's a part-time security guard who comes on duty and watches the live feeds. If there's trouble, he deals with it. He has a little office just off the foyer, opposite mine. You probably noticed it on your way in."

Not me, I thought. I noticed the dirt, not the doors.

Cindy says, "Yes, I saw that office door on the right and wondered what was behind it. What sort of 'trouble' do you get here?"

"Well, as I said, a lot of our clients have addictions, drugs, alcohol, and sometimes their social filters, shall I say, slip and they exhibit inappropriate behaviour for this setting."

She was speaking with so much political correctness I wanted to scribble all over her walls with black magic marker. Instead, I ask, "What do you feel are the main causes of homelessness."

"It's my experience that mental health issues are the main cause. I can only speak about the here and now, the present, what we deal with here. I can't speak to the causes of the mental illnesses, but I think they're what one would expect. Abuse, abuse, abuse with a head trauma thrown in for good measure and perhaps a gene or two."

Well, well, Lydia was certainly going out on a limb there, abandoning the government speak. I might like her after all. I ask, "Any other ideas about the causes?"

"Foreign investment."

"What?" I don't believe her.

"Sure." She leans forward earnestly to expound upon her personal theory. Now I am liking her even more. All of a sudden I see the passion that drove her to work in the centre. She steps into a realm that isn't controlled by her employer. "Foreign nationals come to Toronto, one of the safest cities in the world, and want to invest their millions in our mostly non-violent haven. They get permission to build huge condominium towers, arguing that they are easing the housing crisis. In actual fact, they are creating homelessness. One would think that creating more density would provide affordable housing, but the opposite is true. It's a totally false narrative. The gentrification of poorer neighbourhoods pushes people who are marginally employed out onto the street. They certainly can't afford the condo prices asked in Toronto. Sometimes the foreigners buy existing buildings and instead of tearing them down and building new, completely retrofit them, pitching the existing tenants out of their units. The new term is 'renoviction.'"

"Wow," I say. "I never thought of foreign investment having that kind of consequence. As a Home and Garden reporter I always felt that building a new tower or upgrading a building was a good thing, an improvement, but I can see that it actually causes harm."

Cindy isn't at all interested in this conversation. I can tell by the circles her thumb is making that she's scrolling through Facebook.

"And crime," says Lydia. "It causes crime."

Cindy looks up when she hears her magic word. "How does foreign investment cause crime? In this scenario, I mean."

Well, at least she was listening a little.

"Most of the foreign investors are Asian. When people are pushed out of their homes or their neighbourhoods, they get frightened and angry. They have no place to live. Yes, they end up on the street, but they also become racist. And if their anger is hot enough, and believe me it is, then they lash out in violence, breaking the new windows, painting graffiti on the walls, screaming and ranting at others. Shooting if they join gangs."

Cindy is now very interested and writing like crazy on a notebook that she's dug out of her bag. She usually types her notes on her phone, but I guess she's trying to fit into the non-digital atmosphere.

"How likely is it that these people will join a gang?"

Lydia says, "Very likely. Especially the aged-out kids"

At least I know what that means now.

Lydia continues. "It's not as if they seek out a gang. New on the street, they're really doing their best just to survive. But gangs see they're vulnerable and prey upon them. They promise protection and money, drugs and housing. A sense of family, of belonging. And what's worse, they foster an 'Us and Them' mentality which breeds violence. They build hatred for someone else, another gang, or another race."

I say, "In short, this particular cause of homelessness, aging out, leads to crime. It's impossible to separate the two. Everything is woven together and you can't tease out the parts." Shirley's dictum for two separate articles is looking more and more like a no-go.

"Exactly. And of course, there's the politics. That also is a main cause of homelessness which then leads to violence and crime."

Cindy looks up from her notebook. "What exactly do you mean, 'politics'?"

"To be kind, let's call the government's negligence of people in the north 'environmental extraction projects.' I personally think it's criminal."

"What do you mean by environmental extraction projects?" I ask.

"I use the word 'projects' loosely. Believe me, there are no written plans. No structure that's acknowledged. No written mission statement. But the negligence is so ongoing over such a long period of time, I, like most other social workers, now use the word 'projects.' It is my belief that the government is deliberately creating disgusting situations on reserves so that people will extract themselves, they leave." Lydia's spraying her desk with the force of her words.

I jog my head back to avoid her droplets. Another habit from the pandemic. To my way of thinking, what she's saying could be the truth. Why else have these situations gone on for so long? The thought that people are being forced out of their homes cuts through my heart. I resolve to research this when I get back to the office.

Lydia is now really worked up. "This has been going on for a very long time. It's inexcusable." She slams her palm on her desk. "Decades."

Cindy looks up.

"The people who live there often have no running water, and if they do, it's unpalatable, it smells and is often brown. Undrinkable. Sometimes this water is so toxic that to even bathe in it causes rashes and serious illness. How hard is it to have clean water? There are filtration systems that can purify even the most polluted water. The government funds projects to provide drinking water in countries all over the world. But here? Nada. Nope." She leans back, her face flushed.

I venture, "So people leave the reservation and come to the city."

"Wouldn't you? If you had no drinking water, no local school for your kids, no heat for your home, and food at ten times the cost of city stores? Wouldn't you?"

"It would be overwhelming to not have the basic necessities." I'm trying to remain professional and I think I pull it off, but my stomach is churning. I find it unbelievable that the government would deliberately allow these conditions to remain for years. And yet they have. Environmental extraction projects. Lydia's right, it seems deliberate. I feel slightly sick.

Cindy says, "At least there are safe injection sites." Sarcasm drips over her words.

Lydia looks at her watch and stands up. She smooths out the creases in her pants somewhat zealously, her anger still vibrating in her body. Our time is over. "Sorry, but I have to make sure the lunch is ready. And no, the safe injection sites are at great risk. There are rumblings afoot that their funding is on the chopping block. I think that's deliberate as well."

I ask, "How do you mean?"

Cindy and I both stand up and gather our belongings together while Lydia heads to the door of her office. She turns to us and throws up her hands. Despair colours her words. "It's statistically proven that the sites save lives, that they don't encourage drug use, that they help. But everything about them is expensive. They have to be equipped. They have to be staffed. Rent has to be paid. We've lost several this year alone. The rumour is that the provincial government, the premier, finds it more cost effective to close the sites and let the people die."

Cindy shakes her head. "All in the midst of an opioid crisis."

I ask, "What is the mayor's position on the closing of the sites?"

Lydia tilts her head and raises her eyebrows. "He hates the premier. Hates him. He'll fight this tooth and nail."

CHAPTER 7

LYDIA WAVES GOODBYE TO US as she makes a beeline for the elevators to go up to the cafeteria. When the elevator doors open, the smell of tuna casserole wafts through the foyer stronger than ever. Lunch is ready. Cindy and I go in the opposite direction and head out the front doors. We step around people who are pulling trundle buggies and shopping carts up the accessibility ramp. Some are having fabulous conversations with themselves, their pupils dark pinpricks in bloodshot eyes. I smell alcohol fumes, bad breath from rotten teeth, and ripe body odour, as I weave through these desperate people. They're lining up, waiting to be herded inside on the dot of twelve noon.

I am grateful to see that the drunk leaning against the corner is gone as we approach my car. I'm not sure I could face the accusation in his eyes. I couldn't discern how old he was because years on the street in all kinds of weather had turned his skin a leathery brown. Whatever his age, he was angry. Did he hate me because I had money? Because I was white? Or worse, did he think I was an entitled white supremacist? A supporter of colonialism? I hated being judged by the colour of my skin. Didn't everyone? Wouldn't that be enough to change people's attitudes to each other? I was grateful to get to my car, such as it was.

I push my spare tire behind the steering wheel and do up my seatbelt while I wait for Cindy to get in. I watch the steady stream of people dragging their meagre belongings up the ramp into the centre. As Cindy gets settled, I say, "At least they have somewhere to go. At least there's a meal or two a day and laundry."

Cindy snorts. "You honestly think it's okay?"

I don't know where she's going with her comment. I can't read her tone of voice, but I'm getting an inkling that she's warming up to a tirade. "Why?"

"Do you have any idea what these homeless shelters are like?" She's now a little shrill.

I don't, not really. We certainly weren't offered a tour. I detect more than a little edge in her voice. I spin my wheel and do a U-turn on Queen Street. We bump over the streetcar tracks and bang over the edge of the sidewalk on the far side of the street. I've done this a hundred times and am not worried about damaging my car. The first few times took care of that.

I say after the car calisthenics, "I've never been in one. I was hoping to see inside that centre, but Lydia wasn't very forthcoming about letting us go anywhere but the first-floor foyer and her office." I turn my head, checking for traffic coming up behind me. I've been hit doing a U-turn before, which is why the rear taillight is held on with duct tape. "Look at that lineup, Cindy. So many people use that shelter."

"Robin, think about it. No one gets a door."

I'm puzzled. What do doors have to do with anything? "What do you mean, no door?"

Cindy is impatient. "No *door*. No one has a single-occupancy room. With a door. There's no privacy. None. No doors. Everything is in the open. So, you change your clothes in front of other people. You brush your teeth in front of other people. You eat in front of other people. All day long you're on the street in front of other people, and then, at night, you're in front of other people in beds beside you. There's no sense of privacy. If that isn't soul-destroying, I don't know what is."

"So, no doors."

"You got it. Plus constant surveillance. You heard her. Security cameras everywhere. It's so, so…patronizing." She spits out the word. "It's even worse than that. It's infantilizing."

She picked up that word from Lydia, I'm guessing. "No doors and patronizing. Infantilizing." When Cindy gets angry like this, I do my best to make sure she knows I am hearing her. It seems to calm her down. I feel a bit stupid, repeating what she's saying, but hey, I'm concentrating on my driving in the greasy slush and I want to do more than nod or grunt.

"What are you? A fucking parrot? You sound stupid."

Well, I tried.

"On top of that, there's no oversight for assault. I bet fists fly when the smallest thing goes wrong."

"The smallest thing." I'm taking a risk here, repeating her. I've decided to make it that annoying game of repeating everything someone says before the words are barely out of their mouths.

"Yes, like your bobby pin falls on the floor. Or you leave toothpaste in the sink. You could get punched."

"Punched," I say.

"Don't piss me off, Robin. Stop repeating what I'm saying."

The game is working. "Stop repeating what I'm saying."

Finally, she laughs. Everyone was a victim of this game by a sibling. It's ridiculous. But it diverts her. I didn't want her pounding my dashboard to make a point. It might fall off.

"Living on the edge of society makes one edgy. Volatile. Plus, possessions are stolen. Despite the cameras. One security person sitting in a room, like they had there, is useless. In addition to all this loss of dignity, you have to leave at seven in the morning. Seven! The sun is barely up in the winter. So out you go into the cold and dark. And will they hold that same bed with its thin blanket and grey sheets for you? Not on your nelly. It takes all day, the whole fucking day, just to secure food and shelter. Everything requires lining up. Look at that queue. Halfway down the block. All for some tuna fucking casserole."

So, she noticed the smell as well. Mothers all over Canada knew that smell. "So, not ideal."

"And why wouldn't she show us the safe injection site? What's that secret about? And I wanted to see where people sleep. How many beds did she say they have?"

"She didn't."

Cindy looks it up on her phone. "Oh, for Christ's sake. Twelve. Twelve? What kind of shelter has twelve beds?"

"A small one?" I offer.

She consoles herself. "But at least they serve lots of meals. There must be a hundred people in the lineup."

We drive along in silence. Finally, I say, "I guess if I were homeless, I'd prefer to stay in a tent with my own stuff. I'd feel more in control of my life."

"And if you're from the far north, you'd probably have good camping skills. I know that might be a stereotype."

"I was pretty upset by that whole environmental extraction project business Lydia talked about."

"That's nothing compared to the major environmental destruction you were researching earlier. Neglecting the necessities of life for Indigenous people isn't the whole story."

"What do you mean?" I am focusing on the car behind me. I can't see it very well because my rear-view window is smeared with winter grime, but the shadow of it seems to be way too close to my car. I hate that. Tailgaters are so rude.

"You're the one who researched the James Bay Project. Talk about environmental extraction! That project was actually called a 'project.' All for the sake of hydroelectric power. That's so disgusting, ruining miles and miles and miles of beautiful wilderness for electricity. Somebody should pay for that. No wonder there are so many homeless Indigenous people in Toronto."

"It was almost fifty years ago, Cindy. I'm not sure the effects of that flooding account for much homelessness today." I'd been thinking about it.

"Are you kidding me? Of course it has an impact. They still don't have clean water. They still don't have heat. They still don't have decent schools. They still have to pay a premium for groceries. And they still live on shit land that isn't good for hunting. That's where the government put them, and that's how the government treats them. Like shit."

I was about to say, "Oh, you're right," but my sentence comes out as an aborted squeal. A person has wobbled off the sidewalk into the traffic. The car in front of me screeches to a stop. I slam on my brakes so I don't hit it, but feel a crunch from my rear end. I've been hit. "Oh, for fuck's sake," I say. "That person behind me was way too close. And now I've been hit. That bumper has been hit so many times I'm surprised it's still attached to my car."

Cindy grabs the back of her neck and says, "Oh-h-h, my neck. Whiplash. Insurance."

I know she's kidding. It was just a tap at about ten kilometres an hour. "Knock it off," I say to her.

I throw open my car door and get out to look at the damage. Hard to tell, what with all the dirt and dents. It's nothing. Then I inspect the bumper of the car that hit me. A significant dent in its shiny chrome. The licence plate is bent. The front turn signal light is cracked. I can't believe the damage. I check the car's insignia. A Mercedes? So much for money purchasing fine engineering. My old Sentra came out of that altercation way better. At least it wasn't my fault.

Cindy gets out of the car and laughs when she sees the front end of the other car. "Seems like they got the worse end of the deal."

The driver of the Mercedes is now at the front of his car and rubbing his chin. Maybe he smacked it on his steering wheel. I look closer at his thin, long nose and recognize it. I can't believe it. This is the same asshole with the thin patrician nose and Rolex watch who was tailgating me down Jarvis on the way to work this morning. I'm amazed. What a weird coincidence.

"So," he says, hands clasped in front of him over his navy cashmere coat with shiny buttons, "Looks like your car did quite a bit of damage to mine. Plus, I whacked my chin. Luckily my teeth seem fine. No chips. Your insurance isn't going to be too happy with my claim. Looks like several thousand dollars to me. Not to mention the physiotherapy I'll need for my neck." He rubs the nape of his neck the same way Cindy did a minute ago. What a liar.

I'm flabbergasted. Everyone knows that if you rear-end someone it's your fault.

Cindy stands her full height, which is formidable. She towers over His Smugness. "Nice try, buster. You were driving too closely. You think you own the road? Well guess what? You rear-ended her. That makes it your fault. And you obviously weren't wearing your seatbelt, which is against the law. All this will impact your insurance rates, not hers."

The man ignores her and stares at me. "You look familiar. Do I know you?"

He was that kind of jerkoff. Women were non-entities.

"You were tailgating me down Jarvis this morning and then splashed that woman on the curb. We had words. Well, gestures." I'm still a bit embarrassed by my behaviour.

Cindy walks around his car. "Nice wheels. Too bad you don't keep it clean." She stops at the driver's door and stares wide-eyed at the dried slush. She's making a point. If only she knew. I try not to look at it or laugh.

The man barely acknowledges her and says to me, "I'll need to look at your licence and insurance information."

"And I'll need yours," I retort. "You are at fault, you rear-ended me, and if you want to make a claim your rates will go up. And maybe your insurance company will stop insuring you, being as it is that you habitually tailgate and have likely rear-ended other people before."

He jerks his head back at my words as if I spat on a nerve. I was right. But he quickly regains his fat cat composure, reaches into his pocket, pulls out a fine leather wallet, probably alligator, and snaps it open to his licence. It's one of those wallets that only holds cards, of which he has many in transparent sleeves. He holds it out to me with manicured fingers. Ronald Rowland. I take a photograph of it with my ancient phone and say, "Your insurance?" He tilts his wallet so the next cellophaned section flips into view. His insurance pink slip. I take a picture of that as well. "Thanks, Ronnie," I say, deliberately not using his last name and making fun of him.

All this aggression is making me want a drink. Or a bowl of Cheetos. It really isn't who I am. Sally Josper at six-thirty tonight should help me sort this out.

Ron slides his wallet back into his pocket and curls his fingers in a give-me-your-information gesture. I dig into my bag past my meatloaf sandwich, the candy, beef jerky, and curling iron to root out the plastic card holder at the bottom. I pull out my licence and pink slip and hold them together in front of him so he can snap a photo with his huge fancy iPhone. Probably an iPhone thirty. Of course he has the latest model.

"Thanks, Robin," he says, mimicking my tone, but is at a loss because there's no female child version of Robin. He turns on his heel and oozes into his car, thunking the door shut behind him with that sound only a Mercedes can give.

Cindy is tugging at her car door. "Come on, Robin. Frappe la rue."

I get in beside her. "Frappe la rue?"

"Yeah. 'Hit the road,' en français."

I shake my head.

She says, "That guy was a snake."

"I know. I had a slight interaction with him already today. He was tailgating me down Jarvis."

"I heard. I imagine you gave him the finger?"

"Oh ya, and splashed his car. That mess on the door you were looking at."

"That was you?" she laughs. "Good job, Robin."

"He turned onto Queen, so I think he works for Ontario Hydro. Probably a CEO or something. They make too much money. As far as I'm concerned, no one deserves to make millions a year. Especially when people can't pay their power bills and do without fresh vegetables in the winter so they'll have heat."

"He works there for sure."

Sometimes Cindy amazes me. I had guessed at that this morning, but it was only a guess. She was speaking like she knew the truth. I ask, "How do you know that?"

"There was an Ontario Hydro identification lanyard tossed

onto his front seat. He probably needs to wear it in the building to pass security."

"Security at Ontario Hydro? At their office? Seems a bit extreme."

"Oh, you better believe it. There are all these rumours about foreign actors infiltrating the power grid and collapsing society. The Chinese in particular."

"I thought we were just worried about spying through a 5G network. About sabotaging the internet."

"No, the power grid as well. So that's why he has ID, even to get into the building, even though he's at the top of the heap."

I throw the car into drive and it grumbles like an old woman along Queen Street, sliding on the wet streetcar tracks and lurching into the inside lane. "Where to now, Radisson?" I'm continuing with her French theme.

"There's a food bank on College Street, des Groseilliers. Let's check it out."

"Whereabouts on College?"

Cindy scrolls on her phone. "It's between Spadina and Bathurst. On the north side. You know, around Kensington Market."

"Isn't there a medical building around there?"

Cindy expands the Google street view with her fingers. "Yes, I see it. The food bank is a little bit west of there."

"Do you see a Starbucks around? Or a Subway? I'm starving."

"No, but there are some nice cool coffee shops." She reads a few of the names from her phone.

"Great. Let's get something there. Maybe a muffin."

"Not bran," says Cindy. "Not while I'm in this small car with you. You've already had one bran muffin today and I can only take so much risk."

She knows me so well.

"Don't be vulgar," I say.

"Oh-h-h," she sings, "you are a perfect asshole. You never fart."

I give her a look, head north on Bathurst Street and turn right at College. It's easy to locate the food bank. A long line of ragged people snake along the sidewalk, waiting for their turn to pick up their white plastic bag of rations. One fellow, he could have been twenty or fifty, it's hard to tell with the damage that living on the street causes to a person's body, sits on the sidewalk with his back leaning against the repurposed storefront. He digs into his bag of food, hunting for bits that he can eat right away.

I feel like crying.

CHAPTER 8

I YANK MY WHEEL AND PULL into a parking spot in front of the food bank, but across the road. "This okay?" I ask Cindy. I think I might be too far away.

She says, "Perfect," while snapping photographs through the front windshield of the lineup in front of the food bank. "Not everyone likes their photo being taken, so at least they can't see me do it from here. I'll zoom in when I'm editing them."

"Why do you need photographs? Why do you need to zoom in?" I look at the rundown storefront that was painted too long ago. It's so depressing. I jiggle the car back and forth until it's straight in the parking spot. Every time I throw it into reverse, I hear a gurgle come from the centre console. Transmission, probably. I briefly covet that guy's Mercedes.

"Buzz down your window and lean back," she says. I follow her instructions like a good girl, although I still wonder why she's taking pictures. Cindy holds up her phone and reaches across my chest. Her hand skims my breast and she exaggeratingly jerks it back.

"Oops," she sings.

I roll my eyes and lean back further, out of her reach.

"I'm looking for weapons. If I edit the photo and zoom in, I'll be able to make out bulges in jacket pockets, a bit too much weight in the material, you know what I mean?"

I look at the sad but straight line of people, with their worn-out boots and toques sliding off their heads, their coats missing buttons and hems coming undone. "Weapons? I don't think so, Cindy. These people don't have enough food, how could they possibly afford a weapon? In particular, an expensive gun?"

"You heard Lydia. Gangs prey upon the homeless. And look at these people. Most of them are young, in their late teens and early twenties. I bet half of them have aged out of the system. Or they're runaways. Vulnerable. Ripe for the plucking. Gangs target people with less power."

When she said the word "power," the Ontario Hydro guy flies across my mind again. People with power almost always abuse it, and he had that snickering, pompous air about him. "You see gang activity everywhere, Cindy. These people are just getting food. That's it."

Just then there's a loud shriek. Voices crash against each other in a rising crescendo. The tidy queue falls apart like a line of collapsing dominoes, with people stumbling and scrambling to the left and right. Cindy unsnaps her seatbelt so she can lean further across me. She moves her phone in an arc, now videotaping the action. "This is fantastic," she whispers. "Just fantastic."

I have trouble seeing what's going on because I'm leaning so far back that her elbow is jabbing into my neck. I can't turn my head to look. I squawk. She shifts to the right and then her left shoulder is wedged into my eye socket. I can't see a thing. I whisper back, "What? What's so fantastic? What's going on, Cindy?"

"God, I wish I had my good camera with me."

She's practically leaning out the window.

"Cindy, what the hell is going on?" My voice is muffled by her scarf.

"Nothing much, just a little drug deal gone wrong."

She twists backward out of my window, shoulders her car door open and jumps out. Through the front windshield, I spy a tall skinny guy pimped out in a black hoodie, black pants, and black Doc Martens racing down the sidewalk, away from the food bank. His head is shaved with a tattooed lightning bolt running from the crown to the nape of his neck. A black backpack with reflective tape across the bottom bounces on his bony bum. Another lightning bolt is sewn in the middle of the knapsack. A store-bought decal. He probably was called Flash, or Bolt. Another guy is chasing him. I can hear the unattached soles of his shoes slapping the pavement. The cuffs of his pants flap above his ankles. He runs with one leg held straight, listing to the right like a boat in high seas. One arm is bent behind his head, his hand holding onto a sleeping bag rolled up on top of his knapsack, somewhat secured with frazzled twine. His other hand is deep in his pocket. A gun?

Cindy aims her phone over the roof of the car, following the action. The two guys round the corner at the lights on Major Street and she gets back into the car.

"Should I follow them?" I say, revving the engine and thinking this is a great example of crime and homelessness merging.

"Naw. It's no contest. The guy in black will get away. He'll dodge down an alley. He's the dealer. I think he probably shorted the homeless guy."

"Should we go to the police?"

Cindy looks at me incredulously, her green eyes wide. "Over that? You're kidding me. That was nothing."

"It kind of looked like something, like he had a gun. The homeless guy I mean. Shouldn't we report that?"

"What, and wreck his whole life? Besides, I doubt he had a gun. He was just acting as if he had one in his pocket to scare the dealer."

That didn't make sense to me. "But the dealer wouldn't see that the other guy had his hand in his pocket. He was too far ahead and looking forward. So why pretend?"

"It's hard to fathom the mind of someone mentally ill, Robin. He thought he was being threatening, and that's all that counts. To him."

I know far less about the streets than Cindy and give her the benefit of the doubt. I look back at the line and see that it has reconfigured back into some semblance of order. It's as if nothing had happened. My stomach is in knots. It needs ice cream. I think about that for a minute. Might be too cold. So maybe cheese. I have to get out of here.

"I've seen enough," I say to Cindy. "This has been quite the education for me this morning, but I'm hungry." I look at my watch. It's now almost one o'clock. "It's lunch time. Let's head back to the office."

"Sure, let's take University south, it'll be faster than Spadina."

As we round the corner at College and University, I say, "This is where the fat cat works, at the Hydro building. The jerk in the Mercedes. What's his name? Rowland. Right, Ronald Rowland."

Cindy looks up from scrolling through her pictures on her phone. "Yup. More power to him."

"That's not funny, Cindy."

"Then why are you laughing?"

And I am, it was pretty funny. Although God knows he doesn't need any more power. The traffic going south on University Avenue is fast and loose. We whiz past what I call Hospital Row, aiming for the lake. I turn left and head east to the *Express* building.

Once we're parked at my bra size, we trot to the elevator and then check our phones on the way up. I've missed three calls. I decide that I'll check my messages while I eat and not in the elevator. I jam my phone back into my purse. Finally in the office and seated at my desk, I root in my bag for my lunch and pull out the now squished meatloaf sandwich and my phone. Cindy has veered off to the toilet. Small bladder for such a big human being.

I carefully unwrap the tinfoil on my sandwich and flatten it, making a plate. I then squeeze out some ketchup onto the foil from one of those little sachets that I snaffled from some take out joint and dip a corner of the sandwich into it. Nirvana. As I chew, I tap my phone for messages. An electronic voice tells me my voice messaging service is full. That always pisses me off. It should have infinite space. I listen to the first message. It's from Sally Josper, asking me to confirm my six o'clock naturopathic appointment. I thought it was six-thirty, so I'm glad she left a message. I hadn't texted her back after Cindy read her message to me in the car. I delete her voicemail and quickly text her back, rather than return the call. I'll go. *I have to get my drinking and eating under control*, I think, while looking at my sandwich and wondering where the first half went.

The next message is from my brother Andrew. I have my phone on speaker and quickly lower the volume until his supercilious voice is barely audible. He sounds like a seagull on speed, cawing away in his fake British accent. He thinks if he talks like that it makes him one of *them*, his Rosedale neighbours, who all talk as if they've come from England, the blessed mother country. I don't want people to know I have a brother like Andrew and sense that, behind me, Karen Marumbo has perked up a bit and is listening to my calls. I would likely do the same. I know she's not deliberately eavesdropping; it's lunch and she's just looking around while she munches at her desk after investigating the government's pandemic spending for several hours. It's a diversion, and not a very interesting one. But still. I turn the volume down further.

I missed the first part of his conversation and replay the message. His bleat comes through loud and clear, and I hear Karen's chair move on the tiles. She's probably leaning forward, now actively listening. Our Karen is not only tenacious and talented, she's very curious. All perfect attributes for a really good journalist. Do I want her listening in? Nope. I like and admire her, but this is my business. I need to make a difficult decision. Do I take him off speaker and hold the device to my ear? I decide I have to risk brain cancer. I tap off the speaker function and hold the phone up. The message is short. He wants me to call him with an okay on renting out the family cottage to some of his highly connected and wealthy friends next week and over Easter weekend. The cottage was named Pair o' Dice years ago, and now I wish the dice had been tossed more in my favour. I delete the message with an extra hard tap. It leaves a greasy mayonnaise smudge on my phone screen.

Andrew infuriates me. He's so bossy. A bully, really. He thinks because he's rich and uses Farrow & Ball paint on his front door that he owns the family cottage. There's no asking me if I think it's okay, oh no, he just wants me to put my seal of approval on a deal he's no doubt already made. Well, it's my cottage too, and I need to be consulted before a rental is solidified. I know I'm going to agree to the deal, we need the income to help pay the whopping taxes the Town of Huntsville charges, but out of spite, I'll bug him. It's immature, I know, but geezus, he pisses me off with his holier-than-thou attitude.

I text him a list of questions, giving my dignity muscle some exercise. Who exactly is he renting it to? Is the driveway plowed? Are the winter potholes in the driveway filled in? Has he hired cleaners to get rid of the mouse poo? To make up the beds? To clean the windows? Is the ice out? What shape is the dock in? Should they be told not to use it? How much is he asking?

He texts back in seconds. "Yes, to all of the above."

I can't believe it. That's not an answer. So dismissive. Where on earth did he learn how to be so degrading? To be so demeaning to his sister? I'm fuming. I smash my meatloaf sandwich into the ketchup and snarl off a bite. My tinfoil plate crumples sideways and ketchup drips onto my desk.

"Fuckity fuck fuck," I say.

Cindy looks up from her computer. She's finished her soup. "Robin?"

"My brother," I say as I wipe up the mess.

"Oh." She goes back to writing her article. Cindy knows all about my brother and the way he treats me.

I rip another bite out of my sandwich, grab my phone, and head over to the coffee stand by the north side of the building. I'm going to call the fucker. It's not going to be pretty and I don't want to be overheard. My pit bull jaws pulverize the grainy brown bread as I walk, scrolling to find his number. I connect and wait while it rings. I know he's got his phone right there beside him on his desk. I know this because he texted me right back. He's seen my name come up on his caller ID and is making me wait. He knows he's pissed me off because he did it on purpose. Finally, he answers, just before his answering service kicks in, on the fifth ring.

"Andrew MacFarland." He's pretending he hasn't looked at the caller ID and is acting all professional.

"I asked you a list of questions about this supposed rental and I need them answered before you make the deal. Pair o' Dice is my cottage too."

"Oh hello, Robin. You eating?"

I see red. *Fuckhead.*

He laughs. "The potential renters are clients of mine, so I know they're fine. Three great guys."

"Oh, just like that guy whose money you handled, that rich actor, who murdered a young woman by making a bear attack her? Clients like that?" A couple of springs ago, I discovered that one of his clients was a murderer. It was a front-page extravaganza and Andrew hasn't forgiven me yet.

He pauses. He's been caught. He did have a killer as a client and it's stuck in his craw. "No, these are old Toronto families. Highly connected, politically and economically. You needn't worry. One lives on Post Road and the other is on Dunvegan. Their money is good, trust me."

Why he won't give me their names flummoxes me. "Who? And didn't that actor live on Bennington Heights? Or was it Roxborough?"

He avoids my question, knowing I'm right, that an address is no guarantee of a moral code. I'm out to do battle with him. "They want anonymity, Robin, they just want to get away for the week before Easter and then that long weekend as well, out of the media spotlight and their public jobs."

I let it go. I don't really care and I'm tired of this life-long dance with Andrew. "How much have you quoted them?"

"Oh, don't worry about that either. More than enough to cover all the expenses, the cleaning, the road plowing, and what not, plus the taxes for the whole year."

"So, thousands?"

"Yes, thousands."

"But you won't say how much?"

"You sure are feisty this afternoon, Robin."

I think, *fuck off, Andrew*. He knows I'm thinking it while the silence stretches.

He names a figure. It's unbelievable. I capitulate. "So, you've made all the arrangements to open the place up?"

"Of course I have."

"Of course I have." I mimic his smarmy voice. He means his personal assistant did it. Now it's his turn to say nothing.

"Sounds like a good deal, Andrew. Go ahead. Although you probably already have, given it's Friday and Easter Weekend is next weekend. They're probably already there now, right?" I'm squeezing the words out through my teeth.

"I'm so glad you approve. And yes, they are." He's raised his voice to a miffed loftiness. How dare I question him.

"Goodbye."

I'm so angry at him I could scream. If my phone had been an old rotary dial, I would have slammed the receiver down. It feels so impotent to just tap the little red button and disconnect the call, but that's what I do. But I do it three times. *Tap, tap, tap.* The prick made the deal before consulting me. I walk back to my desk, breathing deeply, trying to dissipate the rage. Derrick Johnston dodges to the left as he passes me in the aisle. He knows what's good for him.

I thrust my chair under my desk. Cindy says, "Better now?"

I answer her with a snort and focus on the article. Causes of homelessness. I have a list and I make an outline for carefully constructed paragraphs around each topic. Hay Hair walks by in her tight, blue satiny pencil skirt, no wet spot now, and tangos into Doug's office on her stilettos. I still can't believe she was homeless for four years. I hear murmurings through his office door. What are they talking about? It goes on for a while. I get to number three on my list, environmental extraction projects, courtesy of Lydia at the shelter.

Eventually, Shirley shuts Doug's door behind her, wiggles across the floor, and stops in front of my desk. She places a blue nail on her chin and smiles sweetly while she pretends to push on a dimple, which she doesn't have. It's her Betty Boop look. "Come into my office, you two."

I glance at Cindy and raise my eyebrows as I stand up. Despite the little girl poses, the highly sexed poses, the Doberman Pinscher poses, Shirley Hay Hair must be obeyed. She's the boss. We follow her through the desks into her office, first me like a shrinking violet and then Cindy like a lumbering Walmart truck, grunting behind me. Hay Hair's perfume and clinging cigarette smoke leave a cloudy trail of chemicals behind her. I pull up my turtleneck as I let Cindy pass me before I shut Shirley's office door. What the hell does she want now?

"Sit, sit," she coos, waving her arm expansively over the files stacked on the two chairs in front of her desk. It's a fake invitation.

We stand.

"Oh, be like that." She sits and crosses her legs. It's an event. Fluorescent lights bounce off her blue shellacked toenails poking through her open-toed shoes as she pumps her foot. "I've just been talking to Doug and he's so right sometimes." Does this mean that she was wrong about something? And who wears open-toed shoes in March? "We talked about the two homelessness articles you were doing, Cindy with the crime angle, and Robin with the causes angle."

Oh, here we go. Cindy shifts her feet. Her back still hurts from the fall.

"Anyway, Doug, I mean Mr. Ascot, thinks it's really just one article. I argued it was two, you know, one for each of you, but he made some good points. So, the two of you are to collaborate."

I pipe up. "Why doesn't Cindy write the article and I go back to roofing?"

"Haha. No." She puts her finger on her fake dimple again and smiles at me. "Robin, you are more...how shall I say it?...more intuitive than Cindy, and although she gets the facts, you get the feeling. I need both of you on the article."

Cindy says, "Oh come on, Hay Hair, I've written lots of in-depth articles. Robin doesn't really want to do this article. She wants to do the roofing one. Shingles versus sheet metal."

Shirley abruptly stands up, turns her back, and looks out her window at the Gardiner Expressway. She says nothing for a full minute, which is a very long time for her, and I see her shoulders go up and down. She's breathing hard. When she turns around, her eyes look moist. "What did you call me?"

Cindy's mouth opens and shuts. She's made a colossal error. Shirley's nickname has become so common, so frequently used, it just slid out of Cindy's mouth. "I didn't call you anything. I was clearing my throat." She demonstrates clearing her throat so that it comes out sort of like "Hay Hair." Shirley looks like she needs more convincing, so Cindy does it again. To give her credit, it does sound remarkably like "Hay Hair."

"Oh," says Shirley, smiling brightly. "Anyway, you two work together. It's one article. Try to think up a good title. Something snappy that will make readers curious about the content." She waves her hand. We are dismissed.

I whisper to Cindy as we head back to our desks, "Good save, Cindy."

"That was a close call."

When I sit down, my phone vibrates and skitters across the desk. It's my daughter Maggie. "Hi, sweetheart."

Maggie is breathing hard, as if she's been running a mile, full-speed. "Mom, didn't you get my message? I called you two hours ago." And this is coming from my daughter who doesn't return my calls for days? "It's coming now. The baby. Come."

Oh, my God. That was the third message. I got sidelined by Andrew's call. I scrunch up my tinfoil plate, find my car keys in my bag, and kick my chair under my desk. "I'm coming right now. Right now. I'll be there in ten minutes." Oh, geezus. Maggie's having her baby.

Cindy is watching me. Her eyes are the startled green of a deer's reflected in the headlights of a car on a country road at night. "What's going on?"

I grab my bag, and say, "The baby," as I race to the elevator.

CHAPTER 9

Maggie's having a baby! Right now! Oh God. It feels like bits of my body are vibrating off as the elevator creeps down to the parking garage. Why is it going so slowly? I search in my bag for the beef jerky. My fingers circle around it just as the doors whisper open. I hoof it to my car, plucking off pieces with my teeth as I go, managing to inhale the whole thing before I get there. I stuff myself into my seat and jab the key in the ignition. Please start, please start. It coughs into life but there's a ding from my dash. A red light. I peer at the little icon of a gas pump. Fuck. I'm almost out. I knew I should have filled up before coming back to the office this afternoon with Cindy. Just shit. Why am I so stupid?

Now I have to really get my skates on. I roar up the three ramps to the garage door, squeal right onto Yonge, take a fast right onto Adelaide, breathe deeply at Jarvis waiting for the damn green light to turn orange so I can turn left, and peel into the station at Richmond and Jarvis. I thrust my credit card into the pump, jam the nozzle into the gas tank which reminds me briefly of Ralph's fun time nozzle, and finally take a breath. I think about my next steps. While the gas fills up the tank, I fill up with dread. I'm missing a key piece of information.

Exactly where is Maggie having the baby?

Christ. I can't believe I don't know this. There was talk about her having it at home. In one of those inflatable tubs that supposedly make the journey into childbirth a little easier.

73

Hahaha. Marketing wizardry that didn't fool me for a second. Was that idea nixed? Right. I remember now. Yes, it was. But did that mean they weren't having the baby at home? *Think, Robin, think.* She had a doula. She had a midwife. Probably at home, then. I decide to go there first.

I zip across the downtown core on Richmond, heading west. She and Winchester have a first-floor apartment in an old Victorian house at the quieter end of Richmond, near Portland. I can't ditch my car on Richmond because I don't know how long I'll be and it's a tow away zone after three. I turn left onto Maud and find a legal spot near the discount hardware store on Adelaide, just a block away. I squelch through the slush to her front door and lift my hand to knock when it opens.

A broad-faced, pink-cheeked young woman takes a step back with her hand on her chest. "Oh, I didn't expect anyone to be there." She's holding a bulging green garbage bag.

"Sorry I startled you," I say. This must be the midwife. "Maggie?"

"Oh, Maggie is just fine. I'm Barbara, her midwife. She's resting comfortably with the baby."

She's had the baby? I've missed the birth? Geezus, that was fast. I'm simultaneously relieved and devastated. Relieved because I really didn't want to witness blood and placenta pumping out of my daughter's vagina. So gross. But devasted because I've missed a miracle. My first grandchild entered the world and I wasn't there to see it happen. If I hadn't been flinging angry words around with Andrew, I would have been here in time. "They're in the back bedroom?" I ask.

Over the midwife's shoulder another person appears. The three of us crowd together in the small foyer. "I'm Christine, Maggie's doula. She did great. It wasn't that long a labour, considering it's her first."

"That's an understatement," says Barbara. She shifts the green garbage bag to her other hand. It must be heavy. "Tons of laundry," she says. "Christine's right. It was very fast. The next time she should call me immediately. It was a bit of a race against time for me to get here," she laughs. "That's one impatient baby."

Just like her mother, I think. "Thank you so much for taking care of her." I'm upset I missed the birth. "I was supposed to be here as well, but I didn't make it."

"No way you could have," says Barbara, soothingly.

She seems kind and I'm grateful that Maggie has a compassionate midwife. "Well, thanks again. I'll just head in to see her now."

I extricate myself from the two kind women and feel my way down the darkened hall, past the doors to their living room and kitchen. I feel a little woozy because the lights have been shut off and the floors are somewhat slanted, being an old Toronto house. When I get to Maggie and Winchester's bedroom, I stop and look through a crack in the slightly open door. Mother and father are sleeping on the bed, a tiny baby on Winchester's bare chest. It is such a beautiful sight, so peaceful, so tranquil. I snap a photo.

"Hi, Mom." Maggie's eyes remain closed. She's heard the click from my phone.

I whisper, "Sorry if I woke you. And sorry I didn't get here in time, honey." I tiptoe to the edge of her bed.

One eye opens, "Oh, there's no way you could have made it. This baby was in a big hurry to get out into the world."

I'm so relieved she hasn't made me feel guilty for not picking up her message. I could have made it. Maybe. "But still. It's a major, life-altering event. I feel badly. Do you need me to get you anything?"

"Don't worry about it, Mom. I know you get really busy at the office. Maybe a glass of water. I've only had ice chips for the past couple of hours."

"Do you want me to warm the water up in your microwave?"

"Sure. That might be better than something really cold. I'm feeling a bit chilled."

"Coming right up," I say, grateful to have something to do. I'm buzzing with excitement.

I let the tap run for a bit to get any lead out of the old pipes and then nuke it for not quite a minute to heat it up. While it's heating, my phone buzzes in my pocket. I check the caller ID. Jocelyn? Andrew's wife? I let it go to messages. She's as bad as he is. Judging people by how much money they make. Wearing her damn pearl earrings. Her off-white woolen suit. Her burgundy pumps with her burgundy clutch bag. Her silky hair. I punch decline and then it rings again. What? Why is she calling me twice? It must be an emergency. Maybe Andrew's twisted heart just twisted into an attack. I chastise myself for my evil thoughts as I pick up. He is, after all, my brother and deep down I think I love him. "Hello?"

"Oh Robin, I'm glad I caught you." Jocelyn's breathy voice wraps around fake British accented vowels, just like Andrew's. Why do they do that? So jolly hockey sticks. So sponge toffee. So Big Ben. So pretentious.

"Hello, Jocelyn." I try to sound friendly, but I'm sure I'm wide of the mark.

"I was just talking to Andrew and he asked me to call you. About the cottage. He's on his way up now."

I'm baffled. "But it's rented," I say.

"Ah, um, there's been a slight problem."

I'm impatient. "It must be more than a slight problem if he's heading up to solve it."

"Well, it is."

The glass of water in my hand is cooling off now. I want to get it in to Maggie and start walking to her bedroom. I also want to get a closer look at that brand new, teensy baby. My grandchild. I don't even know if it's a boy or a girl. My patience with Jocelyn, Andrew's highly accomplished executive wife, but nonetheless eye candy, is running out. "Spit it out, Jocelyn."

"Well, um, one of the renters has died."

I stop so suddenly in the hallway that water splashes over the rim of the glass. "What the fuck?"

"Oh Robin, you don't need to swear."

Maggie calls from the room, "You okay, Mom?" She's heard me yell.

"Fine darling, fine." I get back to Jocelyn. "How did the person die? Was there a bear attack? And who was it?"

"I don't know, Robin. Andrew was in such a hurry to get there, he didn't expound on the information."

"Expound?" Who says "expound" these days?

"And he's on his way up now?"

"That's what I just said." She's such a bitch. My temper flares. I bite my tongue. "Maybe you need to go too." Her voice slides out of my phone like treacle. The bully. "Maybe he needs you there."

Maybe Jocelyn needed to get the stick out of her ass. "He didn't give you any hints? Have the police been called? Are we liable for his death? Was it a he?"

"I really don't know, Robin."

"Just...fuck. I'm at Maggie's. She's just had her baby."

"Oh, congratulations." She doesn't sound cheery. "A boy or a girl?" She let the swearing go this time.

"I just got here, I don't know yet."

Jocelyn repeats me. "You don't know yet?" She says it like I am a major failure. Judgmental bitch.

"Look, I just got here a minute ago and I can't leave to head up north. There are things happening here." Like Maggie's water is getting ice cold.

Maggie whisper-shouts from the bedroom, "Mom?"

I hold the phone away from my ear. "Be right there, honey."

"So, I guess you don't know the baby's name either."

"Just shut the fuck up, Jocelyn."

There, I said it. I've reached the end of my rope with her. Her gasp delights me.

"Really, you shouldn't use that word, Robin."

That was her comeback to being told to shut up? Pathetic. I rip into her. "I am a writer, Jocelyn. I'll use whatever fucking words I want to use to get the fucking point across. Shut the fuck up. Stop blaming me for things that aren't my fault. So, fuck off." I tap the phone sharply to disconnect.

I stand in the hall holding Maggie's now-cold glass of water. I see little ripples bump across the surface. My hand is shaking.

She makes me so angry. Some wine would be good right about now. I turn around and reheat the water while taking calming breaths. When I deliver it to Maggie, she looks at me questioningly.

She whispers so as not to wake Winchester or the baby. "What was that about, Mom?"

"Oh, nothing. Jocelyn rubs me the wrong way. She gave me some bad news. Some guy passed at the cottage." I'm trying to downplay the effect this news has had on me. The word "passed" is kind of calming.

Maggie jerks in the bed. "What?"

"Ya, Andrew rented it out and the renters just got there today. Somebody died. I can't do anything about that just now. Now, you are far more important to me. Tell me, how are you feeling?"

We're murmuring. She points to her crotch and makes a face.

"I know. So sore. I know it hurts. Is the baby a boy or a girl?"

"A little girl."

A girl! I lean over Winchester's body and take a good look at the baby. Her little lips are a small pink bow in a scrunched up new baby face. "She's absolutely beautiful." My heart feels like it's been squeezed. I touch the top of her still damp head very lightly. "Have you got a name for her yet?"

"No, not yet. We're considering a few." She yawns. "I'm pretty tired, Mom. Tell the other kids the baby's come and go deal with the cottage and Uncle Andrew. I'll sleep for a bit. Winchester and I will be fine on our own for a few days. He's got time off work."

I've been dismissed. But I'm okay with that. New parents need their space to bond with their baby. "Okay, honeybun. I'll come over when I can." I do hope that's true, but with a death up at the cottage in Huntsville it might be impossible. If I go, I might have to stay a few days. Should I get on the highway and head up? Andrew would be able to handle it, but my journalist nose twitches. Why hadn't he told me who was renting? And I still didn't know how the person died.

I stagger down the lopsided hallway and make sure the lock on the front door catches behind me as I head into the dreary March day. It seems bizarre that Easter weekend is just a week away. It must be very early this year. Not that I kept track of the holiday, being a Buddhist, but didn't Easter usually fall in the middle of April? When the weather warms up and tulips are beginning to break through the earth? When the world is renewing? When rabbits hop out of caves? I laugh at myself. I know I got it wrong.

I clomp through the wet snow on the way back to my car. It reminds me of brown sugar and I get a sudden craving for oatmeal cookies. *Robin. You are a food addict. You have an eating disorder.* Oh God, I remember my appointment with Sally Josper. I'll never be able to see her today. Not if I have to get in my car and head north. Maybe Ralph will come with me. I can't remember what shift he's on. Was he home last night? Oh, right. I watched some Netflix alone and then hit the hay. He got in after midnight, woke me up clambering into bed. I dwell on the fun time that followed for a moment. This means that he has the weekend off, unless he's been called out for overtime on a major incident of some sort.

What to do, what to do. Should I head up north? Before I start the car, I call Ralph on his private cell phone. He has this thing about not using the police-issued devices for his personal communication. It's not that he's paranoid about big brother, but he's cautious. That's the word he uses. Or sometimes he uses the word "boundaried." Whatever. He knows that I know he works for an organization that wiretaps. When I get settled in the car, I call him.

He doesn't pick up. I try not to imagine why, although thoughts of him getting shot dart like bullets across my brain. I leave a message. "Hi sweetie, I don't want to alarm you, but a person renting the cottage has died. I think I should go up. What do you think? If you think I should, do you want to come with me? I hope so. You'll be a good buffer against Andrew. He's on his way up now. Also, I have some exciting news."

I turn the ignition and head back to the office on Adelaide. My phone immediately rings on the seat beside me. Ralph. I look around for cops and then press the answer and the speaker buttons. The irony that I'm talking on a handheld device breaking the law while talking to a cop isn't lost on me. "Hi, Ralph."

"Maggie? She have the baby?"

I loved Ralph's priorities.

"Yes, a tiny baby girl. No name yet. She's beautiful." I was gushing.

"Congratulations. How was the birth?"

"Very fast. I didn't make it in time."

"You're kidding? That's unbelievable for a first. My first took thirty-six hours."

Sometimes I forget that Ralph had a whole other family. He never talked about it. I knew there was something awful in his past but he didn't want to unpack that baggage in front of me. I often wondered if he ever would. Last summer in Nova Scotia I'd learned he had a restraining order against his wife. And that tidbit of information had to be dragged out of him.

"Ya, it was very quick. But everyone is well. They were pretty much asleep by the time I got there."

"That's such good news, Robin. And what's this about someone dying at your cottage?"

"A renter."

"A renter? Who?"

"I don't know that. Andrew won't tell me. Some honchos. They all have fancy addresses."

"I'm sure they do. He runs with an interesting crowd."

"You can say that again."

I turn right onto University and then a quick left onto Wellington.

"How did the person die?"

"I don't know that either."

"Suspicious?"

"I don't know that either."

"So, you think you should go up?"

"I don't know that either."

Ralph laughs at me. "Well, if you do decide, it's my weekend off. I could come with you. I personally think you should go. It's your cottage and Andrew, well, Andrew is Andrew."

I think Ralph remembers how Andrew doesn't seem able to admit his type of people can be criminals. "You'd come?" I sound like I'm begging. That's because I am.

"Of course, sweetie. But call Andrew and get more information. You know, just so you can decide if you should go and so I'm not walking in there blindly."

"Okay. I will. I'll call you back." Sounded like he already knew I'd be going up.

I call Andrew. He doesn't like to talk while he's driving, which is why he had Jocelyn call me, even though his car is equipped with Bluetooth and everything. Maybe his little pea brain can't cope with driving a car and a conversation at the same time.

"Andrew MacFarland." He sounds panic-stricken.

It must be bad if he answered. "Hi, it's me. I heard from Jocelyn. I am trying to decide if I should come up." He says nothing but I can hear him breathing. I ask, "You okay?"

"Not really. This is a catastrophe. A fucking shit show."

Andrew swearing? Holy smokes. Something really bad has happened. "Andrew? What's happened? Who died?"

Andrew's voice is shaking. "The premier, Robin. The premier of Ontario. Philip Kahn."

CHAPTER 10

THE PREMIER? THE PREMIER OF Ontario? Kahn?" I'm
squealing. And then I'm speechless. Andrew rented our shabby,
ancient Muskoka cottage to the hifalutin premier? And now that
premier is dead? Oh, my God. I have to call Ralph right back. I
have to go north. "Who else? Who else is there?" I'm squawking
now.

Andrew drawls, "Just a CEO of a company and the mayor.
Their wives. Six people all together." Now Andrew was trying to
act all casual.

"The mayor? Of Toronto?" I'm screeching into the phone while
I zoom down University to the office.

"And a CEO of a company."

"Do I know this person?"

"I doubt it."

He was probably right. I don't run in the same circles. Thank
God.

I turn left on Wellington, then right on Yonge. "So, the mayor,
the premier, and this CEO guy. And their wives."

"That's about it."

"And why the hell didn't you tell me who you were renting to?"

"They wanted privacy, Robin. I told you that." He is so
condescending.

"Why? Are they being bribed or something? Or doing
something that's not quite kosher? You handling a questionable
money transaction, Andrew? Why couldn't you tell even your

own sister?"

My reporter's instinct is kicking in. Something is going on. This had to do with money.

"Nothing like that. I've been hired to help raise funds, you know, from my stable of investors, once an agreement between the three partners in the deal is struck."

I was right. This benefitted my narcissistic brother. Damn money. "Spill the beans, Andrew. What kind of deal? What the hell are you into?" Like most very rich people, there was no doubt something shady about this deal. I could sense it. I've had it with him.

"Don't be like that. It's a good thing for society."

I doubted that, not if fat cat conservative Andrew was at the helm. "What kind of deal?"

"They're working on some sort of energy package and they wanted to hammer out the details. In private. I was sworn to secrecy by the CEO of Ontario Hydro. Rowland. But I guess that's changed." He pauses. He's regretting his big mouth. I can tell he's thinking about who he's talking to. A reporter. "You better not tell anyone about the deal. The death is one thing, but not the deal. This is off the record, Robin. Off the record. Do you hear me?"

Andrew had raised his voice. Well, well. Isn't that interesting? And now he's trying to save his ass. I say, "Don't be ridiculous, Andrew. I know that Rowland guy. We bump into each other." I suppress a laugh at my wit. "This isn't cloak and dagger stuff. Energy deals are happening all the time. It's not worth my while to pay attention to them all."

I love putting Andrew down. He thinks he's so high and mighty.

"Oh, don't you believe it. This was a major proposition. Worth billions."

My ears perk up. Billions? A motive for murder? "So, do you think the premier was murdered?"

Andrew laughs outright. "Are you kidding? By who?"

"Whom, Andrew. Whom. By whom." I love correcting him.

"Whatever. But not those guys. Those guys are friends. I hear it was a sudden health incident."

"Heart attack? Stroke? What happened?"

He clears his throat. This is what he does when he's covering up some kind of failing. It's his default signal. He doesn't know how the premier died. The next thing that comes out of his mouth will be uproariously snobby.

"That's for me to know and you to find out."

"Oh Andrew, don't be so childish. Why don't you just say you don't know?"

I can hear his flat run car tires humming on the road as his Porsche speeds through the wilderness to the cottage. Andrew was thinking about how he should play this out without harming himself.

He asks, "Are you coming up?" I can tell he doesn't want me to. His voice has a steel edge that would cut through the most polite of inquiries.

"Oh yes, I think I'd better," I say snippily, dashing his hopes. "Ralph and I will arrive shortly after dinner. I'm sure you need some help with the media." And the police, I'm thinking.

"The media? Really? Just because the premier is kaput?"

Kaput? Using the word "kaput" to describe the loss of a life? Was my brother a sociopath? Probably, but I can't think about that now. I put on my patronizing voice. "Andrew, Andrew. The premier of Ontario, Canada's most heavily populated province, has died suddenly. The media is going to be all over this. So are the police." I wasn't sure about the police, but I liked to bug Andrew.

I could smell the wheels smoking in his little rat brain as loudly as I could hear his wheels smoking on the highway. Now he's seeing there's a personal benefit to him if I'm there. All of a sudden, the tone of his voice changes. He wants me to come. There's that clipped, fake North Toronto British accent again. "It would be nice if you could come, Robin. You could handle the media. You'd be good at that. And Ralph can help with the police." He skips a beat. It cost him to be nice to me and he needs to regroup. "But don't mention the deal. Just say it was a spring skiing holiday. Or something."

"Or something, Andrew." I fake laugh and make no promises. I'm not going to lie for him. "I gotta go. I'm heading into the bowels of my work's parking garage. No signal."

"You've been talking to me while driving?"

"Just like you, Andrew," I shoot back.

"Where have you been?" he asks. Like he cares.

"Maggie's. She's had her baby."

Andrew is my father's son, a racist. But Andrew hides it better by contributing to various Black initiatives. When I told him Maggie and Winchester were married, he said, "That's nice," and changed the topic. He didn't approve of interracial marriages. I disconnect before he can say anything far too polite to be genuine as I drive down the ramp to my office building's parking garage.

When I get to my desk in the newsroom, Cindy looks up. "That was quick." She checks her watch. "You've been gone just over an hour. Everything okay?"

"The baby came wildly fast and Maggie needed to sleep. Winchester and the baby were already out like a light when I arrived. She was so adorable, so tiny, curled up on his chest."

I throw my car keys on my desk. They jangle and skitter across the Formica. I'm still agitated by Andrew's news. Cindy looks at them and then at me.

"A baby girl!" She tilts her head. "Did you want a boy?" Cindy's sensed my mood and is treading carefully.

"No name yet. She sure is a beauty." I start typing furiously. I have to get the damn homeless article done today if I'm going to be away for a few days.

"So-o-o, what's up?" Cindy perseveres.

"Look. I have to get this article written today, or my share of it. I have to go up north. If I don't get it done, can you finish it off for me?"

Cindy isn't fooled for a second. She knows I'm holding something back. And what a something it is. But should I tell her? It's such a scoop. The premier. Philip Kahn. Dead. She'd love it.

Cindy starts fishing. She says, oh so sweetly, "And why is that?"

"Look, Cindy, I can't tell you. It's really big."

"Thanks a bunch. Now you have me really interested." She lowers her voice to a soothing hum. "Come on. You can tell me."

Cindy is pleading. I relent. I trust her. Most of the time. "But you can't tell a soul. Not a soul."

She crosses her heart with her right hand. Her left hand is out of sight under her desk. I'm pretty sure her fingers are crossed.

"The premier, the mayor, a CEO of some major company, and their wives rented our cottage. They got there today around three."

"That's not really big news, Robin." She thinks for a second. "Oh, is that what you were arguing with Andrew about earlier? Renting the cottage?"

Cindy is formulating a timeline.

"Yes, he did it without checking in with me. Anyway…"

"Anyway, what?"

I can't bring myself to say what's happened. My lovely cottage that's been in the family for generations is once again the scene of a horrible event. Last spring, Cindy and I discovered the bear-mangled body of a female stagehand in the woods near our cottage. And now this? Was the place cursed? Would I ever be able to enjoy another relaxing summer there, ever again? God, the whole thing makes me dizzy.

"What, Robin? Now what's happened? Come on, Robin. Tell me. I can't help you unless I know what's going on. And I think it's very bad." She leans toward me, almost touching, genuine concern in her eyes. She knows I am a fainter.

I don't want her help. I have Ralph. On the other hand, she is such a good friend and maybe I do need her help. She probably knows me better than Ralph. But I really don't want her to pounce upon the news like the rabid reporter she is.

"You have to promise me, off the record. This isn't a story for the paper," I lie. Of course it was. The news was starting to sink into my mind and become a reality. I can't believe that the premier is dead. At my cottage. Oh God. The horror of it scuttles in my veins. My feet have disappeared. And my old friend, the snake, is hissing in my ears. Oh God, I'm having a full-blown panic attack. The next step is losing my eyesight, black filigree strands blinding my vision. And then, of course, the faint.

"I already promised. It's off the record." Her left hand is still under her desk. "You okay, Robin?"

No, I'm not okay. My brain is now banging against my skull. Little black specks are floating across my eyes. Air is seeping out of my pores. Am I going to faint? Cindy's voice sounds distant, like she's in another room. Or dimension.

"Um-m-m, Robin, put your head between your knees. You look like you're going to faint."

She knows me so well. I sure am a fainter. I bend over and mumble into my lap, "The premier is dead."

"Pardon me. I'm not sure I heard you correctly. Did you say Premier Philip Kahn, is dead?" Cindy asks as if she is asking about the weather. She rubs my back in long slow loops. To give her credit, her circles didn't falter for a second as she heard the astonishing news.

"Yes. Philip Khan."

"Okay. Don't worry. Breathe deeply. Just breathe deeply." She pauses for a second, trying to relax me as she casually asks, "This happened at your cottage? Today?"

"Yes." The tingling is leaving my fingertips, although the blood still pounds in my ears like waves crashing on a beach. "Jocelyn called me and told me to call Andrew. He's on his way up now. So I called him and he told me. Just now. In the car. Coming home from Maggie's." In for a penny, in for a pound. I might as well tell her everything. "He told me the three men wanted to work on an energy deal in private. He didn't want me to mention it."

"Why not? Energy deals are a dime a dozen." She's still rubbing my back in slow lazy circles.

"He said it was worth billions. Andrew's raising the funds from his investors."

"Billions?" Cindy rolls the word around in her mouth.

I'm feeling better and carefully sit up. "Thanks, Cindy." She pushes her chair back to her desk, her head cocked to the side, assessing me. Coming to the conclusion that I'm out of the woods and won't faint, I see her brain calculating the possibilities of what sort of energy deal could be worth billions.

I pat down my hair and confirm. "Yes, billions. And of course now he's worried the deal will go south if the premier is, as he said, 'kaput.'"

"Kaput? He said that? Your brother is a piece of work."

"Not news, Cindy." I'm feeling so out of sorts.

"It's the deal, isn't it? That's really what he wants to be kept quiet. Not the death." She pauses, thinking. "Well, that isn't going to happen. How long ago did Kahn die?"

I check my phone. It's now almost four o'clock. God, I'll never get that article finished today. "I think around three. Just after is my guess. I have to go up."

"This is hot, hot news." Cindy's eyes are sparking with excitement.

"Yes, it must have been not quite an hour ago. Or that's when Jocelyn called me. Maybe Andrew was told earlier, but it wouldn't have been much earlier, because their rental didn't start until three. Oh, so yes, about three."

"I'm going with you."

"No, thanks, but that's okay, Ralph is coming with me." Ralph and Cindy aren't that great together. Cat fights come to mind.

Cindy's reading my mind. "We get along better now, since Nova Scotia. We worked out our issues. I think I should come. To help."

She's right. They do get along better now. Besides, she's known me for over thirty years. She knows, almost instinctively, what's going on with me at any given time. She can read me like a book. But what kind of help she thinks I need is beyond me. Besides, although she and Ralph get along better, it still isn't always copesetic. I say, "There isn't room at the cottage." I was lying again.

"It's got six bedrooms, right? Six?" I feel my stomach contract. I'd been caught in the lie. Cindy had been at the cottage with me before. Of course she knew how many bedrooms there were. She holds up six fingers and then bends them down as she talks. "One for Andrew, one for each of the guests and their spouses, so that's three more, one for you and Ralph, and one for moi. That makes six."

Clearly, she really wants to come. She's fighting me on it. I try one last time. "But the homeless article."

"We'll do it up there in the off times. Does Ralph know about this?"

"Oh God," I moan, "no, he doesn't. When I talked to him earlier I just said that Andrew was on the way up because someone had died and I thought I should go too. I didn't say who it was. Ralph said he'd go with me. When I talked to him, I didn't know it was Kahn who'd died." I'm blathering.

My phone rings. I hear its muffled tone deep in my purse. I don't want to talk to anyone. But maybe it's Maggie.

"You going to answer that?"

I dig the phone out and see from the ID that it's Ralph. Speak of the devil.

"Ralph," I say to Cindy, holding the phone in my hand.

She spreads her arms, her hands wide in a what-are-you-waiting-for gesture.

I nod, gather my resources, and answer it. "Hi, Ralph."

"Robin, I just heard that the premier died suddenly in Muskoka, near Huntsville."

How did he hear that? God, news travelled fast. "Ah, yes, yes. Big news. There's something I have to tell you, Ralph."

"Can you believe it? The premier. He was so young too. Suddenly dead. Can you believe it?"

I say it again. "Ralph, there's something I have to tell you."

I can tell he is preoccupied, furiously typing away at his computer. Finally, the tapping of his keyboard stops and I have his attention. "Sorry, paperwork. What do you have to tell me?"

"He died at my cottage."

"At Pair o' Dice? You're kidding me. Why was he even there?"

"Andrew rented it to him. And the Mayor of Toronto.

McCormick. And the CEO of Ontario Hydro. Rowland. And their wives."

Ralph takes a moment to absorb the news. "How soon can you get home?"

"I have this homeless article to write…"

"I think the premier's death at your cottage is far more pressing news than your article. Just talk to Shirley and explain the situation to her. She'll understand. We should leave as soon as possible."

"What's the hurry?"

"Remember the police up there?"

He's referring to the semi-literate Huntsville force of cops.

"Why worry about them? Andrew said the death was a health incident. Do you think it's suspicious?"

"All sudden deaths need to be investigated by the police." He says this like he's reading it out of a textbook.

"Oh." Ralph doesn't trust the local police to do an adequate job. "I see your point. I was wondering if the police would be called. I'll talk to Shirley."

"She'll understand."

"I hope so. And Ralph?"

"Yes, sweetie?"

"Um-m-m." How do I tell him? "Cindy's coming."

"Aw, Robin. Don't let her."

"I already said she could."

More tapping in the background. Then silence. "Okay, okay, I know she's a good friend and you're probably upset about another death at your cottage. I understand. You need your friend. But she drives her own car."

He didn't want to spend more time with her than he had to. I laugh, "No problemo, Ralphie."

"Don't call me Ralphie."

"Okay, Ralphesco."

He gives up. "Get home soon, and we'll head up. We can stop for food on the way."

"Good plan." I'm already starving for a highway hamburger.

CHAPTER 11

CINDY STOPS TYPING FOR A minute and turns her head to me. "So, it's a go? We're leaving right away?"

"Apparently. You're to take your own car."

"Really? That's kind of a waste of gas. Oh, let me guess, Ralph's stipulation?"

This is embarrassing. "Well, you know…" I wiggle my hand back and forth. What can I say? They fight. I change the topic. "But I'm worried about the article." My work ethic is a little too strong sometimes.

"Don't worry. I'll just tell Hay Hair that we'll be doing street interviews on Monday and Tuesday. Why we won't be in. That'll be our cover story for being away those days. We shouldn't tell her why. Not yet." Cindy's speaking in her normal, fairly loud voice. I can't believe it. Here she is, planning some sort of subterfuge through a megaphone.

I can't think of any reason why we shouldn't tell her. It is a bona fide story. I turn down the volume on the conversation, hoping she'll get the hint. "I think it's better if you just tell her the truth." I rethink what I just said. Why am I letting Cindy do the talking with Shirley anyway? It's *my* story. *My* cottage. "I mean to say if *I* tell her the truth. My cottage, Cindy. I'll tell her we might be gone for Monday and Tuesday. And I'll tell her why. The premier's death, et cetera. We do need her permission, you know. And Doug's. Your *boss*, remember?"

The smell of cigarette smoke drifts in from behind me. Oh

God. How long has Shirley been standing there? What has she heard? Cindy was always getting me into trouble with my editor. I hope she hadn't heard Cindy calling her Hay Hair again.

"What's this about Monday and Tuesday?" Shirley asks, her words slice the air like broken shards of glass. She's pissed off.

Cindy bolts upright and spins her chair around. She hasn't smelled the smoke signal. "Oh hi, Shirley. Something's happened. Just now." Cindy is babbling, covering her ass in froth.

Shirley steps forward, closer to our desks. She is not smiling. "The homeless article has happened. There's no taking off now for a long weekend. You can have a long weekend next weekend. Easter. I need that article on my desk by five. A space has been booked for it on Saturday's inside front. That's tomorrow."

In the Saturday paper? Inside front? This article must be really important to her. "Okay, Shirley," I say.

Shirley says to Cindy, "And exactly what's this about street interviews? What's that a cover for?"

So, Shirley has been standing there throughout the whole conversation. She's heard Cindy, but I'm hoping perhaps not me. I can't remember what I said, but I hope it wasn't incriminating. I don't know if Cindy is going to tell her the truth. I can see that she is flipping through the mental file containing what the two of us had talked about in the past three minutes. Shirley watches her, chalking up the time it's taking for Cindy to answer. Giving up on her honesty, Shirley turns to me. "Robin, what's happened?"

Although I am getting better at lying, this doesn't seem like the time for a ploy. I can't figure out why Cindy wants to keep the premier's death a secret. It will be all over the news in minutes anyway, gushing on a tidal wave of media excitement, flooding into Toronto from a Huntsville leak. I look at the TV screen in the corner of the room. Nothing yet. No red banner snaking across the bottom of the screen. Besides, Shirley may have heard me, even though I was almost whispering. I come clean.

"The premier died. Suddenly." And then I add the unthinkable. "At my cottage."

Shirley takes in the news at lightning speed. She looks off into the distance and nods rapidly once. Then she spins on her stilettos. "Wait here," she commands with a hand chop.

She minces over to Doug's office and snicks the door shut behind her with a flick of her wrist. Doug is the news editor, whereas Shirley oversees the soft sections of the paper. There seems to be fairly constant overlap and it looks like this is one of those times. The door opens almost as soon as it shut.

"Okay. Doug and I have let the space for the homeless article go. For now. We decided it would be best to let both of you cover this story. You seem to complement each other. It worked out well when you both went to Robin's cottage last spring. That was a great story."

She pauses. Accolades from Shirley were very rare and she is making a point that Cindy and I work well together and produced a good article a year ago, one that sold a lot of newspapers. I suppose I'm grateful.

"I want the two of you to leave right away. Now. Get up there. We need photographs and great copy. Now. Don't just sit there. I want to beat the other Toronto papers."

We quickly stand up and start collecting our things together. I can't find my keys. Cindy sees me looking and tosses them to me. They'd skittered off my desk onto hers when I threw them down.

While pitching coffee cups into the garbage, Cindy says "It'll be dark by the time we get there. Not great for photographs."

Why the hell did Cindy have to say that? We had permission to go. We should just run out of here. But maybe she needs a good excuse if her pictures aren't great.

Shirley looks at her, considering. "Take lights," she says. "They're in the basement. Ask Alison Trent where they are. She's holed up down there." Alison Trent is the whacky, young, but extremely capable woman who does the research for the paper. She knows everything, and if she doesn't know, she knows how to find out. "Cindy, I want fantastic *Express* photos. Preferably of the dead guy."

The dead guy? What's with people? Have we become so jaded as a society that the loss of a life can be treated so casually? *The dead guy is kaput?* I say, "You mean the premier, right? Mr. Kahn? Who has young children and a wife? A family man?"

"Oh Robin, stop it. You know he was an asshole."

I shrug. She's right of course. But still.

Shirley pivots on her spikes and prances to her office. A cigarette has magically appeared in her hand. She holds it dramatically in the air as she flings over her shoulder, "Oh, and Cindy? Don't call me Hay Hair."

There was a vacuum of silence in her wake that was eventually broken by a snigger from Derrick. I glare at him.

I whisper to Cindy, "You gotta admire her."

Cindy fans her face. She's being sarcastic. "Another close call."

We skedaddle into the elevator, our possessions a jumble in our arms. I say as the doors are shutting, "Do you remember how to get there?"

Cindy looks at me as if I'm slightly demented. "Robin, Robin. Of course I do." She taps her purse. "And so does my phone."

I roll my eyes, here we go with her smart-ass comments for a whole weekend. "Well, this should be fun."

"I wonder if that cute young female cop is still with the Huntsville department."

"I thought you didn't like her."

"Oh no, I liked her, it was just that she was so young. But it's been a while since I met her, and who knows, maybe…"

"Cindy, we're going there to work. No hanky-panky." Who am I to say anything? I am already planning my nightly romps with Ralph. So I finish her sentence. "Maybe you'll like her now that she's a little older." I don't add, and so are you. "What was her name anyway?"

"I forget. All their names up there I think were Polish. Or German. They ended in Chucks."

Cindy scrolls through her phone. Just as the elevator doors slide open, she says triumphantly, "I found it. Officer Andrechuk."

"Oh right," I say. "Now it's coming back to me." As we walk into the parking garage from the basement elevator lobby, I remember the Huntsville cops. "Detective Kowalchuk. He was the guy in charge. He knew my parents. And Officer Niemchuk was the one who the bear charged. You got great pictures of that."

"Thanks. But I can't remember her first name. It's not in my notes."

I scrounge around in my foggy brain. "I think it began with the letter K. And I remember thinking it was a sort of a British name." I feel the pieces clicking together. "Kimberley."

"Right. Kimberley. Well, maybe I'll connect with her again."

"You couldn't have liked her that much if you can't remember her name," I say as I grab my car door handle and yank. It opens. "Voila!" A miracle. I never know if it will and am always somewhat ecstatic if it does. "Okay, Cindy, see you up there. I have to do a few things at home, so you might get there before we do. Just explain to the renters who you are. Set up the lights."

She twirls a hand over her shoulder as she heads to her shiny Honda. She gets a new car every two years. Especially if one has been blown up by an under-carriage bomb. Her job comes with certain risks. This one is a sparkly grey that clashes with her red hair, but I don't say anything. Who am I to talk? I'm not exactly a fashionista. Besides, cars aren't usually regarded as matching accessories. She gets in her car and then quickly gets out, frowning.

As Cindy stomps past my car, I shout out my window, "Where are you going?"

"I forgot the fucking lights."

"Oh. See you there."

The traffic is terrible, being a Friday afternoon. I finally get to my quiet street. Amazingly, I find parking right outside my tarted-up old Victorian house in Cabbagetown. Lucky, my cute little dog, starts yapping as soon as I insert my key into the front door. "Stop barking!" I shout through the heavy wood. If I had a penny for every time I said that to my dog, I'd be a rich woman. But wait a minute. The Canadian mint discontinued pennies years ago. So much for hoping to be rich.

As soon as the door opens, I hear Ralph call, "Is that you?"

Of course it's me.

"Robin?" He comes out of the kitchen carrying a shopping bag that looks full. I try to look in it to see what he's packed. Oh good, a whole bar of cheese. "Hi, sweetheart." He pecks me on the cheek. "I'm just packing up some food for the cottage."

My heart does a little happy dance as I behold his long limbs and broad shoulders. His brown hair has silvered over the past two years and frames what I think is the most handsome face I've ever seen. Handsome to me, in any event. He's not Marlboro Man handsome with a square jaw and strong hands curled around a cigarette, he's more like a Hugh Grant kind of handsome, cute and smiley. And he is gentle and smart as well. How on earth this lovely man has come into my life, I'll never know. What does he see in me?

"Thanks, Ralphonso."

He snorts.

I say, "Let's just take breakfast and lunch stuff. We can get take-out or eat at a restaurant for dinners."

Ralph rubs his two fingers together. Money.

I say, "I know it's expensive, but we didn't take a winter holiday this year and I've still got my savings that were earmarked for that. I'll pay."

He shrugs. I often pay. I don't mind. Ralph is still coughing up alimony to his ex-wife. She negotiated a three-year settlement so she could get her career on track. Ralph hasn't told me the names of his children or his wife. Even though we've been together for a while now. I know nothing about them, except for a few sparse details and the nettlesome restraining order thing. I found out about that little tidbit last summer in Nova Scotia. He had to fly back to Toronto for a day to personally open up his storage locker and get something she needed. He has a restraining order against her, which I find totally bizarre. Isn't it usually the other way around? The wife usually needs one against the abusive husband? I am so curious about her that I want to shake him until all the sordid details fall out of his lips. But I don't ever bring his family up. I learned that lesson when I first met him. One morning, before we were even really dating, I was chatting away, my motor mouth in full gear, and asked him about his kids. Big mistake. Every muscle in his face tightened into a hard mask and his lips compressed into a dark slash. I haven't asked him about his family since. Every now and then, I see Ralph gazing into distant memories with deep sadness etched upon his face. Whatever happened, it must have been terrible.

Ralph puts the shopping bags by the front door beside his luggage as I sprint up the stairs to grab enough clothes for four days. Just in case. "I'll be back in a sec to help. It won't take a minute to pack." Lucky chases me to the second-floor landing, his tail wagging briskly. He knows something is up and doesn't want to be left behind. I call down, "Don't forget the wine, Ralph."

I doubt he would. We both like our wine, probably too much. Oh, my God. That reminds me, I have to text Sally Josper and cancel my therapy appointment. When will I ever have time to deal with my addictive personality? The thought, *hopefully never*, zaps across my noodle. My fingers race over my phone as I tap out a quick message. She understands that I am often suddenly called away to cover a news event, but still, I feel badly cancelling, leaving a blank, unpaid spot in her calendar. But I don't feel badly for me. I do love having fun, drinking a glass of wine, and having some cheese and crackers.

Oh, get real, Robin. When was the last time you had a glass of wine? You never have a single glass. You have a whole bottle. Or maybe two. I jam clothes into a green garbage bag and then grab a few toiletries from the bathroom. Soap, toothpaste, deodorant, face cream. I'm not exactly a girlie-girl. I leave that up to Shirley. I pitch the bathroom booty into the bag, tie it up, and head downstairs, Lucky at my heels.

Ralph is on his phone at the bottom of the stairs, scrolling and tapping. "Sorry I kept you waiting," I say.

He doesn't look up. "No problem, just catching up on some

emails before we head out."

"Did you remember dog food?"

He finally looks at me, puts his phone away, and slaps the cloth bag slung over his shoulder. "Right here," he says to me while patting Lucky. "I'd never forget your food, would I, Lucky? I even brought your T-R-E-A-T-S," he spells out. Lucky yips at him.

I laugh. "I swear that dog knows how to spell, Ralphie."

Ralph shakes his head, "Don't call me Ralphie."

"I do it because I love you, Ralphred."

"Oh God," he says. "Here, let me take your fine luggage. You can bring the dog."

"Where's his leash?"

"I think hanging over a chair in the kitchen."

I head into the kitchen, see the leash right where Ralph said it would be, snap it onto Lucky, and follow Ralph out after locking the front door. "Is the back door locked?" I call to him. I'd forgotten to look when I was at the back of the house.

"Yes, I locked it after letting Lucky out for a last pee."

"What car will we take?" I'm hoping he'll say his.

"Mine. Of course."

I laugh. "I think that would be best."

"Duh," says Ralph. And then sensing he's gone too far and hurt my feelings, adds, "My snow tires are still on, and you never know. It's still very early in the spring and we are heading north where it's colder."

"Good save," I say. He knows I love my car. Besides, he is right, I don't have snow tires. I remember sliding in the slush, my car missing Rowland's Mercedes by inches.

He opens the back door of his Corolla and Lucky jumps in. His whole body wiggles as he ricochets off the front and back seats. And then Ralph opens the front passenger door for me, bowing at the waist and sweeping his arm toward the seat.

"My lady," he says.

"Are you sure you don't want me to drive?" I ask, bending over and cramming myself into the low-slung seat. I'm just being polite. Ralph is a great driver and I love having the freedom to

POWER: A ROBIN MACFARLAND MYSTERY

look around at the scenery.

Ralph ignores my fake offer and settles into his seat, cranking it back to accommodate the boots on his long legs. He checks the time on his dashboard clock. "We should be there by six-thirty," he says.

"Traffic," I say. "Rush hour. More like seven-thirty."

"I'll go up Highway 27 to avoid the Barrie commuters. We'll make it by six-thirty."

"Betcha." There's no way we will be there in two hours and fifteen minutes.

"You're on."

"Five bucks," I say.

"Ten," he counters.

"Ten, then." It's his loss.

Lucky barks twice as we pull away from the curb.

CHAPTER 12

MY STOMACH IS GROWLING LOUDLY by the time we stop at
Paul Webers, the famous take-out joint on Highway 11, for two
of their delicious hamburgers. We savour them in their parking
lot, along with ketchup-drenched french fries and thick chocolate
milkshakes before getting back on the road. Ralph breaks off a
piece of his burger and gives it to Lucky.

"Don't give him junk food, Ralph. It's not good for him."

He gives me a look and rubs his stomach. I laugh.

If I were alone in the car I would eat while on the move, but
Ralph, being a cop, can't risk being pulled over for distracted
driving. He is ridiculously moral and always obeys the law,
including driving at the speed limit. It drives me nuts. Who
drives at one hundred kilometres an hour on the highway? Even
the cops cruise by us at a higher speed than that. Not that it
makes that much of a difference today, being a Friday and so far,
the traffic has been stop-and-go in spots, even on Highway 27,
especially around Barrie. The journey is taking far longer than
Ralph thought it would. I'm secretly pleased. That ten-dollar
bet for the ETA being at least seven-thirty is looking like a win.
The stop at Webers will add at least fifteen minutes. To stretch
out the time, I don't gobble my food. I use great restraint and I
chew slowly, carefully, watching the seconds tick by on the car's
dashboard. Ralph, being the perfect gentleman, won't leave until
I'm done.

I take the pup out of the car to do his business. He sniffs

around for discarded fries and then lifts his leg on the garbage bin behind the take-out shed. When we pull out of the gravel parking lot, I see that a few random snowflakes are dancing in the headlights, looking like lost stars that have fallen to earth. I am lulled into a sense of peace with my body full of comfort food and the slow hum of the tires on the still dry highway. The light snowfall swirls in eddies above the pavement, like the brush strokes in a whitened Van Gogh painting. I drift off into that lazy and slow land between being asleep and awake.

My mind wanders over the past year, touching down on major events. It's been months and months, almost a full year, since I've been at the family cottage. The horrible murder that May traumatized me so badly that I stayed completely away over the summer. My family, Ralph, and I had a week of bliss on a beach in Nova Scotia instead, although that happy time went south after a couple of murders out there. One of the dead was a Black woman, a community leader from the South Shore. Systemic racism runs deep in the east.

And now there's been another death at my cottage. So much death. Am I cursed? It doesn't sound like a murder. Andrew had said something about a health incident, but Premier Kahn was a young guy and there were lots of money negotiations floating around by the sounds of it. After the morbid death of last spring that looked like an accident but was a carefully planned homicide, my mind seems wired into being suspicious. As the car floats along the highway, with lazy snowflakes drifting from the dark into the car headlights, I wonder: *Will I ever be able to enjoy the cottage again?*

As we get closer to Pair o' Dice, I feel myself heading into an even-further-away nostalgia land, remembering some lovely summer moments I've spent there with my young family. My heart feels restricted as my thoughts drift into the past. The memories bounce over my life with Trevor, my now-dead husband, who had criticized and controlled me whenever he could. But that dark spot in the family holidays is overshadowed by the whoops of delight as kids leapt off the dock into water and ran through the woods at dusk, playing forest games before bedtime. Finally, I doze off as these dreamlike recollections swirl around me. The next thing I know, I'm being poked in the arm.

"Robin, Robin." I slowly surface. "We're here," Ralph says while driving around slushy puddles of snow. The car's wheels are being sucked into deep ruts of mud on the driveway through the woods. "You fell asleep."

"No, I didn't," I say. I'm feeling grumpy. I look at my watch and perk up. Seven-thirty on the nose. "And I win."

"Yes, you did. And yes, it was a longer than normal trip. The traffic seems to be getting worse every year." The car jolts and Ralph jerks the wheel to correct the steering. "The ruts are terrible. Looks like a lot of activity has gone on here. The road's a mess."

"Andrew said he had the potholes filled."

"Andrew."

I know what Ralph means, of course. Andrew wasn't above lying when he wanted to look good.

I peer ahead through the darkening forest, towards the cottage and see bright white LED lights flickering around the tree trunks. Cindy must have arrived and set the lights up. She probably didn't stop for food. As my eyes become adjusted to the dark, I think I see a shadow moving from tree to tree in the woods to my right. "I see someone in the woods," I say to Ralph. The figure disappears. "Maybe." I'm not sure if the shadows are playing tricks on me. These woods by the road have always given me the creeps.

"Probably the police, searching for evidence."

"The police?" I didn't think that furtive shadow was the police.

"They have to investigate all circumstances surrounding a sudden death. You probably saw someone canvassing the nearby forest."

"What on earth do they expect to find?" I say this while searching the woods, looking for that dark figure jogging from tree to tree. The sun has gone down, but there's still a little light in the sky. The shadows from the spotlights shift in the breeze.

"You never know. Bits of fibre on a tree branch. A discarded gum wrapper. DNA on a cigarette butt."

I wonder if Ralph is making fun of me. "You've been reading mystery novels," I say.

"No," he says, "I get all my info from TV shows."

I snort.

Ralph pulls up beside the cottage and slides the car between two police cruisers. Their rotating lights are splashing bright red blood on the cottage's white siding. From my low-slung seat in the Corolla I can see the uniformed legs of three or four cops standing under a tarpaulin. It has been nailed to the side of the cottage about eight feet off the ground, and then tied to the backs of what I recognize as our cottage kitchen chairs, creating a makeshift lean-to. I guess Andrew had given them permission to bring out the chairs and to nail into the wood siding. But what a strange place to die, right at the base of the cottage. What was the premier doing there?

I scrunch forward so I can see under the tarp better. Squinting my eyes, I see a pair of legs in white jeans standing close to the cottage. Those must belong to Cindy. Only she would wear white jeans in mud season. I guess that's why I hadn't seen her when I first looked, as her pants are the same colour as the bank of snow behind her. The legs are moving and then she appears from under the tarpaulin. When she sees Ralph's car, she waves her camera high in the air and smiles broadly. She must have gotten great shots.

I bang my shoulder against the car door and launch into the air when it springs open. I'm so used to the rusty hinges on my car that I forget that not all car doors need to be manhandled. "Hi Cindy," I say, dusting myself off and recovering my composure. "What's up?"

"I got great footage of the kaput guy."

Geezus. She'd said that to bug me. It worked.

Ralph has already made his way over to the cops under the tarpaulin. Lucky is now barking his head off in the back seat, thinking I've forgotten about him. I open the door and grab his leash before he leaps away.

Cindy gestures to the tent, "Other than that, not much. He's pretty dead. Just kind of lying there. Not much blood."

She seems remarkably unfazed by looking at a dead body, but then, I guess she's seen a few. I say, "Any idea of why he died?"

"They're saying he was leaning back in a chair and fell, whacking his head on the side of the cottage. That's what it looks like anyway."

"I don't get it. He was sitting in a chair beside the cottage? Why was he sitting in a chair beside the cottage?"

"The go-to theory is that he was catching some spring sunshine, sitting out of the wind."

"Didn't anyone ask the other renters exactly what he was doing?"

"I don't know. I got here too late for that. But I think they asked his wife why he was sitting outside, you know, right by the house. That's what the cops are saying anyway."

I'm dying to look under the tarpaulin, but a cop is now wrapping crime screen tape around the legs of the chairs and nailing it to the side of the cottage. Andrew won't like all those nails being hammered into the siding. He'll be out with a tube of Dap in the morning, lips pursed. I wonder where he is and look around. His BMW is parked over by the trees.

"How did you get under the tarp to see Kahn?"

Cindy smiles like a cat who's eaten a canary.

"Oh." It dawns on me. The potential girlfriend. "Kimberley, right?"

"Yup. She's still working in Huntsville." Cindy lowers her voice. "She's under there right now."

"Lucky you."

"I wish she were under me," Cindy whispers. I groan.

Lucky hears his name, stops sniffing the ground, yaps, and starts straining at his leash. He's desperate to get into the woods. I say to Cindy, "Cops in the woods looking for evidence?"

She looks puzzled and shakes her head. "Nope, not since I've been here. They're huddled under there," she says, thumbing at the tarpaulin, "Looking at the toppled chair and Kahn lying on the ground. I don't know what Lucky is trying to get to."

"So, no one has gone into the woods to do a search?"

"No. I don't think so."

Lucky tugs hard at his leash. I look to where he is trying to drag me. "Well, someone is over there."

"I doubt it. It's probably just a deer." She pauses. "Or a bear."

She's trying to spook me. I laugh it off and say, as I try to see in the woods, "Or a rabbit."

But I don't think so. I'm pretty sure I saw a figure sliding through the trees earlier. I try to replay the images that were in my brain as we drove down the driveway. I'd just woken up and perhaps I wasn't all that aware of the reality around me. Maybe it was nothing. Maybe it was just the lights from under the tarpaulin making shadows. There was still a slight wind wafting through the trees. Maybe that was making flickering shadows in the forest. *Oh Robin, you're trying to convince yourself. You know you saw someone in the woods.* And if Lucky has the right instincts, that person is still there. I shiver.

I turn back to Cindy, "Maybe it's one of the renters. Do you know where they are? You know, the mayor and the CEO?"

"And their wives, the unpaid labour," she says. Cindy is always ready to make a political point. "They were gone by the time I got here. Apparently, they didn't want to hang around longer than they had to. Especially the wife of the premier. The cops said that she was almost catatonic. I think they booked into the Holiday Inn outside of town and left in a hurry. Or maybe they just went home. Back to Toronto."

"That's what I want to do. Go back to Toronto. This place is spooky in the dark."

"It's not that dark."

She's trying to reassure me, but it comes out as argumentative. I say, "So basically, the place is empty. They didn't even sleep in the beds."

"I haven't been inside yet so I don't know how much they made themselves at home. Maybe there's food in the fridge. But the cottage isn't empty. Andrew is in there now."

Which explains not only where he is but also why she hasn't gone in. Cindy feels the same way about Andrew as I do. He's to be avoided as much as possible. I'm not looking forward to spending the night under the same roof, but needs must. I certainly won't be going to book into a hotel.

By now Lucky is frantic, his nails scrambling in the grainy snow, trying to get me to go into the woods. What on earth does he smell?

Cindy looks at him. "Maybe we should check out the woods. Do you have a flashlight? Not that we need one, there's still enough light to see."

"You're nuts. I'm not going in there."

"Oh, come on, Robin. Bears sleep at night. Besides, Lucky wants to see. Let's go look." She's already walking in the direction Lucky's nose is pointing.

"Wait a sec. I'll get a flashlight. Here, hold Lucky for a minute." Cindy walks back and takes the leash out of my hand. "Ralph always keeps one in his car."

I get back into the car and rifle through the glove compartment. No luck. I feel under the seats. Not there either. And then I stretch over the driver's seat, get jabbed in the belly by the gearshift, and scrabble in the side pocket of his door. Bingo. By the time I find the flashlight Cindy is at the edge of the woods, Lucky leading the way.

I hurry as much as I can through the icy mud and grass while turning on the flashlight. "Wait, Cindy." She stops and puts her hands on her hips, tapping her foot, putting on a show of impatience. In the glare of the flashlight, her white sweater looks neon. "That's not nice." I say to her. "And bears sleep whenever they want, not just in the night."

"I knew that."

I was making it up. I had no idea when bears slept. "Here, give me Lucky."

Cindy hands me the leash and against my better judgment, we follow the dog into the woods. I am consoled with the thought

106

that if we don't return in good time, Ralph will come looking.

"If we're lucky the bears will still be hibernating," I say as I step into the bush.

The last time I had ventured into these woods was almost a year ago. Cindy was following me then too, and complaining bitterly about the blackflies. We had come upon a disgusting pile of flesh and bones weighted in place on the earth by a frayed woodsman's jacket. I am hoping against hope that we won't find a dead body today. I don't like what I'm feeling. Not that I am a witch and can sense stuff, but I am certainly sensing another person. There is definitely someone in the woods. I whisper-shout, "Hey, Cindy, wait up." I don't want her to get out of sight.

Lucky starts to sneeze. He does that when he's walking behind the exhaust pipe of a car, or if he's on the couch when my son lets one rip. We laugh ourselves silly when he does that, and of course, it encourages the kid to fart more. And Lucky is sneezing now, trying to rid his nasal passages of some obnoxious odour. I stop to sniff the air. What is Lucky smelling? And then the sweet, almost skunk-like aroma of weed floats into my nostrils.

I doubt a policeman would be smoking weed while on the job. Although, one never knows in Huntsville, which is a distribution centre for all kinds of drugs to the far north. I didn't know if the town had any legal cannabis shops, not that it mattered. People everywhere are pretty loyal to their dealers. The costs are about the same, if not less from a dealer, and the quality of the product seems to be better. So, if not a cop, who is smoking weed in the woods?

"Cindy," I say as I catch up to her, "do you smell that? I think someone's smoking up."

She stops walking and holds her head up, sniffing the air. "No, I don't think so, not right now. I can smell weed, but I don't think it's smoke."

"What do you mean?" I try not to sound crabby. You either smell it or you don't.

She sniffs the air again. "No, it's the smell of weed on someone's clothes. Sort of wet, woolly weed."

I stop to sniff the air again. She's right. There's a faint undercurrent of that distinctive smell of wet wool. I'm surprised that I didn't notice that right away, being sensitive to wool and always having my antennae up for allergens. Lucky is pulling on his leash, forcing me to follow him deeper into the woods. The light has almost completely faded and we are relying totally on the washed-out beam of the flashlight to see our way over fallen logs and around boggy mounds of leaves. Suddenly Lucky stops, looks at me and whines. His feet are standing on something.

I can't quite make out what he's found and I don't want to go closer. Maybe it's a large parcel or something. There's a shimmer at the base. Is it part of a person? Last year we found a headless torso. I am starting to feel sick. Was I going to faint? There's a ringing in my ears and my vision is fading in and out. The snake is hissing loudly. I whisper, "Cindy?" She's miles ahead. I try to shout. "Cindy?" I feel frozen to the ground.

She turns around and focuses on me, yelling back, "What?"

I beckon with the flashlight, making a circle with the beam until it lands on the black lump. She perhaps senses my panic and comes hurrying to me, her feet stirring up wet dead leaves. "Don't faint, Robin. What has Lucky found? Don't faint, Robin. Breathe. I'm coming."

She bends over Lucky and pats him. "That's a good boy. Now move away." She nudges him aside with her elbow and inspects what he's found, bending closer to take a better look.

I marvel at her bravery while feeling the Weber hamburger churning in my gut. "I think I'm going to be sick." I look around for a bush to barf behind.

"Well, puke over there," she gestures with her arm. "Don't contaminate the evidence," she says while picking it up.

"What on earth is that?" I ask. One thing I know for sure, it's not a body part. My stomach settles down, my eyesight returns, and the hissing in my ears subsides. But I can't make out what Cindy has pulled out of the earth. In the half-light it looks like she's holding an octopus with numerous arms and legs.

Cindy laughs, "It's a backpack, silly."

CHAPTER 13

A BACKPACK? WHAT ON EARTH IS a backpack doing here, in the woods? On my cottage's property? Cindy turns it over, gives it a small shake, and inspects the zippers. She balances on one foot, lays the backpack on a raised knee, and tugs at the main zipper. Bits of dirt are lodged in the teeth but eventually it opens. She plunges her hand inside. I hear her fingers rustling around, probing the contents, until she finally pulls out a large zip-lock bag. It's stuffed full of broken up dried leaves. I'm wondering why a bag of oregano is in a backpack in the woods.

"Ta dah!" she says, holding it into the beam of my flashlight, as if she's conjured a rabbit out of a hat. "That's not just a wee bag of weed," she laughs.

Oh. It's weed. Clearly, I'm no connoisseur of cannabis. I shuffle forward to take a better look. The bag holds tightly packed crumbled dried leaves and there are some roundish seeds rolling about on the bottom. "Why do you suppose that's here?"

"Beats me," she says, "but I think we'll have some fun tonight."

"I don't smoke. Asthma." I don't want to appear uncool so I add the caveat. Alcohol on the other hand...

"I can make a good dessert with this." She shakes the bag in my face.

The last thing I want is to get high with a dead body lurking at the side of the house. "Not for me. I'm not eating dessert these days." That sounded lame, even to my ears.

"You lie. You just don't want to. Are you a scaredy-cat?"

What was this? Peer pressure at the age of fifty-eight? "Back off, Cindy. No. It's not something I do. Besides, it's not ours."

"Finders keepers, losers weepers," she sings.

I turn my back and cross my arms. I know I'm acting immature, but whatever.

"Oh, c'mon. Way easier to carry dope around than ten bottles of wine, Robin. Alcohol is pretty passé these days."

She has a point, even if she drinks like a fish as well.

"I have asthma," I reiterate.

Lucky starts barking again, straining at his leash. He pushes hard against the muddy snow, lunges, and wrenches my arm. I stumble on a small mound of ice and give it an annoyed kick as I find my footing. I'm a little pissed off. I don't want to be here. I snap, "I don't know if you should be handling that, Cindy."

"Why the hell not?"

She doesn't like to be criticized.

"Well, what if that bag has something to do with Kahn's death? Maybe it's evidence."

"Oh, get real. And shut your damn dog up."

We're both a little cranky. I say, "I think we should go back."

"Are you kidding me? Lucky wants us to go deeper into the woods. Look at him. I bet the person who this belongs to is somewhere out there. Right where Lucky's cute little nose is pointing. Right, Lucky?" Lucky barks happily and lunges again.

Traitor.

"And it's 'to whom this belongs to.'" Cindy snorts and stumbles through the bush, following Lucky. As if I want to go chasing in the dark woods for a drug dealer who's lost his stash. "Call me crazy, but I'm not sure that's a good idea."

"We've come this far, we might as well go a little further, and see what we can see. Here, give me Lucky."

She turns and snatches the leash out of my hand before I have time to object and takes off into the gloom. I watch as she hooks one strap of the dirty backpack over her shoulder. It leaves stripes of dirt on her white sweater. How can she be warm enough in that? It must be about ten degrees now that the sun has slipped below the horizon. Her red hair shines like fire in the beam of my flashlight as she charges into the woods. Lucky's tongue is hanging out as he gleefully pulls her along. I mutter a *fuck* under my breath and follow her.

As we bumble along in the dark, over stumps and small saplings, I feel anger bubbling in my chest. My feet are tripping over mounds of crusty snow. Clumps of mud are sticking to the bottom of my boots. There's no way I can keep up with Cindy. Her legs are ten feet long. I'm panting. I do not want to be doing this. I'm cold and these woods scare me. They are full of animals. Coyotes. Bears. Owls. Plus, the backpack is bothering me. I feel like I've seen it before. Did it belong to one of my kids from when they were younger? Was it stolen from the cottage and then used by some thief? But no, it couldn't have been one of my kids. They didn't like having logos on their stuff. They said it made them look like they were part of the white, privileged elite. Which they were.

I look carefully at the backpack slung over Cindy's shoulder. It definitely has a logo. I can see the reflective sweep of a checkmark bouncing on Cindy's back. It also has a sewn-on decal of a fluorescent lightning bolt, which, according to my kids, was a dorky thing to do, although they wouldn't use a word like dorky. I remembered when I suggested to them that maybe they'd like to dress their backpacks up, they'd looked at me like I was from another dimension. Eventually, they patiently explained to me that if one had to do something to look cool it was definitely an uncool thing to do. My memory jogs around images and suddenly I see the knapsack on Cindy's back superimposed on the knapsack I saw on the guy being chased in front of the food bank. Ridiculous thought. That was hundreds of kilometres away.

"Wait up," I yell. Cindy travels fast on her gazelle legs and she is now five hundred metres away from me. She doesn't slow down. "Cindy!" I bellow. "Slow the fuck down. I don't want to be stuck in the woods by myself."

She looks over her shoulder at me and gestures with her arm.

"Hurry up."

To my relief I see it's getting lighter in front of her. We're coming to the edge of the forest. Finally, Cindy stops.

"I've come to a road," she yells.

"That's the road that leads to town. It's the road you turn off to get to the cottage. Do you see anyone?"

I catch up to her and look through the deepening dusk. Far ahead I see some movement on the road. "Is that a deer?" The far-off dark shape has the same bulk as a deer.

Cindy says, "Where?"

"Up there, where the road rises up the hill."

"I can't see anything."

"I do." I point. "Up there. I can still see something. I think it might be a person. A man. It's too tall to be a deer."

Cindy squints her eyes. "Maybe it's a person." She shrugs. "Well, whatever it is, it got away."

The rapidly moving figure is swallowed up by the dark as it gets further up the hill. I'm actually very grateful. I don't want a confrontation with anybody, here in the bush, so far away from people.

"Look," I point a few metres down the road, "You can see the sign for Pair o' Dice just up ahead. The driveway is a few steps past that. Let's walk home that way and not go back through the woods."

"Sounds good to me. Here, you take Lucky." She hands me the leash and bends over to pat him. The backpack swings around off her back and falls off her shoulder. It narrowly misses Lucky's head. She doesn't notice. "You're very cute, but not a good tracker."

I yip, "Hey! Watch the knapsack, Cindy. Don't let it hit his head."

She quickly straightens up. "Right. Sorry about that." She shoves the knapsack back onto her shoulder. It swings around and nearly bonks me. "Wouldn't want to hurt you, cutie pie." She's talking to the dog.

Lucky wags his tail and prances to the driveway, all sense of urgency evaporated. Whoever it was is long gone.

Cindy and I traipse along the muddy driveway in silence for a bit. I swing the beam of the flashlight back and forth in front of us, so we don't sink into any of the muddy ruts. Lucky runs from side to side, nose to the ground, sniffing invisible prey. I feel the fear and anger settle down in my chest.

"I wonder who was in the woods." Even to me, my voice sounds reasonable.

Cindy thumps the knapsack. "Whoever it was will be missing their source of income."

"What? You think it actually belongs to a drug dealer?"

"Oh, no doubt about that. I pulled out just one bag. There must be at least twenty in there."

I let that sink in.

"Twenty?"

"At least."

"Is the bag heavy?"

"Why do you think it swung off my shoulder like that? It's not light, that's for sure."

"So…"

"So what?"

"So what are we going to do with it?" I have to confess, my dark side was fighting with my light side. We could sell the stuff and make a killing.

"I know what you're thinking, and I have the connections, but no, we are going to hand this backpack over to the police. It obviously belongs to one of the Bolts."

"The Bolts?"

"Ya, a Toronto gang. That's their logo." She jerks her head over her shoulder at the decal.

"The guy at the food bank had a knapsack with this logo on it."

"I know. But it's a huge gang. Stretches all the way up to North Bay."

Cindy knows her gangs.

"I'm not so sure about giving it to the town police."

"I will hand it over to Kimberley."

"No, I think it should go to Ralph. I trust him." Oh God, did I say that? Out loud, in public? I wasn't ready to say stuff like that to Cindy. She already felt threatened enough by my relationship with him. Jealousy. I back pedal. "I mean, as a police officer. He's very moral."

"I found it, it's my say-so."

"You didn't find it. Lucky found it. My dog, not yours. And I smelled it first." It feels good to be bickering with Cindy. "You just want to impress Kimberley."

"So? What's wrong with that?"

"Look, watch out. Here comes a car." I could see the high beams heading toward us. "We better get to the side of the road."

Cindy and I split up, her going to the left, me to the right. She stands behind a tree. I climb over a hump of snow and pull Lucky in close to me as the car roars up the driveway. It sways in the mud as it slides to a stop beside me. I look through the window. Andrew. Ugh. He buzzes down his window. "Hi, Andrew." I smile as nicely as I can, but I feel my lips pulling tight across my teeth in a grimace.

"Hi, yourself. What are you doing out here?"

None of your fucking business. He always acts like he has the right to control my activities. "Oh, just having a walk. Taking Lucky out for some exercise."

"I see." He doesn't believe me. "Unbelievable what happened. I guess I'll have to refund their money."

Really? That's what it comes down to? A murder reduced to a refund? Andrew is such a jerk. The premier lost his life and Andrew is bellyaching about losing a deposit? "I guess so."

"Everyone's left."

"The death of the major player tends to put a damper on things."

I hear Cindy stifle a guffaw. Andrew's head swings around to the passenger side of the car. She's still behind the tree so he can't see her through the far window. I hide my smile.

"What was that?" He looks a little alarmed.

"What?" Little Miss Innocent.

"I thought I heard a noise."

"Probably just an animal scurrying in the undergrowth."

He nods, somewhat satisfied with my answer. But not totally. He's a coward. I guess I shouldn't judge. He says, "How long are you staying?"

"Ralph and I will hang around for a few days. You?"

"I'm just heading to town for some dinner. I'll bring back some coffee for everyone. I'll stay here overnight and make sure the police put everything back the way they found it. Then I'll probably leave in the morning."

That's great news. Just one night with him. "Did you tell Mom and Dad?"

"Tell them what?"

I can't believe it. "Tell them a man died on their cottage property."

"Oh, right. That. No." He thinks. "Why don't you give them a call and let them know?"

It's just like Andrew to preserve his relationship with our parents, letting me do the dirty work. "You were in charge of renting it out, so you tell them."

"C'mon Robin, it's your turn."

"My *turn*?" This is heading into a full-blown fight, I can feel it.

"I had to tell them about the last time you were here. When you found a dead body in the woods."

"It wasn't a body. It was a body part. A torso." I'm just revving up. "A body that had been murdered by *your* client. That was *your* job, not mine, just like this is *your* job, not mine."

He spits, "Oh, fuck off, Robin. It wasn't my client this time that murdered anyone. The premier simply leaned back in a chair, hit his head, and died from the blow."

"You sound so sure of yourself."

Andrew's version of events resonates in my mind. It doesn't make sense to me. Lots of people fall back in their chairs, hit their heads, and don't die. They don't even get a concussion. "They were your clients that were here and you did the rental agreement. Without asking me, I might add. So, this is your

115

fucking show, fuckhead."

"Oh, now you're resorting to name calling, are you? And you, the writer. I'm not telling them. Not this time." He stares straight ahead and grits his teeth. I watch his jaw muscles tighten under stretched skin.

As I look at his angry profile, the thought crosses my mind that Andrew might be a psychopath. He seems to have no empathy, no sense of others' feelings. Everything he does, he does for his own advantage. Why had he really rented the cottage to these people? What was his interest in an energy deal? The thought that he might truly have a hand in this gives me a shiver.

"And that's final," he says, his eyes glittering as he challenges me.

I hold my ground despite what I see sparking from his eyes. "I guess they'll have to read about it in the paper, then."

"No doubt a story you'll write, Gobin. I hope that makes you happy." What a child. He's reverted to being six when he made up his stupid nickname for me. He pushes his foot down on the gas. Globs of wet earth fly out from behind his car as he takes off. I breathe heavily in the wake of the confrontation, wanting to hit him.

"Gobin?" Cindy is laughing. "Gobin?"

CHAPTER 14

"WHAT A DICKFACE." I TAKE a deep breath. I am so angry I could spit. "Fucking brother."

"Luckily I don't have that problem," says Cindy. "But I have to say, I think sisters might be worse."

I wasn't sure about that, given my relationship with Andrew. "Probably. I've heard there's a lot of sibling rivalry between kids of the same sex."

"You mean of the same *gender identification*."

She had to be so damn politically correct. But then I think about it. She's right. "That makes sense, I guess."

"Of course it does. "Fights over clothing. Fights over products in the shower. Fights over boys. Fights over affection from parents. Fights over who gets the most attention from friends. And grandparents. Even the family dog. Fights over the size of a slice of pie. And the list goes on."

"Sounds like you had a pretty rough go of it, having a sister."

"A sister?" Cindy is sounding a titch shrill. "I had *three* sisters. There was enough estrogen in that house to keep osteoporosis at bay for a century."

Why didn't I know Cindy had three sisters? I thought she only had one. What kind of friend was I if I didn't know this basic information? "I'm sorry, Cindy, I thought you had just the one sister."

"I do now."

She does *now*? What does that mean? Had two died in a tragic accident I knew nothing about? Or have I stumbled into a hornet's nest? I don't know what to say. I ask the most innocuous question I can, trying to make no assumptions. "How did that happen?"

Cindy sighs. "It's a long story. My parents were way older than yours. My mother died when I was in my late thirties and my father a few years after that. I was forty-two."

I had to put my two cents in. "In a way you were lucky." My parents were a tad difficult.

"Ha. I know you have some issues with your parents, Robin, especially now that they're older. Anyway, my father made me executor of his will and I guess I handled it badly because now two of my sisters won't talk to me. They disagreed with everything I did, including the sale of the house and especially how the contents were divvied up. Tiny knickknacks caused huge battles. 'I want the egg cups. You can have the carving knife. I must have that painting.' So much bullshit. There was incredible bitterness. So, I haven't spoken to two of my sisters for over fifteen years. On the other hand, my younger sister, Carla, thinks I did a great job."

I try to figure this out. There's a lot written about birth order and it might help me if I knew where Cindy fit into the family dynamic. I make a guess. "So, you had two older sisters?"

"Yes. I do miss them. Despite all our squabbling, I loved them so much." Cindy looks so wistful; my heart goes out to her. I, on the other hand, never really liked Andrew. He was always holier than thou. A bully.

"I don't get it. Why were you made executor if you weren't the oldest?"

"That was part of the problem. They didn't like that."

"No, I wouldn't either. And I imagine Andrew would go ballistic if I were executor of my father's will. He already hates me. So, I guess you were between a rock and a hard place."

Cindy sighs again. "Families."

"Ya," I say. "Families."

We trudge up the driveway in silence through the mud and

patches of snow. My anger at Andrew has been stoked by this conversation and I try to calm down my fury by doing a few internal Buddhist chants. It doesn't work.

Thoughts swirl in my mind. Was Andrew somehow involved in the death of the premier? How could he be? But there was that awful look he gave me on the road. My stomach flips and contracts. It seemed so *evil*. But he is my brother. How can I think things like that about him? My mind churns. I hope against hope that Andrew had nothing to do with the premier's death. It was probably impossible that he had. The premier had fallen backwards and whacked his head on the wall of the cottage. Right? That is the supposed cause of death.

Not that I believe it. I want to take a look at the wound. I know all about head wounds after having four kids. I know when to take a kid to the hospital. I know the difference between a bad injury and one you should be able to walk away from. Three of my kids fell backwards before they learned not to lean too far back. Evelyn has always been the cautious one. But the boys? Maggie? Daredevils. I don't see how that particular hit could kill someone. I'd really like to look at it.

The flashing red lights of the police cruiser bleed through the trees. We were getting closer to the cottage. I say, "Do you think I could somehow get permission to go under the tarp? I'd like to see what everyone is looking at." I also want to hear what they were saying.

"Sure, I think I can arrange that." Cindy taps on her phone. "I'll just text Kim now and ask her if you can go in." A few steps later, her phone dings with the answer. She doesn't tell me. She's reading the text and licking her lips. God. I walk over the mud, dead leaves, and tiny bits of remaining snow, waiting. From a distance.

"Well?" Why Cindy doesn't tell me is fueling my bad mood. Oh God, now she's giggling. Nothing is as disturbing as a middle-aged woman giggling. "What are you giggling about?"

"Oh, nothing."

Right. Probably some sex thing.

Cindy reads from her phone. "She says, 'Sure, this is a good time to go. The other officers are hanging around outside the tarp, waiting for Andrew to come back with some coffee.'"

"Great. Thanks for arranging that. But I'm surprised they let Andrew leave the property. In fact, I'm surprised they let the others go as well."

Cindy is puzzled, her green eyes wide. "Why do you say that? It's not like they have to be interviewed extensively. Or held as suspects. There was no crime. It was an accident."

I shrug. "Still, maybe it wasn't. I've never known someone to die from falling back in a chair. Have you? Didn't your kids ever do that? And they didn't die."

"You're right." Cindy mulls it over. "Maybe he had a thin skull. There's some kind of phenomenon about that. Or maybe he was just a numbskull."

"Well, we know he had no brain, but a thin skull? The more I think about it, I have to wonder. It doesn't make sense. I even knew an old, bent-over woman who'd had too much to drink and fell off her chair, hitting her head on the corner of a wood stove, not even on some wooden boards. She was fine."

"Was that your mother?"

"No, an aunt."

"I wondered because your mother isn't that fine."

"In more ways than one." Cindy knows how worried I am about my mother's declining brain power. She even has trouble speaking these days, often looking around the room as if the word she's seeking might magically appear from thin air.

"No, she isn't but not because she had a brain injury."

"Well, all the cops are signing off that the cause of death was an accident."

I won't let it go. I can't. "There's just not enough momentum in that kind of fall to cause death. Maybe someone grabbed the two front legs of the chair and threw him backwards."

Cindy rolls that around in her head for a minute. "No, if your theory is that there isn't enough force in that kind of fall to kill, then I doubt someone would be able to hurl him back hard enough to create a fatal force. It's too awkward a movement, you know, bending over, grabbing the legs, hoisting them. Surely the premier would have kicked an assailant that was in front of his face like that."

I persist, "Did they search for footprints in front of the chair or around the premier?"

"By the time I arrived there were hundreds of footprints around him. The ground was soggy anyway. Footprints would have disappeared in the oozing mud."

I shake my head. Stupid cops. "Maybe it was soggy only because people had tromped all over it. Anyway, they ruined any possible evidence."

"I think they could get fingerprints off the two front chair legs if they thought that was a possibility."

"Really? Off wood?" The things I don't know.

"They can get fingerprints off skin these days. Wood is a piece of cake."

"Did anyone look for fingerprints?"

"Not while I was there. And I doubt they did before I arrived because I didn't see any of that dark powder they use to lift prints."

"Was it light when you arrived?"

"Pretty light, but eventually they were grateful for the lights I brought from the paper."

"They don't have spotlights here?"

"Small town, Robin. Small town."

"You're telling me. If this had happened in the city, this situation would have been handled with far more care. It would have been treated, first and foremost, as a suspicious death. Here they just assumed it was a simple accident."

"Maybe it was, Robin."

"Naw. I don't think so. There's something about the energy deal. Plus, he had enemies. I want to look at the head wound."

"Oh, so you're a forensic scientist? A coroner? A doctor?"

She's pissing me off. I say, "I'm a mother of four active children who skateboarded without their damn helmets. Who played hockey on backyard rinks with no protective equipment. Who fell off the jungle gym in the school playground. On their heads. I saw lots of head injuries, so this one must be much worse if it was bad enough to kill."

Giving up on arguing with me about this, Cindy turns away. "Oh look, there's Kimmy."

She's changing the topic. "*Kimmy?*" I whisper to her. "Aren't you moving a bit quickly?" Cindy's boundaries have always been a little wonky. I wave at the cop. "Hi, Kim," I shout. "Nice seeing you again." Not really, but I'm polite. Kim bugs me, although I don't know why.

She skips over to us, waving her slender arm like a flag on crack cocaine. She looks about ten years old and I feel so sorry for Cindy. Her heart will be broken, yet again. She can't seem to find a suitable partner anywhere. And then I have a revelation. Maybe she doesn't want someone permanent in her life. Maybe she subconsciously chooses impossible relationships that could never in a month of Sundays work out.

"Thanks for letting me take a look at the premier," I say. No harm in being gracious. Get more with honey, et cetera, et cetera.

"No problemo," titters Kim. "It's not really my call, but the big guys over there are all busy chewing the fat."

When she says this, she looks at my waistline while thumbing over her shoulder in the direction of the cops, who are standing in a gang around their vehicles. So, little Kimmy is judgmental of people's bodies from her lofty height of superiority. There is a streak of cruelty in her. There'll come a time when I have enough voice to stand in my power and address someone mocking my body, but not today. Today I'm seeking out Ralph. When my mind turns to him, I admit to myself that I don't really care what someone like Kim thinks of me. She can take her polished abs and shove them. Ralph, on the other hand? His opinion matters to me. He loves my extra this and that. He says it gives him more to love. Besides that, he loves to chew my fat.

Robin, don't let your mind wander. Focus. Dead premier. Focus. Dead premier.

Finally, I see Ralph, gabbing away, in the centre of the group of cops. He's cozied up to them in only the way a gregarious man like Ralph can. I wonder what they're saying. Is he chastising them for not being more careful, or has he swallowed the accident theory hook, line, and sinker? Knowing him, he's probably dancing around what he's seen, expressing concern for all the stress the local guys are under, policing a huge area with minimal staff, before he says what's really on his mind. There's always a bit of bad blood between local cops and intruders upon their territory, especially those from the big city, so it's important to be diplomatic.

In the meantime, Cindy is making google eyes at Kim. I want to give my head a shake. Kim must be thirty years younger than Cindy, cruising in at about twenty-five years old. How on earth is that ever going to work out? By the time Kim reaches full womanhood, Cindy will be retiring and drinking tea in her housecoat.

I think about that vision for a minute. Naw. She'd never do that. Not the type.

Besides, there's the distance. Huntsville is a good two and half hours from Toronto, on a good traffic day, so unless Kim has applied for a transfer to the Toronto Police Service, the distance will eventually snuff out the relationship. On top of all this, it's irritating that Cindy has been taken in by such surface attributes. As far as I can see, the only thing Kim has going for her is that she's female with a tight, energetic body. With firm tits.

Whoa, Robin. This isn't your business. What Cindy wants and what you want are two different things. Cindy isn't your child and she can take care of herself. So why am I so hostile toward Kim? Why does she annoy you so much? *Robin, you old cow, I think you're jealous.*

I rumble with this thought. Jealous? Me? Of my friend, who's having fun flirting with a much younger woman? Shouldn't I be pleased for her? What is wrong with me? Am I sexually jealous of Cindy? No, I don't think so. The thought of going to bed with her has zero attraction. So, it's not that.

Maybe I'm just plain worried about my friend. I know Kim's

type. Sure, she's just a kid, really, but I can tell she's developing those kinds of traits that cause people harm. She's a user. Not a druggie user, but a people user. She's letting me go into what I think might be a crime scene without clearing it with her boss. In a police force, that just isn't done. She's acting like she has the authority to do that. And she's probably doing it to win favour with Cindy. So, Kimmy darling is a user. Whatever. I'll take advantage of it. I start to walk to the tarpaulin when I hear a car engine and turn around.

Andrew. He slides to a stop in the slush and gets out of his low-slung vehicle. I notice with some satisfaction that there's mud on his car's shiny chrome and he's got mud on his tasselled loafers. He's clamping a box of Tim Horton's donuts under his arm and balancing two tiers of large coffees in those cardboard trays in his other hand. Smiling away, as if to say, "Aren't I a good boy, look what I've brought you all."

I sure am crabby today. After all, it is nice of him to go all the way into town and get everyone a snack. He's handing them out to the cops like a talk show host distributing prizes to all the contestants in this little drama. The spotlights even make it look like a TV set. He approaches me with a smile fixed on his face. It looks sort of grotesque in the glare of the fluorescent lighting and I wonder again what his part is in all this. Cindy and Kim interrupt their goo-goo talk long enough to take a coffee and donut. Andrew turns to me.

"I thought I saw you heading to the tarp."

He doesn't miss a trick. "So?"

"Well, I'm not sure you should go under there."

I raise my eyebrows while snaffling a maple glazed from the box. My favourite. "Why not?"

"There's blood, Robin."

I'm surprised at this. "Blood? From hitting a head on wood siding?"

"He was a big guy. Probably hit it really hard." And how did Andrew know there was blood?

"Still..." I take a sip from a cup of coffee that somehow

magically appeared in my hand. I don't remember taking it out of the tray. Andrew does that to me. I miss bits of life. It's probably a PTSD thing, although I can't recall any traumatic details of the things he did to me. That lack of recall might be a PTSD thing as well. Oh, the irony.

"Would you like me to go in with you?"

"Fuck off, Andrew. I'm perfectly capable of looking at a dead body on my own."

"Robin, I don't think so. You're a fainter."

Cindy muscles in between us. "Hi Andrew, thanks for the coffee," she says, her tone mocking. I know she prefers Starbucks and shuns Timmies. She's after something. "It hits the spot."

He reluctantly turns to her. "You're welcome. And who's this?"

"This is the rising star of the Huntsville police force. Kim..."

Oh God. That's hilarious. She's forgotten Kim's last name. While Andrew is bent over, politely waiting for the rest of the introduction and Cindy is digging through her brain cells for Kim's surname, I think this is a good time for me to sneak away. I hear Kim's voice pipe up her last name as I turn and walk to the tarp.

I lift it up with some trepidation. Andrew is right. I am a fainter and already I can hear my old friend, the snake, hissing in my brain. I take a few deep breaths and feel my feet going numb. Oh, maybe it's just an anxiety attack. I wait a second. Nope. Black spots swim in front of my eyes. I grab the back of a kitchen chair to keep myself standing. I reach out for the tarp. It feels like the slimy underbelly of a fish. I jerk my hand away. I will not faint.

The scene is bathed in a ghostly white light with a blueish tinge reflected from the tarpaulin. The plastic undulates in the slight breeze, making me slightly seasick, and prickles form on the back of my neck. I take a step back to the chair, hold the side that doesn't have the tarp tied to it, and breathe deeply again. I am not going to faint. I am not going to faint.

Lying on the ground is a toppled chair and the premier, his head somewhat askew. Not enough to indicate a broken neck, just slightly off to one side. I guess this makes sense because he's almost, but not quite, lying on his side. One arm is under his body and the other is flung almost straight out. His grey Columbia ski jacket is wide open and the bottom zipper edge is embedded in sludge that's seeping up through the grass. The premier is definitely a big man. His shirt buttons are stretched to their limit by the belly hanging over his belt. His legs are curled up in a semi-fetal position, one on top of the other. The bottom leg is covered in mud and his shoes are caked with it.

I feel steadier on my feet now that I've acclimatized to the scene and take a few brave steps forward. I really want to look at the wound that killed him, supposedly sustained by falling backwards. My feet squelch in the muck as I walk around to the premier's head. Andrew is right. There is definitely blood. A deep gash slices through skin on the back of his head. I can't tell how deep it is because his head is just slightly turned. I look around me and under the tarp. There are no legs near me. I know I shouldn't touch anything in case this is truly a crime scene but I just can't resist. I poke at his head with my boot to turn it so I can get a better look.

The premier's head lolls to the side and his nose hits the mud. I feel badly about that but if I lean over, I can see that there is a significant gouge running from the crown of his head for about a full inch. No fall caused that kind of damage. I know I eventually have to return the premier's head to its original position, but I don't know how I can possibly do this. I wasn't going to touch it with my hands. No way. I don't touch dead things. Plus, what if there really is foul play at work?

Again, I am shocked by the lack of care in the treatment the police gave to this death. Nothing about this makes sense to me. They say he hit his head on wood siding. If this is true, there should be a dent in his head, not a gash. And there is certainly a gash. I think a deep wound like that would kill him. But the side of the cottage is a flat surface. I trace my fingers over the wood where I think he might have hit his head had he been sitting in front of the wall and fallen backwards. Nothing. Not a sharp nail sticking out and not a scratch in the wood. There's nothing at all protruding from the wall that would cause a cut like that. A sharp sliver of wood or something. Something pointed. And certainly, to my untrained eye, there's no blood on the wall, although I don't have one of those special blue lights that reveal even tiny specks. The wall is unmarked.

What on earth is going on?

CHAPTER 15

I LEAN AGAINST THE COTTAGE WALL and think about what I know, what I don't know, and what my next steps should be. Should I tell anyone my suspicions? That all is not what it appears to be? Would they believe me? I hear a low murmur of voices drifting under the edges of the tarpaulin. Ralph's laugh punctuates the various comments the local cops are making. I know he's doing his best to fit in. I also know that that's a waste of time. He would always be "from away." Nonetheless, they all think this premier situation is a slam dunk. An accident, pure and simple. Goofing off, probably punching each other in the shoulders, guffaw, guffaw.

Would this in-crowd ever believe there was something amiss? I doubt it. They don't want to. They want a neat and tidy little bow around the death of Ontario's political leader. The media would be here shortly and press releases would be handed out like candy. Death by accident. A bad fall. Nothing untoward. He simply fell out of his chair. Some would take that symbolically. Like me.

Not that he'd deserved to die in the prime of his life. But no, I don't like Kahn much. My mother always told me not to say the word "hate," so I won't, but I *really* don't like him. Nope, not after what happened to all those seniors in long-term care homes during the pandemic. So much death. Not when he crowed that all of those same homes now had a cooling station for the brutal summer heat in the province. A single cooling station.

What? He expected all the elderly residents to wheel their chairs around a single air conditioner? He thought this was a major accomplishment? And I especially don't like him, not after he cut back funding for education. During a pandemic. When kids needed more space in the classroom, more compassion, more supplies. HEPA filters. This is all especially disgusting now that I have a darling grandbaby. How dare he compromise her future? Geez. I better calm myself down. Here I am, getting all revved up, forgetting that this guy has a wife and kids. And now, he's dead.

Would anyone believe me that this was a death worth looking into? Cindy might. Or, I think she will. But one never knows with her. Cindy can blow hot and cold sometimes, besides, she wants to be in Kimberley's good books. And I know *Kimmy* thinks this is an accident, just like her cop buddies.

But I know for certain that there's no way the premier died from a backward fall. Something else happened to cause that deep gash in his skull. I know he was murdered. But by whom? And why? Why was the premier of Ontario killed? Who would have a motive to kill him?

That's the easiest question of all. A no-brainer. Plenty of people want him out of the picture. He was ditching injection sites. Cutting back on homeless shelters. Slashing publicly funded mental health care. Hacking away at education budgets. Chopping up infrastructure projects. Selling off public corporations. Pushing at laws to build on the sacred greenbelt around Toronto. And here he was, in cottage country, working on a secret energy deal. He was schmoozing with the mayor of the country's largest city and the head of Ontario's power company. Talk about a meeting of the elite. All in secret. Pick your enemy, there were hundreds.

But wait. Didn't that woman at the shelter Cindy and I visited say that Mayor McCormick hated the premier? Could the mayor have killed Kahn?

I gaze at the premier and shake my head. No way was this an accident. I crouch down to take a closer look. Gooey blood has mixed with mud around his left ear. I cock my head sideways to examine the wound. I peer deep into the crevice. I can see bits of bone. It's fascinating. In a gruesome way. The tiny white pieces look like broken shards of a fine bone china teacup. That thought makes me feel a little sick.

Is fine bone china made from bones? I remember something about horses and teacups. Some connection. I'll look that up later. It will make a good House and Garden article someday. Sometimes words lose their meaning when they are frequently used. Not that "fine bone china" is all that frequently used, but still, the word "bone" in that context didn't make one think of bones.

Then, the word "bone" makes me think about Ralph. *Stop it. Robin, you are sex crazed.*

Despite these thoughts, my stomach is now doing a little tap dance right around the bottom of my esophagus. *Don't barf, Robin.* I swallow and keep looking at the wound. It must have bled like a pig. *The pig bled like a pig. Haha.*

The ground is wet with blood; it looks almost pinkish with streaks of brown dirt in it. Sort of diluted by the melting snow. In fact, it looks wetter than it should. I would have thought it would be more viscous. I find a stick and stir it up a bit. I was right—it *is* way wetter than just blood and mud mixed together. There must have been a snow drift that had melted right where he was sitting.

I take out my phone and snap a photo of the sticky mess under his ear. While I'm at it, I take pictures of the wound from several angles. *Snap snap snap.* Bizarrely, at this exact moment in time, I don't feel like fainting at all as I move in closer to the destruction. I feel detached, off in another world. In a far-off universe. A universe that was getting further and further away. Specks of black float across my vision. Uh oh, *now* I feel faint. I take a deep breath and straighten up. Again, I hold on tightly to the back of a chair and wait for the specks to float away. I make a tuneless humming noise to calm myself.

What on earth would cause a slash like that? Not a knife. A

knife wouldn't penetrate his skull. I know quite a lot about knives, my job ensured that: porcelain versus stainless steel, flick versus fixed, serrated versus saw, and so forth, and there's no doubt in my mind that the point of any knife would break off before it broke through bone. I bend down again to take a closer look at the wound. I don't see anything that could be shiny metal imbedded in the matted hair. No tip of a knife amongst the tiny shards.

An axe? No, an axe would leave a longish gash, and this wound is just about an inch long and kind of round. Besides, the centre of the wound looks deeper than the rest of the cut. *A lot* deeper. This cut was made by something sharp and pointed. My face is so close to his head I can smell his brain. It smells like shit. I have a little laugh about that. *Hey, Premier Kahn, you got shit for brains?* I *really* don't like the guy. I remind myself that he's dead. I focus again on the hole in his head. *Hey Premier Kahn, you got holes in your head?* I'm getting giddy. *Smarten up, Robin.* Be respectful. The guy deserves some dignity. *Hey Premier Kahn, you got mud on your face?* The snickers bop around in my chest, threatening to escape.

And then they actually do. I'm consumed by a fit of the giggles. I do my best to stifle them, but it's like trying to rein in a runaway train. And when I think of the people outside the tarpaulin hearing me laughing my head off, I only laugh harder. They must think I'm nuts. They must think that there's a madwoman under here. I must sound like I'm crazy. Oh God. I'm going to wet my pants. *Get a grip, Robin.* I slap my wrist. *Stop laughing.* I slap it again. Stop it. *Slap.* Okay. Deep breath. I settle down. I have to think about this. If the guy was murdered, what was the murder weapon? Not a knife or an axe, but definitely something pointed and heavy.

I take yet another look. Maybe a chisel? Chisels have a pointed end and are much thicker than knives. The point wouldn't break off. Something like a chisel could have made that mess of his head. I imagine someone striking his head and I realize it probably wouldn't work. A chisel doesn't have quite enough heft, enough weight to it to crack through bone. I imagine a strike from a chisel would simply be deflected off his skull. *Boing.*

What about a pickaxe? *Now you're talking, Robin.* A pickaxe would do the job. Heavy. Sharp. Pointed. But was a pickaxe too unwieldy? Too heavy? Could someone aim one accurately? If you missed the head, you'd only wound, not kill. So, if your intention was to kill, you'd have to be really strong to aim the pickaxe and strike the top of the head. And this gash was right at the top of his skull. So, a very strong murderer?

The other problem with a pickaxe is that it wouldn't fit easily under a coat. There's no disguising it. A pickaxe is huge, with a very long handle and large metal head. The head of a pickaxe has a sharp blade on one end and a sharper point on the other. One couldn't just saunter up to someone nonchalantly with a pickaxe in hand. The element of surprise would be non-existent. One would definitely see it coming. From a mile away. A guy like the premier would be savvy enough to be careful about his security. He would run like hell to get away. Or maybe not, in his case, given his fat cat weight issues.

Hey Premier Kahn, did someone pick your brain?

The giggles threatened to erupt again. *Slap.*

How long have I been under this tarp? Way too long. It's time to move on. But I sort of like it under there. It's kind of cozy, if you forget about the dead body. Kind of like a tent or playing house. I don't want to go out into the melee. How should I act? It's just me against the whole group of them. How much credibility could a Home and Garden writer have with all these cops? They despise all journalists, but maybe my subject matter would make me a little more acceptable. Unlike Cindy, the crime reporter. Cops can't stand her. Except for googly-eyed Kim. *Kimmy.*

Oops. I almost forgot. Before I leave my little cocoon, I have one last thing to do. I have to put his head back where it was. I look under the tarp, see no one approaching, and hook my toe under his nose. God forbid I should touch him with my hands. I flip my toes upwards but his damn head flops about in the mud. *Fuck.* I try again, but it jiggles right back to where I'd moved it.

His eyes are staring at me and my arms go a little weak.

Come on, Robin. He can't see you. He's dead, dead, dead. Gone from this world. Pushing up daisies. But what if there's an afterlife? What if he's watching me, like from above or something? God, he'd be so angry. No, that couldn't be true. Could it? Oh, no. Now I really am going to throw up. *Robin.* Take a deep breath. Stay in the here and now, no more wandering into another universe.

I have to get out of here.

But how to put his head back? I have to do it; it's obvious that he's been moved. But I refuse to touch his head with my hands. I have a thing about dead things. I can't touch them. When the kids were little, I always got my husband to unhook the dead fish. The dead hamster. The dead bird. I pick up a long twig and slide it under the premier's chin, digging one end into the mud under his cheek and placing the middle of the stick carefully so it's embedded in the folds of his double chin. I leverage the top of the stick and lift it slowly and to the right until his head is back to where it sort of was. I don't think anyone would notice the centimetre difference in the angle. It's not like anyone took photos of him, unlike me.

Photos! Just to make sure I've got the placement of his head right, I compare his body position with the photo I took when I first came under the tarp. It looks pretty good. I know I shouldn't have moved the corpse, but hell, it's not as if anyone else took his death seriously. And now, job done, I have to re-enter the world. I walk to the edge of the blue tarp, crouch down, and hope for the best. I've decided to say nothing about my suspicions until I have more information.

The world appears to be much the same as it did before I went under the tarpaulin. I look left and right. It seems as if I have wandered into a hifalutin cocktail party, uninvited, with information that no one wants to hear. People mill about, chatting, eating donuts and drinking coffee, courtesy of Andrew. He's off in the far corner of the yard, yukking it up with some of the cops. I wonder what he's up to. Andrew isn't much of a social butterfly; he must have an ulterior motive. For a moment, I wonder how strong he is. Strong enough to wield a pickaxe? Ralph is in the centre of the yard, nodding wisely in agreement with one of Huntsville's finest who was pontificating about something. Cindy and Kim are off by themselves, deep in conversation, their bodies too close for my liking. Am I still jealous? I pick my direction and move forward, heading away from the grisly scene behind me. I do my best to look like I'm merely sauntering over to the least formidable group, Kim and Cindy, and not racing. I set my face into the most impassive look I can muster. *What, me? I have no secrets.*

"Hi, you two."

Kim glares at me—was *she* jealous?—while Cindy's face breaks into a wide smile.

"Hi, Robin," she says. "Where've you been?"

She knows, of course, I'd been under the tarp. After all, she's the one who'd organized it. Why would she ask me that? Oh, for the audience. One of the cops in Ralph's group is listening in, his head tilted slightly so he can hear better. That's probably why Kim is staring at me, willing me to cover for her.

"Nowhere special," I loudly lie. Kim's fierce look softens; she knows I won't give her away. *Hmmmm, so darling Kimmy knew that she'd violated due process by letting me under the tarpaulin.*

My ethics have warped as I have gotten older and started writing crime articles so I admire her subterfuge here. My low estimation of her has gone up a notch. But it slides down again when I realize she was probably just trying to get in Cindy's good graces by giving me permission. Whatever. *Not my pig pen, not my pig.*

My mother used to say that. *Not my pig pen, not my pig.* Her lips were usually compressed when she said it, highlighting her judgment of the situation, whatever it was. She doesn't say that now. Now, she hardly speaks. I'm flooded with a momentary wave of sadness. She'd be devastated if she understood that there had been two deaths at her beloved cottage, one a couple of years ago, and now another this spring.

My father would probably want to sell the place the minute he found out about this current death. It would be too much for him. How do I feel about that? It's complicated. My kids love it. But still, I'm not really comfortable coming up here anymore. It feels jinxed. *Not that I really believe in that woo-woo stuff,* I lie to myself. Andrew wouldn't allow it to be sold, that much I know. He certainly doesn't have a finer appreciation for nature, that's not the reason. He loves the status symbol of having a cottage in Canada's most wealthy cottage country. He and his wife are like that. He'd hold onto it tooth and nail.

Cindy takes my elbow and walks me away from the cops. Kim trails behind until Cindy sees that we're being followed and says, "I have to talk to Robin about some confidential work stuff."

Kim has the good graces to at least paste a compliant look on her face, but her voice betrays her. "No problem, Cin." She turns sharply on her heel and heads over to the gaggle of cops, the edge of her voice cutting the air behind her. Clearly, Kimmy doesn't like rejection much.

Cindy ignores the tension and keeps walking me further away. Lucky trots behind her obediently. I say, "What's up?"

She lowers her voice. "That Kim is getting on my nerves and I needed a bit of distance."

I don't resort to "I told you so," but I think it. I feel badly for Cindy. It's so hard finding a partner. "She's awfully young and you do live miles away from each other. But someone will show up, someone who you'll find really charming."

Cindy looks off into the woods. "I don't know, Robin. I've been single for so long now that maybe this is just my karma."

"You can change your karma."

Cindy laughs, "No, you can't. That's what karma is. Fate. Whatever you might like to call it. It's permanent, destined by the universe."

"No, you can absolutely change it."

She looks at me. "It's one of those Buddhist things, isn't it?"

I leave it alone and say, "People usually get what they want."

She starts to hum that old song, "You Can't Always Get What You Want."

I laugh. "So, what were you two talking about?"

"Oh, nothing much. Just the death of the premier and what's going to happen next. I told her that there's going to be a shitstorm of media interest and coverage. And then likely an election for a new leader of the Conservative Party."

"It's not an election year. The party will just have a leadership campaign and there'll be a new premier to fill in until the next election in a year."

"Aren't you the savvy one, knowing your politics."

"Listen, Cindy, there's something I have to talk to you about."

"What? My relationship failures?"

"No, that isn't my business. It's about the premier."

"What about him?" She flicks her thumb over to where he lay under the tarpaulin. "He's pretty dead. Good riddance. What's more to say?"

I hem and haw. Should I say anything? Talk about my suspicions? Oh God. There's so much more to say. So much that I suspect. But can I trust Cindy with any of it? To keep it under her hat and not write a sensational story?

CHAPTER 16

I DECIDE THAT IT'S BEST TO bounce my ideas off Cindy. She's the experienced crime reporter, not me. She'll have a better take on this than I ever could. She'll be more insightful, more probing, more educated about it.

I say to her, "Remember how I said earlier that there was a lot of motivation to murder the premier? Well, um, what I saw under that tarp confirms my suspicions. I'm not sure it was an accident." So much for my resolve to break my thoughts to her in a roundabout way.

Cindy shuffles her feet and shakes her head. "Oh, fuck. Don't do that, Robin—"

So much for her expertise. She's going for a personal attack. I try not to be hurt and keep my tone light. "No, really. If you look at that wound in his head, it couldn't have happened by whacking it against the wall." I speak really quickly. As if speed will give my words authority. "It's really deep in the middle of the cut and I think something sharp stabbed him. Like a knife or something." I'm thinking pickaxe.

Cindy stands stock still as she listens to me and processes all the information.

"Robin? Wait a sec. How did you *see* that? The wound was at the back of his head."

Trust her to think of the one fly in the ointment.

"Actually, it was at the top of his head."

"Again, how did you see that?" She pauses, looks at me

sideways and puts her hands on her narrow hips. Or at least narrow compared to mine. "Did you move his head?"

"What, me?"

She cants her head in admiration. "Wow. You'll make an excellent crime reporter yet. I hope you put it back to where it was."

"Never touched it." I laugh. So, at least now I know that she's on my side.

"If this is true, you're talking about murder. Wow. Just wow. What a story. I have to check this out."

"Ask Kim for permission to look again."

But Cindy is already hightailing it to the tarp. She flicks her fingers in the air as she walks. Kim is persona non grata. I run after Cindy and take Lucky's leash out of her hand. "Here, give me Lucky," I say. "God knows what he'd do if he's up close and personal with a dead person." I have this vision of Lucky shaking his head with a dead squirrel in his mouth.

Cindy looks over her shoulder as she lifts the tarp. "Cover my back, will you?" And then she scoots under.

I stand guard and face the cops. With my arms crossed and standing stock still, I feel very Buckingham Palace.

Kim sidles over, a quizzical look on her face. On her, it isn't a good look and borders on a sneer. "Where's Cindy? She was here a minute ago."

"She's gone under the tarp to um, take some photos. She won't use them for publication, they're just to refresh her mind when she's writing the story up."

Geezus, I'm turning into such a good liar. And then I hear the sound of sucking mud coming from under the tarp. Oh God, Cindy is moving Kahn's head. I laugh loudly to cover the squelching. Kim looks at me, frowning her confusion, her lip curled the way one would as if I'd done something truly bizarre, like shove feathers or cement into my mouth. Or like I had two heads.

I gasp, pretending to hold my belly, "Sorry, this is just how I handle tension." I laugh again to illustrate my point. And then

I hear the snake hissing in my ears. Lying always comes with a toll. This is all too much for me. I take a deep breath. *Don't faint, Robin. Don't faint.* More mud sucking noise. I laugh again. Loudly. What on earth is Cindy doing under there? If she gets caught by Kim, this will turn into a very bad day.

Kim cocks her head, listening. "What's that noise? Is it coming from under the tarp?"

As if on cue, Lucky starts happily jumping about, his little paws sploshing in the wet earth. I look where he's looking and see Ralph approach. I say, "Oh, that's just mud. Lucky's making the sound. My dog," I clarify, gesturing at his dirty paws. "There's so much mud around."

Ralph is now within talking distance. "Hey Kim, Robin, what's up? Did you get some coffee and donuts?" He seems relaxed, but I can sense there's an underlying strain. I can see it in the way he's holding his shoulders. They're a tad higher than usual.

"Hi, Ralph," I say. "I think you know Kim." He nods at her. "Did you get reacquainted with everyone?"

He takes a deep breath and looks around himself. "It's so nice to be here, even under these circumstances. Poor guy. Sitting on his chair, catching some rays in the spring sunshine, enjoying a few z's, and whack, life's over."

I look at him, trying to ascertain if he's really fallen for the story. It looks like he has, but there's that tension in his shoulders. So maybe not.

I say, "So, you really believe, hook, line, and sinker, that this was an accident?"

"Don't you?" He looks at me as if I'm nuts to think anything else.

I lift a shoulder and do half a shrug. This feels better, calmer than shrieking, "Are you fucking kidding me? Didn't you look at the wound?" Instead, I merely say, "I don't know Ralph. He had lots of enemies."

Kim speaks up, having been watching this exchange, "You're joking, right?" She sounds pissed off. "Around here he was really admired. Everyone loves—I mean loved—the premier. He was doing a great job."

Ralph and I look at her as if she were from another planet. He says, "Where's Cindy?"

"Under the tarp," I reply. "Kim said she could go." I look at Kim for confirmation to my fabrication. Kim had been nowhere around when Cindy went to look at the corpse. I'd covered her back, so she can cover mine now. Luckily, Kim nods. "She's just taking some photos."

Ralph says, "But the *Express* doesn't publicize dead bodies. Too graphic."

"I know. She's just taking them for reminders of the story. For when she writes up the article."

Ralph puts on his interrogation face. I know it well. "I thought it was your article, Robin. Didn't your editor assign it to you? At least, that's what you told me in the car coming up."

Shit. He's just too smart for his own good. "I took some photos too," I say, hoping he won't notice that I'm not actually answering his question. God, this being a lying crime reporter sure is tricky. My ears start hissing.

Ralph turns to Kim and growls, "You gave permission for people other than cops to go under the tarp? Civilians? The *media*?"

This isn't good.

Kim smiles sweetly, but she isn't fooling Ralph for a second. "Sure. It's not as if it's a crime scene."

"But still. In Toronto, all sudden deaths are investigated carefully. As if they are a crime scene."

He's picking a fight; might be good one. Kim looks like a scrapper.

"In Huntsville," she pauses, giving emphasis to the town's name, "we use our limited resources carefully. If it looks like a duck and quacks like a duck, it probably is a duck."

Ralph snorts, "The word 'probably' is concerning." So much for playing nice with the locals.

Just then, Cindy pokes her head out from under the tarp. She takes a look around her, her eyes wide in the sudden gloom after being in the bright lights under the tarp and seeing what she's just walked into, hustles backwards. Wise move.

"Perhaps," Ralph says, "you and I should go talk to your superior officer."

Kim smiles, "Oh sure, no problem. He'll back me up."

I'm not so sure about that, but she's a good actor and gives no indication that he might not.

Ralph heads off to the conglomerate of chortling police with Kim following. She looks over her shoulder at me, grimaces, and crosses her fingers. Oh? So now I'm complicit in this? I guess so. This whole thing isn't really feeling like a winner to me.

No matter what I thought about Kim, I don't want her to get into trouble. She'd done me a favour. On the other hand, she's a bit too flip. Despite the fact that I had wanted to take a good look at the head wound, and was grateful that she had said I could go under the tarp and get up close to Kahn, I'd known it wasn't kosher. A doctor hadn't even pronounced him dead and a coroner hadn't come by to pick up the body. I knew there'd be an autopsy. There always is in sudden death. Those are the Ontario rules.

I watch the two of them as they approach Huntsville's Chief of Police. I'm too far away to hear the ensuing conversation, but I can tell by Kim's cocked hip that he has, indeed, backed her up. Unbelievable. Ralph turns and looks at me with raised eyebrows. We'd be talking about this later. It was complicated. I had benefitted from her lack of following due process. Ralph would feel he'd have to do some sweet talking to get me to see his point of view. And I would have to explain why I took advantage of the situation.

I suddenly feel very hungry. Or in need of a drink. The whole evening is slipping away before I've even had a single glass of wine. What a waste of good drinking time. I hear movement behind me and Lucky tugs at his leash. Now what? I turn toward the sound, hoping it isn't another shady character lurking at the side of the house. That guy in the woods had definitely spooked me. It's Cindy, looking out from under the tarp. Now that the coast is clear, she bustles out and rushes over to me.

"Robin, I hate to say it, but I think you're right. That gash wasn't caused by a fall. No way. It's way too deep. Besides, the wall where he allegedly hit his head is unmarked. It has no jagged bits that would penetrate his skin. Nope. He was definitely hit. And now the crime scene has been compromised."

"Did you move his head?"

"Of course I did. I had to see the gash."

"Did you put it back?"

She nods. "I used a stick. Can't touch dead bodies."

"I get that. Me neither. It was pretty gruesome, right?"

"Did you notice all the bits of bone? In the wound? Like tiny shards?"

"So gross. What should we do?"

"I don't know about you, but I'm going to tell Kim what I think."

I grab her arm before she can take off towards the cops. "Cindy, she won't believe you. They are convinced the premier had no enemies and no one would ever want to kill him."

"Really? That's nuts. Everyone hated him."

"Not around here. Around here, if you painted a goat blue they'd vote for it. It's a Conservative town, through and through."

Cindy says, "You'd think they'd change their tune after all those long-term care deaths during the pandemic. I lay those deaths at the Conservatives' door."

"Be that as it may, they also value their tourism industry way too much to sully it with another murder involving a well-known person. The media coverage would be brutal if the premier of Ontario was murdered. Here. It would make international news. Headlines about the murder would be plastered on all the major papers in the world." Then, I make a ghastly quantum leap in my mind. "There would be connections to the first murder at this cottage. My cottage. Can you imagine? We will never be able to sell it. The reporting would be awful. You know this, right?"

The last major murder in the town had been perpetrated by a famous actor who had killed a young woman because she was about to report him for sexual abuse. It had put the town of Huntsville on the map for all the wrong reasons. The town briefly had become known as the centre of cottage country with out-of-control murders. This of course wasn't true, but sounded the tourism death knell for the next little while.

No wonder the cops want this to be an accident. They knew what side their bread was buttered on.

But it isn't. I'm sure of it.

"Let go of my arm, Robin."

"Oh, sorry." I drop it like a hot potato. I'd been gripping Cindy's arm so tightly while the thoughts of the last murder at the cottage pinged off the sides of my brain. "But no, you can't bring the police into this, not yet."

"Oh, c'mon."

What could this be about? Cindy hates the police. She must still be trying to win Kim over. I guess she really doesn't know what she wants. She'd been so ambivalent about her just a few minutes before. "You want to impress Kim, don't you?"

"Not really. Okay, yes, I do. I feel like I'm coming and going with her."

"Not yet," I laugh.

"You know what I mean."

I say, "But still, don't tell her. I think we need more evidence."

"Or at least some."

Ralph and Kim were marching in our direction, lifting their feet high in the mud. "Oh God, here they come," I moan.

"No, look again," Cindy tells me, "it's just Ralph. Kim has veered off to talk to her chums."

"*Chums?*"

"What? You don't like the word? I grew up in North Toronto. 'Chums' is a perfectly legitimate word."

If Ralph's cheekbones were any sharper they could split open the skin spread tautly across his face. His mouth is a thin white line. "So, you two. It appears that going under the tarp and inspecting the body was an okay thing to do. Here in *Huntsville*." His voice is stretched in an effort to appear calm.

He's pissed.

"Yes," Cindy says sweetly, "I wouldn't dream of going near a corpse without permission from the cops in charge. Good thing Kim was around so I could ask her."

The lie slides off her tongue.

Ralph's left eyebrow slants downward as he gazes into the distance. He's replaying in his mind the last ten minutes of what has happened here. His inner film reel rolls to a stop and his eyes regain focus. "You're lying. Kim was nowhere near here when you went under the tarp."

Oh God. I have to speak up. "No, she was here. I heard her ask." So much for honesty in relationships. But the three of us have to live together for a few days and I need to avoid a war.

He looks at me. "Okay, if that's how you're going to play it, fine." He knows I'm lying and he must know why. He glares at Cindy. "The disgusting things you'll do to get a story." He turns his head to include me in his wrath.

Cindy doesn't flinch. "It's Robin's story. The editor assigned it to her. I'm here simply for fact-checking, research, protection, photos. That sort of thing. This isn't my file."

"Nice try," Ralph seethes. He hates being lied to. He looks between us, his anger flaring. He knows we are in cahoots.

Where does that leave me? In the middle, caught. That's where. I really need to smooth this over. "Okay. You're right. I had permission from Kim. She probably shouldn't have given it, but she did. And because she did, Cindy just skipped over the step of asking her. But Kim would have said it was okay if she'd asked. Cindy had already been under the tarp. Remember? When we got here? So, nobody's at fault here."

"You knew better, Robin." He's still simmering, but at least the smoke was dissipating.

"I know. You're right." Although it cost me some inner brownie points, sometimes it's better to capitulate. "I knew it wasn't the right thing to do, but I wanted to see. I was revved up by that weird guy in the woods and wondered if he had anything to do with the premier's death."

That suddenly puts Ralph on high alert. "What weird guy?"

I don't answer him. "I told Cindy my suspicions that the premier had been killed after I'd looked at his body. That's why she went in to check out the scene under the tarp."

"Exactly what did you see?"

God, I don't want to get into this. If I do, the fact that I'd moved the body might come to light. But maybe Ralph won't make the connection. Not if I set out the facts correctly. "I saw a really deep gash on the top of his head. Not the back. If he'd hit his head on the wall, the wound would be on the back of his head. It would likely just be a goose egg. No blood. It was on the top. Blood."

"What? You moved the body?"

Oh God. He's figured it out. Immediately. I say, "I could easily see the top of his head." I don't add, of course, after I'd jostled his head around. "There was a deep cut."

"So, you went under the tarp, knowing you were entering what you thought was a crime scene, and then you moved the body, the body of a person who you thought could have been murdered, and now you're lying to me about all this? What on earth is wrong with you, Robin?"

Cindy's angry green eyes gleam in the blue light emanating from under the tarp. "Look, wise guy, if we hadn't gone in and looked, if we hadn't moved the body, there'd be no way this information would be revealed. The locals," she spits out the word—so much for her loyalty to Kim—"were completely prepared to write this off as an accident. It wasn't."

CHAPTER 17

RALPH JERKS HIS HEAD AROUND so he can look directly at Cindy. "Okay. Let's let all this unethical shit go. And you're right. Those cops really want this to be an accident. But I want to be clear, Cindy."

Oh no, here it comes. He's going to berate her.

But all he says is, "You think the same thing as Robin? That he was murdered?"

Huh?

Well! That wasn't so bad. He could have lit into her. But one thing about Ralph, he doesn't hold a grudge. When he says, "Let's let this go," he means it, he really does let it go, and he moves on to the next thing. I'm not quite like that. I tend to replay things over and over in my mind until I've had enough to drink to wipe it out. Wine as an eraser. Maybe that would be a good article for *The Express*. Title the article: "White Out." No, that was already taken. The lawyers wouldn't like that. So, "Wipe Out White."

Geez, I really need to deal with my slurping issue.

Cindy looks at him, feigning shock. "You're asking me? Lowly crime reporter me?" She jabs her thumb into her chest.

Exasperated, Ralph holds his hands out, palms up. "I do respect your opinion, Cindy. Despite your attitude, you do have a lot of experience with crime and know a fair bit."

Should I be insulted? Does he value her opinion over mine? Does he think that I know nothing because my expertise is rugs and refrigerators? Tea towels and toilet brushes? I stand up for myself. "I spotted it first." God, I sound like a three-year-old. "I went in first, I spotted the discrepancies first, and it was only after Cindy looked that she agreed with me. We both think he was murdered."

Ralph looks at me with a thought dawning in his eyes. He has offended me. "I know you saw this first. I only asked Cindy out of politeness."

No, he hadn't.

Realizing his misstep, he directly asks me, "Any opinions on the murder weapon?"

Here, I'm a step ahead of Cindy. I had spent a little time thinking about this. "It had to be something sharp, you know, pointed, given that the wound has a very deep centre."

"Something sharp?" he asks. "Like a knife?"

"No," says Cindy. *Bossy pants.* "A knife isn't heavy enough. This weapon, whatever it was, penetrated his skull, smashed a small hole in it and shattered the surrounding area into bits."

She's stolen my thunder, but I don't want to fight, not now, so I add: "I'm thinking a pickaxe."

Ralph laughs in disbelief. "Oh, right. I can see it now," he says, his voice dripping in sarcasm. "Someone just walked up to the premier carrying a huge pickaxe concealed in his winter coat and took a swing at him."

He's pissing me off, making fun of me. I counter, "Well, it had to be something heavy and pointed. Go take a look yourself. See what you think."

Cindy says, "Robin's right. It probably was a pickaxe. I can't imagine it being anything else."

Ralph shuffles his feet in the mud. He doesn't know whether he should look. On one hand, he's naturally curious. On the other, this would be treading on the local cops' shoes. Then again, on the third, totally existent, hand, he has already made it quite clear he doesn't think it was a pickaxe. As his feet sink deeper into the mud, with all this hemming and hawing, it's a good thing he's worn boots. All this time, shifting his weight, trying to make a decision, he's sunk into the muck, ankle-deep.

"Hm-m-m," he says.

I challenge him. "Go on, Ralph. Take a look. You'll see what we mean."

Cindy pipes up, "'Hm-m-m?' Oh, nothing." She has a twinkle in her eye as she pauses for comedic effect. She stands her whole height of six feet and looks Ralph straight in the eye.

"What?" he asks.

"Take a look. You'll see there's no doubt about it. For the last time in his life, someone picked his brain."

We all hoot at that, the tension in the air floating away on the sounds of our laughter.

"No, no," I pant, "It's not funny. The guy is dead. We need to be respectful." The other cops turn their heads, looking at us, wondering what we could possibly be laughing about. But I just can't help myself: "Ralph, go take a peek-a-boo. Or should I say '*pick*-a-boo.'"

His mind made up, he says, "Okay, I will."

He heads to the tarp.

"Don't you have to get permission?" Cindy stage-whispers to his retreating back.

"I have a certain amount of authority here," Ralph retorts. "I'm not a civilian after all. Unlike some people."

"Oh, fuck off," mutters Cindy under her breath, just loud enough for him to hear her.

Once Ralph is out of earshot, Cindy says, "It's fine and dandy that the premier was knocked off, but the question remains: why? Who would want to do this to him?"

"I think it was something to do with why he was here in the first place. Whatever that conference was about. Andrew will know. I think he said it had to do with power. Or maybe it was something to do with that guy in the woods. That was definitely a drug deal that had gone wrong." It all comes pouring out of me, my mind runs a mile-a-minute, making connections; my mouth struggles to keep up. "Cindy, you remember when we were watching the lineup at the food bank and there was that commotion? Remember? The guy took off and then that other guy chased him?"

Cindy looks at me askance. She's struggling to keep up with my quick changes in topic as well. She's still thinking about pickaxes and chipped bone. I watch as her thoughts coalesce and change direction. She focuses directly on my face, away from the tarpaulin. "Ya, sure, I remember. What about it?"

"I think he had the same symbol of a lightning bolt stitched onto his knapsack. Just like the one in your hand."

Cindy raises the frayed knapsack to her eye level and smooths out the fabric on the back of her knee."

"You might be right about that, Robin. I didn't really notice the city guy's knapsack, but now that I think about it, yes, it could have been the same symbol. Wait a sec."

She pulls out her phone and starts scrolling with her thumb.

"What are you doing? Looking for gang affiliations? Groups of kids that have lightning bolts as identifying gangdom?"

"No, I took a photo of the guy as he was running away. It was a great action shot. I want to see if there was a lightning bolt on his knapsack."

She doesn't believe me?

I watch as she squints at the photo while enlarging it with her two fingers.

"Yup. You're right, Robin. You have a good eye for detail."

Is that supposed to be an apology for doubting my word? "So, what do you think?" I ask. "Same person? Is there any way the fellow chasing the guy in Toronto was the same person we saw in the woods?"

Cindy compresses her lips as she adds up all the facts and then flicks the thought off with her fingers. "No way. First of all, he wouldn't have a car and the bus service here is sporadic. Secondly, why would he be here? In the middle of the woods?"

"The guy we saw didn't have a car either. Plus, Muskoka isn't really wilderness anymore, Cindy."

"You know what I mean. Oh look, here comes Kim. We can ask her about the symbol."

Kim picks her way through the mud, placing her feet carefully on clumps of grass. "Hi you two." She looks around, her eyes searching the area. "Where's Ralph?"

"Under the tarp. Just checking out the wound."

A look of distaste passes over Kim's features. "It's just a wound. Why would he want to look at that?"

At least she hadn't challenged the legitimacy of his taking a look.

Cindy thrusts the knapsack in Kim's face. "What do you think about this?"

Kim reaches out for the knapsack and looks at it closely. "What's this? Where did you find this?"

Cindy gestures widely with her arm. "In the woods. Over there."

"This probably belongs to one of the kids from a local reservation. That's their symbol. It means power. Years ago, some members of the band in Quebec had been displaced by the flooding west of James Bay."

I interject, the symbol making sense, "To create a huge hydroelectric power plant."

Kim nods. "Right. Some of these people migrated to Huntsville. Or further north. Some went to Toronto. They wouldn't go to Montreal, even though it was the closer city and many of them spoke French or had married into French Canadian families, because it was the Quebec government that had cost them their homes. The lightning bolt is their symbol of power. You know, the electric power in lightning. They're sort of reclaiming their power, if you know what I mean."

She seems to be at sea, trying to grasp the innuendo of the metaphor.

I say, "I get it. But that doesn't explain the baggies of weed."

"Weed? That's interesting." She unzips the bag and rustles inside it. "Wow. Baggies of it. But it doesn't really explain why the guy was in Robin's woods," she says. "I'm going to take this as evidence of something, but I'm not sure what yet. I don't think anything illegal was going on here. He was likely just stocking up his stash."

"It's a bit much for personal consumption."

Kim laughs, "Not around here it isn't."

Kim walks toward a cruiser, pops the trunk, and throws the torn bag into it. No evidence bag. Even I know that evidence always goes into a sealed bag. Whatever she's doing, it doesn't seem like something quite above board. Is she taking the weed for herself? Then, she wanders off to her colleagues, leaving Cindy and me to ourselves. So much for camaraderie.

Just then Ralph emerges from under the tarp. He ambles over and says, "Well, that's the premier all right. He's got mud on his face."

I laugh politely. "The joke's been done, Ralph." I'm still a little pissed off at him for him believing Cindy over me.

Cindy says, "So, what do you think? Accident or murder?"

Ralph sighs, "Unfortunately for the local cops, I think you two are probably right. He definitely didn't get that gash from hitting his head on the side of the building. I like the idea of a pickaxe, it sort of fits the evidence of the wound, but I really don't see how anyone could get away with that. Kahn would see it coming for sure. Those things are too big to hide. But if it was a pickaxe, it's my guess he knew the person."

Cindy twirls one of her curls, thinking. "Right. It was probably someone he trusted. So that narrows down the field."

"Yes, but why would they be carrying a pickaxe? I mean, how would he, whoever it was, explain why he was carrying it?"

"Or she," I say.

"Naw. A female isn't really strong enough to heft up a pickaxe and then carefully direct it to the top of someone's head."

God, he's getting on my nerves. It's so unlike him to dismiss me. He has a hair up his butt for sure. "Why do you keep discounting what I say?"

He looks genuinely puzzled. "I do?"

"Ya, first you dismissed my assertion that he was murdered and then asked Cindy for her thoughts, and now this."

"Oh. Sorry. I really didn't mean to. I value your opinion very highly, Robin, you know I do. I listen to you. I'm so sorry it didn't seem that way. It was non-intentional. I'm just trying to get to the truth."

"Cut it out, you two," says Cindy, sensing the tension between us. "We're trying to figure something out here. Let's work as a team and not get into one-upmanship about who had the best idea, the first idea, the smart idea. I think it was likely a man, not a woman, because men are typically stronger, pickaxes are heavy, and aiming one at the top of someone's head would take more than talent or luck. It would need brute strength."

I concede the point, although privately I think it could have been a very strong woman. "Sure, let's move on. The question is, why would the premier trust someone approaching him with a pickaxe?"

"Good question," says Ralph.

Is he being patronizing? Or trying to win brownie points?

I continue, "I mean, I really don't know. Maybe there is a legit reason. Like something was stuck in the frozen ground. That makes sense. Something was frozen in solid and needed to be chipped out. Maybe that was the person's excuse." I'm still a bit rankled about the gender business so I refuse to say "he."

Ralph likes that idea. "I see what you mean, Robin," he says. I watch him consider the idea. Whenever he's thinking hard, he rubs his eyebrow; I see him doing that now.

So, he hadn't been patronizing. He was really listening to me.

"Do you have a pickaxe anywhere on the property? You know, somewhere conveniently at hand?"

He has me there. "I have no idea. I can't recall seeing one around, but I haven't been here for a few seasons. Andrew would know for sure. He's the one who keeps tabs on the maintenance and maybe he's purchased one in the last little while. Speaking of which, he'll be mightily ticked off about the ruts in his beloved grass." I kick at a clump of semi-frozen mud.

"And, drum roll, speak of the devil, here he comes."

Andrew stomps across the yard, his lips pulled back from his capped teeth in what is supposed to be a smile. Lucky growls at him.

He holds out his hands in a welcoming gesture. "Robin. Cindy. Ralph."

He must have been at some leadership convention and learned to identify all members of a group by name upon approach. What a bad actor. It was like watching a slug trying to be cavalier.

"What?" I say.

Lucky strains at his leash, teeth bared, a low rumble emanating from his throat. He *hates* Andrew.

"Put your dog in your car, Robin."

"He won't hurt you and his paws are too muddy for Ralph's car."

Andrew stops a good three metres away. He's trying to act all nonchalant while I tug at Lucky's leash, reining him in.

Ralph takes a step closer to Andrew. "Do you happen to have a pickaxe around here anywhere?"

"Why? Is something stuck in the ice? Your tires?"

The helpful host.

Ralph improvises on the fly. He won't give his thoughts and suspicions away that easily. "A pickaxe would be good for chipping out a car embedded deeply in ice," he says, glancing at Cindy and me. "Do you have one?" he repeats. Does he suspect Andrew? I know I have my doubts.

"Sure, in that shed over there." Andrew hitches his thumb over his shoulder toward the back of the cottage. He sees my surprise and says, "I just got one in the fall. I was hoping to spend some time here this winter and one never knows when one might need a pickaxe."

He seems to stumble over his reasons for getting a pickaxe. "Why did you think you needed one? What for? I certainly wouldn't try to chip out tires with a pickaxe. That would be too risky and likely puncture the tire. I would use salt and melt the ice around the tire."

Andrew guffaws. "Salt loses its effectiveness at about -10 degrees, Robin." He's *actually* looking down his nose at me.

He's right, though. Of course. I know that, too. My bad.

"So, I thought I should get a pickaxe to cover the winter

temperatures here in Muskoka. Just in case."

Ralph is itching to look at it. "Let's go take a look."

"Why do you want to see it?" Andrew demands. He's acting so strangely. What could he be hiding?

Ralph lets the cat out of the bag. "Maybe it was a murder weapon." He watches Andrew carefully, gauging his reaction to this tiny bit of news.

"A murder weapon?" someone asks. Kim had approached us from behind. She'd overheard Ralph. "Who was murdered?"

What an airhead.

Cindy is far more patient than me. "We were just wondering, Kim, if maybe someone hit the premier with a pickaxe."

Ralph and Andrew had already started walking to the shed, so Cindy and I hurry to catch up. Kim trails behind us.

"Naw," she says. "He hit his head on the wall when he fell back. There was no weapon."

Andrew comes out of the shed, holding a brand new pickaxe in his hands. The blades glint in the ambient light and the handle is smooth and varnished. Ralph bends over and peers closely at the tip. "Here Andrew, hold it up while I shine my flashlight on it."

Ralph aims the laser-like point of his phone's beam at the shiny tip of the pickaxe. It's easy to see the thing has never been used. Not a speck of anything on it. No matted hair, no blood. Not even a smear.

"See?" says Kim. "He wasn't murdered with a pickaxe. He simply fell. Whose idea was it that he was murdered?"

Cindy and I say each other's names simultaneously.

Kim laughs, "Oh, you media-types. Always looking for a story. Even where there isn't one. He simply fell."

That isn't true, I know it isn't. I'll just have to find whatever was really used to kill Kahn to prove it to them.

CHAPTER 18

As KIM HOOKS HER ARM through Cindy's to drag her over to the gaggle of cops, a large grey van pulls into the clearing.

Andrew looks puzzled. "I didn't order a plumber."

Geez. It's always about him.

Ralph states flatly, his anger in check, "It's the coroner's van, Andrew. It's come to take the premier to the morgue for an autopsy. The dead premier." Ralph digs in his heels. "The premier, the political leader of Ontario, who died."

Andrew dismisses all this with an offhand wave of his arm as he turns his back and saunters over to the cottage. I watch his back fade into the darkness and wonder why he is being so cavalier, so glib. Is it all an act?

But with his departure, Ralph and I are finally alone. "Listen," I say, "About earlier…"

"No, it was my fault, sweetie, you always have good ideas. I was trying to be extra careful with Cindy—we do have to live together for a few days—and it sorta backfired."

"You think?" I still feel a little irked.

"I am truly sorry. What else can I do so you won't be mad at me?"

I smile at him and waggle my eyebrows. "Oh, I can think of a few things."

He laughs and pulls me into his arms. We would be okay.

Ralph says to the top of my head, "I'm one-hundred percent sure he didn't die from hitting his head. Sure, he was banged with something on the top of his head. You are right about that. But not with Andrew's pickaxe. Or at least not with the one he showed me."

"What? You think Andrew's involved somehow? That he banged the premier with a second pickaxe?"

Ralph lets me go and shrugs his broad shoulders. I watch his coat stretch across his chest and have a few thoughts about getting banged myself.

Ralph says, "It's pretty obvious to me that he's hiding something. I just don't know what it is."

"I was thinking the same thing, Ralphie. He's definitely being secretive. No, not secretive. He's being *elusive*. I mean, where is he right now? He's disappeared. He used to do that as a kid. He'd hide if he'd done something wrong. And that's how I know he's being secretive."

"'Elusive'? That's a pretty big word around us dumb cops."

I laugh.

"And don't call me Ralphie."

"Okay, Ralphie."

He fake-frowns at me.

The van doors open and two men and a woman step into the muddy yard. Ralph strides toward them. "Ralph Creston. Detective from Toronto. Hello." He'd left out the word "homicide" from his credentials, probably to be diplomatic and leave the cause of death verdict open. Or perhaps he's just a humble guy who doesn't need to impress anyone.

The woman stomps across the yard and meets him halfway. Her voice is almost mechanical, sort of like the whine of a food processor. "Dr. Sherk. Where's the body?"

Hmmm. Not a smile, not a greeting. All business.

The two guys who had arrived with her fling open the back doors of the van and wheel out a gurney. A couple of cops stride over to the action. It's as if the yard has turned into a fast-forward film, going from static groups to high-speed movement.

I recognize one of the officers from my—shall we call it "escapade"—last spring. Niemchuk. He had been a rookie then, but seems much older now. Aged by a bear charge, I guess.

"Hey, Dr. Sherk."

I watch as Niemchuk approaches the doctor. Clearly, he knows her and wants to be friendly. Sherk isn't buying it.

"Niemchuk." She makes it sound like a swear word. Nope, she doesn't like him much. Or maybe this is just her way.

"You've come for the body?" He's making conversation. He knows why she's here.

Dr. Sherk doesn't roll her eyes, at least not visibly. She shakes a few strands of blond hair off her face. "Was it you who called this in to my office, saying it was an accident?"

Niemchuk puffs himself up. "Yes. I called as soon as I was alerted by the premier's wife that her husband had died while sitting outside. That he'd hit his head on the siding of the building."

"Be that as it may, I'm the one who determines cause of death, not you, not his wife, not anyone else. Not even the Queen." Her hands are slotted on her hips and her head pulled back indignantly.

Her bitchiness is growing on me. I kind of like it. So much confidence and authority.

Niemchuk gives the other cop, a red-faced guy with a button nose—what was his name?—a *whatever* look, and says, "Sure. We know that. But it's pretty obvious he fell backwards and hit his head."

Dr. Sherk looks at him disbelievingly and huffs. "I have never heard of anyone dying from falling backwards and hitting their head against a wooden building. Heads are constructed to withstand blows like that. Skulls are incredibly strong. So don't tell me how to do my job."

Niemchuk shakes his head and gestures a "let's go" to Mr. Button Nose beside him. He turns on his heel, snorting. "Geez. *Women.*"

Now Dr. Sherk rolls her eyes and heads for the tarp. "Under here?" she asks Ralph.

"Yep."

I try to look relaxed as I race behind her. "Mind if I come with you?"

She stops, pauses, looks me up and down, and says, "Yes, I do mind."

Although this pisses me off, I have to admire her boundaries.

"Okay, no prob."

I smile to let her know that there are no hard feelings. She doesn't care.

Dr. Sherk bends her lanky body into a paperclip with the ease of someone who does yoga at least twenty times a day and slides under the tarpaulin. I can see the beam of her flashlight through the translucent covering as she walks toward the premier. First, it aims at what I imagine is his head. Then, it travels all over the wall of the cottage. In a few short minutes, she emerges from under the tarpaulin and gestures Ralph over. I follow at his side. I want her to know that I'm not to be so easily dismissed.

"Tell the cops to get over here."

Ralph, who isn't used to being ordered about, looks at me and then tilts his head. He can't decide if he should be graceful or exert his authority. I press my lips together, trying not to smile at his discomfort. I give an almost imperceptible nod. *Do what she says.* He takes a few steps in the direction of the group and shouts, "Hey! Hey, folks. Dr. Sherk wants to talk to you."

The cops look up from their ad hoc coffee klatch and amble over. Kim and Cindy are with them. Andrew is still nowhere to be seen. He was likely inside. Hiding?

Dr. Sherk doesn't look happy. In fact, she practically has smoke coming out of her ears. I don't know, maybe this is a typical look for her. I had her pegged as a bossy bitch, and given what I've seen so far, she was living up to my estimation. The cops sense her anger and lumber around, hands in pockets, looking like sheepish children who'd been caught doing something inappropriate.

Dr. Sherk spits at the group, "The death of this very important man was not caused by him leaning back in his chair and falling backwards, to then hit his head on a wall behind him. Why you said his death happened like this is beyond me." Her eyes flash in anger as she looks at each officer in turn and then settles in on Niemchuk. "On top of this, I can see that you *people*," she hisses out the word, "didn't treat this scene with any respect at all."

"I set up a perimeter and covered the body." The name of the small-nosed cop I couldn't remember flies into my mind as he speaks. I now vividly remember him from two years ago. *Kowalchuk.* Mr. Button Nose detective sure is defensive. "Nobody went under the tarp to look at the premier. The scene is pristine."

Oh boy. Is he ever wrong. Hadn't he heard how the chief had supported Kim for her letting Cindy under the tarp? I watch the chief's mouth slam shut. I watch Sherk as she processes her thoughts to this obvious misinformation.

Spittle explodes out of her mouth. "Do you take me for a fool?"

Kowalchuk looks defiant. He still thinks he's right. Kim and the chief, Cindy, Ralph, and me all know he's wrong. And so, apparently, does Dr. Sherk.

"You couldn't be more wrong. There are footprints everywhere around the body. Everywhere. Up by his head. Down by his feet. Around his arm." Her voice has taken on an icy calm as her arm chops the air around her body to illustrate where the footprints had been. No spittle now. "There was a stick to the left of his head with blood on it. Blood! Someone had used this stick. Someone here, right now, had used this stick to poke at the premier's head. To move him somehow."

Oh God. Was I ever in deep shit.

All the cops look at each other, shaking their heads. *Wasn't me, wasn't me.* They all lean back on their heels as if that would deflect her wrath.

She continues, her voice raised, "The dead body was moved, was touched, was walked around. How on earth do you *people* expect me to do my job with a scene as compromised as this? If there were any clues to what had happened here, to this very important person, they are now gone."

Kim Andrechuk speaks up. She sounds a bit timid. She should be, given it was her who had allowed various people to go under the tarp and take a gander at Kahn. Would she confess? Probably not. If she did, she'd likely lose her job. If a person outside the force knew what she had done, they would definitely report it to her superiors. To operate so wildly outside of protocol would be a cause for employment termination. I see the police chief move closer to her. He's at fault as well.

The body language of all the cops is a game-changer for me. One by one, they step toward each other, banding together. They huddle together, barely a foot apart, forming a big black wall. The black uniforms of the OPP all meld into one. It's disgusting and somewhat frightening. How could the truth come out, when that pearl of truth was embedded in the clamming up of the force? There's no way any one of them would admit to any wrongdoing or not support any one of them who was accused of a misstep. I was witnessing the force of a cover up. Right before my eyes. Thinking all this, and coping with my feelings about it, I completely miss what Kim was now asking.

Dr. Sherk says, "Yes, it could have been a murder, but I think it was more likely an accident." The surrounding officers listen to this with relief and "I told you so" expressions on their faces. "Looking at the scene, or what remains of it, I believe that an icicle fell on his head, killing him instantly and knocking him over."

So, Kim had asked if the coroner had thought this was a homicide.

But wait. What had the doctor said? An icicle? He was killed by an icicle? It was an *accident*?

The coroner points at the roof of the cottage. Several huge icicles, larger than the world-famous stalactites in Brazil, hang from the eaves. There are about five in all, long, hard, pointed spikes suspended from the roof, forming a line of pillars. Between these five are the remains of several broken-off icicles. Clear drops of water slowly trickle from each one as they melt in the spring temperatures. The drips punctuate the quiet in the vacuum of silence that has been created by the coroner's announcement. It certainly looks as if this was in fact an accident, caused by the random falling of an icicle.

I look up and see that there is one missing right above where the premier had been sitting. Like a six-year-old's missing tooth, there's a gaping hole in the row of columns above his head, the flat edge of where the icicle had broken off, now dripping, and a smaller icicle beginning to form in its place.

The meaning of her pronouncement in conjunction with the visuals dawns on me slowly. What a ridiculous way to die. Talk about bad luck. There was the premier, sitting in the sunshine, enjoying his moment of peace, rocking a bit on his chair, maybe humming a little tune to himself in the pretty spring afternoon, breathing in the fresh country air, and then—*WHACK*. Dead.

I catch Ralph's eye. A smile plays around the corners of his mouth. He finds this all as funny as I do. The premier of Ontario, the leader of Canada's most populated province, has been killed by a melting icicle. Who would have thought? What a bizarre thing to happen. Talk about karma. Talk about the weirdest accident around. Who needs an assassin when you have icicles? I imagine the editorials. The headlines.

I notice that Cindy is madly tapping on her iPad. She was already writing up the story.

I'd have to talk to her about that. It's my story after all, isn't it?

Recently, I had been questioning my memory. It could be a little addled by wine, and I had experienced some gaps in my thoughts. Shirley did say that, didn't she? That this was my story? I go over the conversation I'd had with her right before I headed north with Ralph. Yes! She did say it was my story, and mine alone. I can hear her clearly in my mind, her throaty rumble saying it was mine, not Cindy's. That Cindy was just along for the ride. For safety. For photographs. So now, why was she trying to steal my thunder? She got great stories all year long. Me? I got to write about sponges, sea versus vegetable cellulose. I stride over to her, ready for battle.

"What are you doing? Stealing my story?"

She looks up from her device, her eyes wide, her stance fluid. "I'm not stealing your story. I'm making up captions for my photos."

"Sure you are." I know Cindy. She lies all the time. Anything to get her name in print.

"I am. See, look." She thrusts her tablet at me.

Oops…She is actually telling the truth. This time. I read, "Premier gets iced." And "Premier gets the point." And "Pointed towards death."

"Hey, those are pretty good. I'm not sure the legal department will like your puns, but you never know. I'd go for it. No one liked him much."

Kim raises her head. She'd been working on her phone too. "Oh c'mon. I don't know why you keep saying that. He was doing a terrific job. Especially during the pandemic."

"Are you kidding me?" I say. "So many people died because of him opening up too soon. Because he had cut back on funding for long-term care homes. And some of those elders still don't have air conditioning."

Kim shakes her head. The ropey muscles on her neck stand out. She's winding up to a rant, I can tell. No wonder she and Cindy get along. Cindy could rant with the best of them.

Except, this time, she doesn't fight at all. My friend says, "He did the best he could with the expertise he had. With the budget he had."

What? Cindy supporting the premier? Oh, the power of love.

I'm incensed. "Oh, right. Even I knew at the time, in the middle of the pandemic, he was opening up too soon. The numbers were going up and restrictions were easing. Two days and numpteen deaths later, he shut everything down again." Cindy knows this was true. "And you want to talk about budget? What about those fancy superfluous million-dollar vaccination clinics when pharmacies and Shoppers Drug Mart could do the job better?" I'm on a roll. "And even I know that an air conditioner is only a couple hundred bucks from Canadian Tire. What would that cost if every senior in care had one? Peanuts, compared to all other budgets. Peanuts." I'm really getting into this. I can feel my head jutting forward.

Cindy sidles between us. "Okay, okay, let's just move on. Everyone has different politics."

I can't believe it. Cindy is such a socialist that she sometimes verged on communist. How could she even begin to entertain a relationship with Kim? How could she even say she agreed with her on something she doesn't even believe in?

"Right," I snort and stomp off, back to Ralph. I'll talk to Cindy about this later.

As I walk away, I look up at the roofline of my cottage and wonder briefly if someone had knocked an icicle off and used it as a weapon to kill the premier. What a perfect murder weapon. It would melt and leave no trace of the killer. Fingerprints would simply dissolve into the earth. A trace fibre wouldn't be visible in the mud left behind. What if someone had broken off the icicle in the morning with say, the pickaxe, before the renters arrived? The person could easily do that while standing on a chair. What if then later, when the premier was basking in the spring sunshine in the same chair left conveniently outside in a good whacking location, that same someone picked it up and thumped him over the head with it? Someone like that kid with the backpack. Or my brother.

What? Do I really think that? No, I quickly dismiss this line of reasoning. The wound, which I wasn't supposed to have even seen, had a deep indent in the middle of it. The premier had taken a blow with a sharp object to the very top of his head. The icicle had definitely fallen right on him. He hadn't been hit by the side of the icicle, no, it had been the pointed tip. But an accident?

I have to think about this. Could a falling icicle do the job? Could it kill? How heavy was an icicle anyway? They look pretty light, being transparent, but water is heavy. Is an icicle heavier than water? Probably not. So how much water made up one of those huge icicles? I carefully size up one of the remaining ones and imagine how many buckets it would fill if melted. I would guess maybe two of a regular-sized bucket, maybe two and a half. How much does a bucket of water weigh? I had never carried a bucket of water, but I had carried a bottle of wine. In fact, I'd carried a week's supply of wine in one bag. It had been very heavy. Twenty pounds? At least. But then again, there was the thick glass of the bottle to consider there. Would seven bottles of wine fill a bucket? These deductions aren't getting me anywhere. Probably because it's long-past time for a glass of wine. All I know is that an icicle of that size would no doubt weigh enough to kill him.

When I reach Ralph's side, I say, "So, what do you think about Dr. Sherk's icicle theory?"

He looks at me and says, "I think it has merit. Too bad about the scene being contaminated though. But I guess it doesn't really matter, given it was an accident."

"Maybe. I'm not so sure."

"Really? Why do you think that?"

Why, indeed. It's just a feeling I have, how do I explain that to Ralph? "I don't know. I'll think about it. He was so hated."

Just then, under Dr. Sherk's supervision, her colleagues begin to wheel the body of the premier toward the coroner's van over the rutted terrain. One of the guys keeps his hand on the black body bag to keep the premier from rolling off the gurney. They trundle him up a small, corrugated ramp and slam the doors of the van.

"The iceman cometh," Ralph says.

Then, there is a loud resonating boom, like a crack of thunder right by my ear. Or a gunshot. Ralph pulls out his gun and drops into a crouch, sweeping one arm at me to hold me back. He aims his weapon from left to right over the dark landscape. I follow his trajectory and see nothing. Then, I look up and see in the shadows of the spotlights, a jagged line of broken teeth along the eaves of the cottage. The remaining icicles had all fallen at once. And under one of them lay Niemchuk, moaning.

CHAPTER 19

NIEMCHUK LIES ON HIS BACK, barely conscious. His right arm sticks out at an angle never intended by nature and his shoulder is about two inches lower than it should be. It doesn't take a genius to know that his collarbone has been snapped by a falling icicle. The evidence lies shattered around his head. He whimpers like an injured animal, his feet writhing and digging into the mud, as if he was trying to get away from the pain.

The van doors fly open and Dr. Sherk runs across the yard toward him, her shoes sucking in the mud. "Is he dead?" she shouts.

Ralph is already kneeling in the dirt beside Niemchuk's head. "No, but badly hurt. I think his collarbone is broken."

I can hear Niemchuk weakly whispering, "My arm. My arm."

I run over and join Ralph. The officer isn't looking good. He's paler than pale and despite the chill in the air, sweat beads on his forehead. That poor man. "You'll be okay," I say soothingly, although from the look of him, I wasn't so sure.

I take in the scene and wonder why the huge icicle hadn't killed him as it had the premier. Then, I see on his right shoulder a small tear in the thick material of his bulletproof vest. I've seen Ralph's vest up close, so I know that the covering is made of the strongest fabric around, a canvas of sorts interwoven with metal threads. The vests weigh a ton. A lot of cops don't like to wear them, especially in rural areas where crimes are far and few between. Usually.

Luckily, Niemchuk had obeyed the new rules that required the wearing of a bulletproof vest at all times while on duty. The straps to the vest go over his shoulders and although the heavy-duty plate of armour in the vest stopped above his heart, the tough material of the outer coating probably saved him from losing his arm altogether, or worse, his life. It looks to me as if the icicle hit, making a tear in the shoulder, but didn't continue on its gravity-fueled journey downward because the metal-infused material on the strap, in combination with the angle of the hit, had deflected the blow. Nonetheless, it had caused a lot of damage. In addition to the broken collarbone, he'd probably dislocated his shoulder. No wonder he was moaning in pain.

Dr. Sherk leans on her haunches in the mud beside him and runs her hands surprisingly gently over the area and pronounces, "Broken clavicle, dislocated shoulder." To Niemchuk she says, "No point in complaining. You'll live."

Such a hard ass.

In response, Niemchuk's eyes roll up into his head. He's fainted. For some reason, I'd thought people couldn't faint lying down. Guess I was wrong.

"Not made of the strongest stuff, this one," Sherk says to no one in particular.

Geezus. Maybe I should dislocate her shoulder and see how she likes it.

She gestures to the two guys from the van to come over. "Get the gurney and bring it here. We'll take him to the hospital. An ambulance would take too long."

One of the fellows objects, "The premier is on the gurney. We only have one."

She unfolds her tall thin body from her crouched position and speaks to them as if they were children. "Put the premier on the floor of the van and bring the gurney."

The two guys look at one another, then back at her. They don't want to do this.

"Now!" she snaps.

They don't move.

Exasperated, she tells them, "Niemchuk needs medical attention now. The premier's dead. He doesn't care. He'd want a person in trouble to have the gurney."

Not the premier I know, but whatever.

The two fellows open the back of the van and I watch as they lift the, um…carcass of the premier onto the floor of the van. The body bag is bursting at the seams. I watch, horrified, as it lolls to one side. They step gingerly around the lump on the floor and efficiently collapse the gurney so they can carry it across the yard under their arms. When they arrive beside Dr. Sherk, they put the gurney on the ground and assess the situation. One of the guys carefully holds Niemchuk under his left arm while sliding his other hand to the centre of his back. As he lifts, he cradles the injured arm in the crook of his elbow. The other guy hoists his feet. They gently slide the unconscious Niemchuk onto the metal surface, raise the gurney up and roll him slowly over the bumps in the yard into the van. The Chief of Police and Andrechuk trail behind their fallen comrade. The doctor follows the procession and climbs into the driver's side of the van. Through her open window, I can hear her arguing with the Chief of Police.

His voice cuts through the night air. "Why didn't you call an ambulance? He needs to be with trained paramedics. What if he has a broken neck? Your untrained guys lifted him. They could paralyze him. And the premier on the floor? The dead should be treated with respect."

Dr. Sherk defends her actions with clipped sentences. "He needs medical attention quickly. He may have internal bleeding. That may be why he fainted. We can get him to the hospital in Huntsville long before an ambulance would even arrive here. Budget cuts."

By the premier. So ironic.

Kim leaves the back of the van and drifts back to Cindy's side, who was working her way toward Ralph and me. Kim says, "We should have called an ambulance."

Cindy interjects, "You heard Dr. Sherk. It would take ages for a bus to even get here."

Kim says nothing.

I can't resist jabbing my two cents in. "How ironic that the guy who cut back budgets to health care is compromising the care of one of your colleagues."

"Shut up," she hisses.

Oh, wow. Little Kimmy has a temper.

Cindy, shocked, takes a step away from her, as if distancing herself from a snake that had poked its head out of its hole. Ralph looks at me and raises his eyebrows. I turn, look directly at Kim, and say in my best mother beast voice, "Oh-h-h. Nice talk."

The van slithers out of the driveway with its cargo.

One of the remaining police officers finishes the work Niemchuk had begun and bundles up the rest of the makeshift tent over the fallen chair, tidying up the scene. The noise of the tarp being scrunched up into a ball crackles through the night like a rattler's tail. Ralph grabs the pickaxe from where Andrew had dropped it on the ground and heads over to the shed. I pull the fallen chair out of the mud and carry it to the back porch of the cottage. Andrew would have a fit with the dirt on the floor. I try to wipe some of it off, but it was still wet and sticking to the legs. Where was Andrew, anyway? Ralph returns from the shed with a hammer in his hand. He methodically begins pulling out the nails that had attached the tarp to the cottage's siding. Every nail groans through the night as Ralph tugs at each one. A car starts and takes off into the dark, the echo of its engine rumbling through the deepening dusk.

Cindy joins me on the porch.

"Where's Kim?" I ask.

"Left."

There's an angry red flush creeping up Cindy's neck.

"So," I say, "what's up?"

"Nothing."

Her arms are tightly crossed. "Doesn't look like nothing," I venture.

She takes a deep breath and attempts a smile. "Kim."

I'd gathered that. "Oh?"

"She said a few things that I didn't like."

"Um." I try to give Cindy lots of space. She'll come out with it when she wants to.

"She said that I was the same as all journalists. That all I wanted was a story. That the premier's death was just an accident. That I was trying to manipulate the facts. Plus, she told you to shut up."

"What did you say?"

"I said that she shouldn't have let people under the tarp. That it could have been a crime scene."

"You were right. Plus, I'm not sure it was an accident. The scene has an off smell to it." Cindy wrinkles her nose. "I mean figuratively," I add.

"I know what you meant."

"Never mind. Let's go inside."

Cindy follows me through the door. "Have you unpacked yet?" I ask her.

"Nope. I haven't even brought my bags in."

"Neither have I."

The whole cottage is in darkness, which is strange because I'd seen Andrew come inside. I flip on the kitchen light with the switch beside the door. "Hey, Cindy, look at this."

"What?"

I point at the light switch. "There's a new light switch beside this one."

"Big deal."

"No. I wonder what it's for."

I hear rustling in the living room and turn my head. Andrew is sitting on the couch and scrolling on his phone. In the dark. "Oh, hi Andrew. What's this switch for? It's new."

"No, it's always been there."

He's lying. Whenever he lies, his eyes float to the left. "No, it hasn't. I've been coming here for my whole life and I know this is a new switch. What's it for?"

"It's nothing, really. It's just attached to some wires on the roof."

"What wires on the roof?"

Andrew hems and haws before he stands. He gestures above his head. "Just some wires."

"What are they for?" Something's going on here. Andrew was acting like a kid who'd peed his pants in school and was trying to hide it.

"Well, I told you I bought a pickaxe, right?"

"What's a pickaxe got to do with wires on the roof?"

"Well, I'm just saying. I want to start coming here more, as I said, maybe retire here with Jocelyn, and so I'm slowly making the place more liveable in the winter."

"First of all, you can't just announce that you're going to start living here. This is my cottage too. And I say no. Secondly, what are the wires for?" He's being so evasive.

"Cool it, Robin. Have a drink."

I can feel my temper bubbling like a hot geyser in the pit of my stomach. Soon I would be spewing steam into the air. He's using a tactic he's used all his life. He'd learned it from my father. He was dismissing me by pointing out one of my flaws. Well, I don't fall for that shit anymore.

"Don't patronize me, Andrew. You drink as much as I do. What are the fucking wires for?"

He changes tact. "We pay good money to have someone come shovel off the roof every winter."

"I know that."

Cindy sings, "I think I'll have a glass of wine." She opens the fridge and takes out a chilled bottle of white. "Andrew? Robin?"

We both say, "Sure," at the same time, making my point about the drinking.

"And what does that have to do with wires on the roof?" I ask.

"They melt the snow."

"So, why didn't you say so. Sounds like a great idea."

Andrew takes the glass of wine from Cindy and sips it slowly, peering at me over the rim of his glass. Something shifts behind his eyes.

I was missing the point. But it seems that Cindy wasn't. "How many people did you tell about this switch, Andrew?"

He presses his lips into a tight line and raises his eyebrows while he shrugs. "I didn't tell anyone."

"Okay." She doesn't believe him either. His eyes are looking far left, out of the blackened window. "There was no snow on the roof when I got here, so when did you turn the wires on?"

"Well, I asked the cleaners to flip the switch this morning, after they cleaned and before people arrived. I didn't want feet of snow tumbling off the roof while people were here."

Cindy's getting at something here. "And did you turn them off?"

Andrew looks like a cornered rat. "I didn't turn them off. When I checked in with the cleaner around ten this morning, she told me the snow had melted off the roof and only icicles remained. The wires work pretty quickly. I bought a top-of-the-line system from a company in Vermont. They know their snow." He mentally pats himself on the back. "So, I told her to turn the wires off. I didn't want to waste the power. She told me she'd already turned them off."

"When you arrived, was the switch up or down?"

"I can't remember. It was a busy time, you'll recall, with the premier lying dead outside."

"Andrew, stop lying," I say. "You obviously do remember if the wires were on or off when you arrived."

"You can't tell me what I remember and what I don't."

"What? Your brain has been pickled by alcohol?"

"C'mon, Robin."

"You don't fool me for a second. You were always the best at memory games. You could remember every single item on the tray at every birthday party you had. In fact, I think you wanted that game played so you could show off your superior memory."

"Children," Cindy says. She puts her hands on her hips and towers over Andrew. She's doing her amazon act. I'd seen her pull that on her kids. It always works. "Andrew, was the switch on or off when you arrived?"

Andrew takes a step away from her. "Oh, wait. I remember now. It was on. Right. The switch was in the up position. When

I came into the kitchen, I remember reaching up and turning off both the kitchen light and the wires."

Ralph stands in front of the switches and peers at the one for the wires through a magnifying glass. I briefly wonder where he'd picked that up but then remember my father always had one sitting in a mug on the desk in the living room. Ralph had caught on to the same thing Cindy had. There's something about this switch. A malfunction, perhaps?

"So," says Cindy, "if the cleaners turned the wires off, who turned them back on?"

Ralph speaks up. "It looks like there's only one set of prints on the switches, from what I can see. But it's a regular light switch, and prints don't really show up with a magnifying glass. I bet there'd only be one set of prints on this switch if we dusted it."

"Well…" Andrew picks up his glass and takes a very small sip, looking at me. "It was probably an accident. Somebody turned both switches on to turn on the kitchen lights."

I'm finally catching up to what Cindy and Ralph were getting at: the turned on wires had melted the snow off the roof and created massive icicles. Because the wires were turned on even after the snow had melted, the icicles had melted at their base and fallen.

But what Andrew had said didn't make sense. "Why would anyone turn on the kitchen light? When the renters arrived, it was still daytime. There was no need to turn on lights."

Cindy looks at me appraisingly. "Good point, Robin." She turns to Andrew. "So, it was no accident. Someone deliberately turned the wires on. Who knew about the switch?"

Andrew lies again. "Just the cleaners."

First things first. "Who were the cleaners?" I ask.

"I used the people we always use, that Indian girl from town, Emily Eagle, and her son."

Cindy snaps, "The *Indigenous woman* and her son."

The backpack with the lightning bolt makes sense now. The kid was helping his mom. But why had he still been around the cottage many hours after the cleaning job was done? What had he been doing? And his running away from us had been odd. What was he hiding?

"And who else?" I ask.

Andrew's eyes now keep flitting toward the recycling bin. It's empty except for one crumpled sheet of paper. What is he trying to hide? I pick up the paper and smooth it out on the kitchen counter. It's the instructions we always leave behind for the renters.

Cindy reads over my shoulder. "Look at number four. Right below the information on turning on the fridge." She reads aloud. "'There are two light switches beside the kitchen door. The left one is for turning on the kitchen light. The right one is for turning on the roof wires that melt the snow. Only turn on the roof wires if there's a storm, but don't forget to turn them off.'"

I look at Andrew. He's puffing out his chest and staring down at me, daring me to call out his lie. I say, "Where did you leave this note?"

"On the kitchen counter."

"So, anybody and everybody could read it. Including the family members of all the guests. The wives in particular. The head of the hydro company. The mayor of Toronto. Even the premier. Not to mention Emily Eagle and her son." I wish I could remember his name.

Cindy picks up the note and waves it. "In short, everyone knew about the wires and this switch."

He puts his glass of wine down on the counter. "Yup," he says, unwilling to give anything else away.

CHAPTER 20

I AM INCENSED. "YOU LIED TO us! You said no one else knew about the heating cable except the people who came to clean the cottage. Obviously, a lot of people knew." I brandish the crumpled note in the air.

Andrew gives his body a little self-righteous shake. "I didn't lie. I said I didn't *tell* anyone about the wires. And I didn't. It was *written* down. In the note."

Cindy looks like she wants to shake him. "Oh, so now you're being a lawyer, splitting details into tiny morsels to get yourself off?"

Andrew gives a smug smile. "Well, I didn't *lie*."

I throw up my hands, almost knocking over my glass of wine. "What? Are you six?" I can't believe that I'm actually related to this asshole.

"Come off it, Robin. No need to name call."

I shake my head. I hadn't even name-called. Was he gaslighting me? "Okay, well now we know the truth. Everyone who was here knew about the wires. And one of those people deliberately turned the cables on while the premier was sitting outside. Likely in the hope that an icicle would fall and kill him."

Andrew snorts out a laugh. "Oh, Robin, get real. You are living in a fantasy world. As usual. How on earth could anyone determine which icicle would actually melt and fall directly on him? You saw how they all fell at once just now. You're wanting him to be killed because you vote for the New Democratic Party.

Or because you are greedy for a story."

Cindy chops the air between us. "Children, children. Stop it. This is getting too personal. Clearly someone turned the wires on. The question is, was it deliberate, or was it accidental. And, of course, who."

"That's my point," says Andrew. "It doesn't matter. No one could be sure that an icicle would fall directly on the premier. Any one of those icicles could fall, not just a specific one. Not just there. On the premier. There's no way to control that. There were at least ten icicles left hanging from the eaves. Any one of them could fall. Or all of them. As we saw with that cop."

He's protesting too much. I don't believe it had been a random hope on the part of a killer. I know that if someone wanted to murder, they would resort to anything to make it happen. I just don't know how. Not yet. But I would figure it out. My brain whizzes around the facts. Unfortunately, the facts are in grim supply. "We'll see."

Ralph puts down his wine glass on the kitchen counter and says, "I've got to talk to the local police." He turns toward the door, clearly in a hurry.

"Why, Ralph? What are you thinking?" I try to ignore his look of impatience as he swivels back to me, his hand on the doorknob.

"There's just one set of prints on the switch. They're probably Andrew's from when he turned the switches off when he arrived." With that, he flies out the door.

I don't know what's the matter with my brain today but I can't follow him, I simply can't see the significance of only one set of prints on the switches. I look at Cindy and raise my shoulders. *What?*

"Robin," she says, her mother voice in place, "If there's just one set of prints, that means the switch had been wiped down. The cleaner's prints should be there as well. Or, the prints of whoever turned the wires back on, plus Andrew's."

"Oh, right. Of course." I'm embarrassed to not have made that connection. To cover it up, to make myself feel better, I say,

"Whomever. Not whoever."

Cindy says, "Don't be like that, little Miss Grammar Cop. You didn't understand because you just don't have a devious mind. But you're getting there." She pats my arm. "Don't worry about it. You don't need to correct my grammar. And besides, I think 'whoever' is correct."

I really don't know if whomever was correct or even why I'd said anything about it. But I guess it's nice of her to reassure me that I'm not stupid just because I hadn't caught on to the up-and-down switch and fingerprint business.

"Hmm," I say, thoughtfully. "This is starting to look like someone deliberately turned the wires on and then deliberately wiped their prints off the switches. There was no accident."

Andrew purses his lips. "Ya, well, I doubt it, Robin. As I said, no way could anyone ensure the right icicle would fall at the right time. Maybe Emily Eagle didn't turn the cables off. Maybe she wiped down the switches because she's a *cleaner* and then forgot to turn them off. Maybe she lied to me. You know what Indians are like."

"Geezus fuck, Andrew."

"Just saying."

"Well don't say shit like that around me. You are one racist dumbfuck." I'm furious with him.

Andrew simply polishes his wire-rimmed glasses.

Ralph flings open the kitchen door, looking irate. "They've all left the office." He shakes his head. "What a way to treat a sudden death. I can't believe it. There isn't even any tape up where the premier fell. Not that it matters, given how many people sloshed in the mud around his body." He looks accusingly at me and then Cindy. Me and then Cindy.

Cindy laughs in his face. "Ra-alph." She draws his name out into two syllables. "You looked too. You walked around the body too."

Ralph shrugs, his jaw thrust forward. I wonder what's eating him. He's being so adversarial, for Ralph. What had happened in that phone call? A bitter administrator?

I say, "Anyway. Ralph, has the whistle-clean light switch made you suspicious about the premier's death?" I don't know if my question will make him more ornery or tamp his bad mood down.

Ralph looks out the window. "It does make one wonder. Although Andrew has made a good point. How on earth could someone ensure the right icicle fell at the right time at the right place?"

Andrew daintily fixes his glasses around his ears. "That's what I've been saying all along. Of course this is an accidental death. Random."

I don't think so. Too many people hated the premier. I look at Cindy and see that she has her doubts too. Andrew doesn't notice. How on earth am I going to write a report of this event when I have so many doubts and concerns. But report I must. I heave my huge bag onto my knee and start pawing through it. Where the hell is my iPad?

"What are you looking for, Robin? Some brains?"

I look up at Andrew's face set in superior stone. "My iPad. I've got a story to submit now. Some of us work around the clock." Not that I often do, but every now and then I had to.

"Well, don't write it while you've been drinking. Wouldn't want you to be spreading your fantasies about murder."

He has a point, but still, I could kick him.

"Anyway," he says, "I'm going to head back to Toronto now. Seems that the excitement has died down." He shoots his cuff and looks at his Rolex. "Let's see, it's eight-thirty. I'll be home by ten-thirty if I skedaddle."

Good riddance. Maybe he'll get a speeding ticket. "Really? You're not going to stay overnight?"

"Nice try, Robin. I know you'd be happier without me here."

He's sure right about that. I say, "I'm just concerned the roads will be slippery and a two-hour trip means you'll be going fast. Might be safer to wait until the morning."

"Nope, I'm out of here."

With that, Andrew buttons up his coat, puts the flaps down on his fur-lined aviator hat, and strides out the door. What was he running from?

Ralph waits for the slap of the screen door shutting and says, "Your brother is such a dickhead, Robin. He really puts me on edge. His politics alone…"

Oh, so maybe that's why he's been so crabby.

"Well, he's gone," I say as I hear his fancy-schmancy car skid down the muddy road. He'd put on a fart box so he could look sporty and young. Childish attempt for a sixty-plus guy. "Let's just forget about him."

Cindy sidles out of the kitchen, grabs her suitcase from the middle of the living room, and says, "I'm going to unpack. Should I go to the same bedroom I had when I was here last?"

I mentally review where I'd put her. I don't want her close to me and Ralph just in case we make some noise. "Sure, that's great. You can have the same bathroom as well."

After she thumps her suitcase up the stairs, I say to Ralph, "So, do you want to get settled now as well? Unpack? Maybe make a fire and have a glass of wine?"

He runs his fingers through his hair. So agitated. "I'm wondering if I shouldn't go along to the police station and tell them about the prints. I feel it's important that they know. I know they've left, but someone will be there for the evening shift. And maybe they didn't answer because they saw it was me."

So much for a quiet evening. "Sure, if you feel that's the best thing to do, then you better go do it."

He must sense my disappointment. "I'm sorry," he says. "But it will give you time to write up your piece and submit it. I shouldn't be long, maybe an hour at most. The night will still be young by the time I get back. We can relax when I get home."

Then, his phone rings and he frowns as he looks at the screen. "Oh, I'd better take this," he grunts as he holds the phone up to his ear and walks out the door.

"Bye," I mutter, as the screen door slams behind him.

Who could be calling him at this time of night? His work knows he's off-duty, not that that ever meant much. He often gets calls while off-duty. There aren't that many homicide detectives on the force, maybe ten good ones, and he's one of the best. He'd get calls in the middle of the night if a complicated case arose. But still, his work knows he's out of town. So, it couldn't be work. Is he having an affair? Is that why he's so on edge? No, Ralph is too principled, too moral, too honest, too *Ralph*, to have an affair. And he doesn't sound too happy about the call. Maybe it is just being around Andrew. He'd put anyone off their food.

The door opens and Ralph throws his suitcase and my bag onto the kitchen floor. He's definitely mad. "Here, sorry, I should have brought these in earlier. I've got hold of the chief and he's going to meet me in town. I won't be long." He smiles and blows me a perfunctory kiss as he disappears behind the shut door.

What a roller coaster. Brisk then breezy. Whatever. I grab the bags and call Lucky off the couch. "Come help me unpack, Cutie Pie," I say as I walk past him.

Cindy is coming down the stairs, but she turns on her heel to go back up. "Sure, Sweetie Darling."

"I was talking to the dog."

She makes a sad face. "I can always hope."

I laugh. "Come talk to me while I unpack."

"Sure." She leads the way to the bedroom I'd stayed in not that long ago, while she and I had been the only ones here, plus a dead body.

I heave the bags onto the bed and say, "At least the beds are made up and the place is ready to go. I imagine the people Andrew rented to will be trying to get their money back, considering they were only here for a few hours, not a few days."

Cindy sits on the edge of the bed while I pull items of clothing out of the bags. "Exactly who did he rent to?"

I say, "Exactly to whom did he rent?"

"Knock it off, Robin. I'm sick of the Grammar Police routine."

I tick the people off on my fingers. "The mayor of Toronto, The premier of Ontario, the CEO of the provincial electric power company, and all their wives. Why?"

"Well, I think someone killed the premier and that person is probably one of the renters."

"What do you think about the Indigenous angle? Emily Eagle and her son?" I ask as I pitch socks into a drawer.

"I'm sure the police would like to blame Emily Eagle or her son. I mean, the kid does belong to that group who are trying to regain power after their land was flooded by the Quebec power company to create a dam. And now that the dam is being replaced with solar power, I would say that would be enraging. Enraging enough to kill?" She cocks her head to one side as she considers the likelihood. "Naw, I don't think so."

"I am worried about it. The majority of people in Huntsville vote Conservative and they would be inclined to first believe that no one *white* would hate the premier enough to kill him, so therefore it must be 'the Indian' who would do it." I slam the drawer shut. Prejudice makes me so angry I could just spit.

"Andrew did make a good point though. How on earth could someone make an icicle fall at the exact right time at the exact right place."

I look out the window and gaze into the dark. My mind wanders over everything that has happened. I think about all the trees and wildlife in the woods. I am happy here, or at least I was, but now the undercurrent of violence in the landscape is troubling. I really believe in morphic resonance, where the environment holds memories of events, both good and bad. Would I have to have the property smudged to eliminate the impact of the murders? Would that work? What would I say to the children, who loved the place, if I wanted to sell?

"Robin?"

Cindy's voice cuts through my reverie. "Oh, sorry. I was just thinking about how I feel about this place. Even though we aren't that far from the city, there's still an abundance of wildlife. Birds. Deer. Otters. Weasels. Ground hogs. Turkeys."

"You forgot the beavers."

I turn to her. "Actually, we did have trouble with beavers for a while there. Right by the water's edge. They nibbled and chewed and gnawed away at the base of an old tree and then it came crashing down into the lake. Created quite a mess."

Cindy scratches Lucky behind his ears. She looks straight into his eyes and asks him, "Do you like beavers, Lucky? Do you chase them? Do they slap their tails on the water and splash you?"

I laugh, "Those destructive beavers from a few years ago drove him nuts. First of all, they're quite large and secondly, they scared me. I didn't want him to catch one, they have such big teeth. I was afraid one bite would take his leg off or leave it dangling by a string."

"Did you like the beavers?" Cindy croons. Lucky wags his tail and licks her nose. "Well," she says, "at least someone around here likes beavers."

I frown dramatically. "Don't be rude."

Just then, we both hear the downstairs door bang shut. Cindy and I jump at the sound and look at each other in fear. Having a recent murder on the property makes us skittish. I run out of the bedroom and call down the stairs, "Who's there?" Lucky races between my legs and crashes to the living room.

"Oh, it's just me, Robin."

"Ralph?"

"Yup."

I head down the stairs. "Oh, what are you doing back? I thought you'd be gone much longer. I haven't even begun to write my story."

"I called the station halfway into town, you know, just to make sure someone was there and got the chief. I told him about the fingerprints."

Cindy had followed me down. "What did he say?"

Ralph shakes his head and looks disgusted. "He didn't say anything. He just grunted. Like it wasn't important."

"Well, I think it is."

"So do I," Cindy echoes.

Ralph digs a bottle of wine out of the fridge, "Not my pig pen, not my pig."

Does he know my mother? I know he really doesn't think that;

this case is eating at him. Ralph feels a heavy responsibility for everyone, no matter whose jurisdiction they're in. I take the bottle from him and pour three tumblers full. "Let's relax for a bit and then simply go to bed. We can decide what to do in the morning. It'll only take me a minute to write the story. In fact, I'll do it right now."

I grab my iPad out of my bag, tap furiously, and have Cindy email me a photo that isn't too gruesome. I attach the photo to my article that announces Premier Kahn's death and add the line that more information about the cause of death is to come. Send.

"There. That's done." I take a huge gulp of my wine, smack my lips, and say, "Time to relax."

That night, while spooning in Ralph's arms and not falling asleep, I keep thinking about the beavers. The beavers mean something, but I don't know what.

Ralph, probably sensing that I wasn't heading into dreamland, asks me, "What are you thinking about honey?"

"Beavers. You know, in the woods by the lake." His hands wander over my belly and head south.

"Guess what?" he laughs, "I'm thinking about beavers too."

So much for trying to puzzle out what my mind was thinking.

CHAPTER 21

THE NEXT MORNING AS I brush my teeth, I inadvertently squirt Ralph's toothpaste onto my brush. Although I use the cheapest tube I can find at No Frills, Ralph always goes to the fancy health food store and purchases the fluoride-free brand that has a cute little beaver on the tube. Spearmint. As I brush away my morning breath, I watch the water trickling out of the tap and thinning out to a point as it travels toward the drain. I love the taste of his toothpaste. It's far more refreshing than the usual commercial peppermint I buy. The scent of it makes me think of the willow trees by the water's edge because at the base of the trees there is a patch of mint. And right beside this pretty grove there is that old maple tree I was telling Cindy about, the one that a beaver had gnawed, leaving behind a pointed stump covered with tooth marks.

All of a sudden, all the images collide together. The point of the water, the point of the tree stump, the beaver on the toothpaste package, the beaver chipping and gnawing away at the tree. In a blinding flash, I realize I know exactly how Kahn was killed, how a specific icicle had been made to fall on the premier. I'd gotten the point. I'd figured out how someone could make a precise icicle fall. In the whirl of images—the water thinning as it ran out of the tap, the tree stump, the beaver references, and the mint toothpaste—I'd gotten it. All one would have to do was chisel away at the base of the icicle so that it would have less volume to melt than all the other icicles hanging off the edge of the roof.

Holy shit! What a brainwave. I spit out the toothpaste, wipe my mouth, and run downstairs to the aroma of brewing coffee, expecting to see Ralph in the kitchen. Needing to tell him my idea. He's so good to bounce things off of. Plus, he would help prove it.

Except he isn't here. I try not to show my disappointment when I see my tall, lanky friend hovering over the stove. "Hi, Cindy. Good morning. Where's Ralph?"

"What? I'm chopped liver?"

She'd picked up my disappointment. I laugh and give her a hug. "No, I'm happy to see you too, but I know how the premier was murdered. I need Ralph to help me prove it."

"I can help you."

Her nose is out of joint; she's peeved. "No need to be jealous. He's a cop. He has access to tests and stuff. Of course you can help me. But not like he can."

She puts her hands on her hips. Pissed off. "You want coffee?"

Oh dear. "First of all, where is he?"

"Out walking Lucky."

"Okay. And yes, I would."

As she pours me out a mug, she turns her back. "So, how was he murdered? That is, if you want to tell me."

As she talks, I look out the kitchen window at the grove of willows and the stump beside it. Tromping into my line of vision is Ralph, talking on his phone and tugging Lucky away from a long, skinny green worm of goose poo. Clearly the Canada Geese had migrated back to Ontario. "Here comes Ralph. I'll tell you both together."

Who was he talking to?

I can sense that Cindy doesn't quite know how to react to that. On one hand, it makes her equal to Ralph. On the other hand, she's always wanted to be more important than Ralph. God, the games we play. I whisper to her, "Someone must have chiselled the base of the icicle to thin it out so it would melt faster than the others and therefore be the only one to fall on the premier's head."

She nods, her eyes flashing understanding as Ralph opens the door. "That's brilliant, Robin. How on earth did you figure that out?"

"Figure what out?" asks Ralph, kicking off his boots and neatly placing them on the rubber mat beside the door.

Lucky bounds towards me, tail wagging. I bend over to pat him. I get a head rush from a lurking hangover. I say, "How the premier was killed."

"Really? That's amazing. I think I need coffee to absorb the news."

Is he being sarcastic? What on earth had gotten into him? He looks at me over the rim of his mug, his eyes dark and impatient.

I say, "No really, I think I figured it out."

Cindy pipes up, "I think she did. It's ingenious."

"Tell me," says Ralph. Now, he looks pretty interested. Perhaps I had misinterpreted that crabby glance of his. It had been so fleeting, maybe it hadn't happened at all.

I begin my recital. "If one is a killer, one would have to solve the problem of getting the icicle to fall at the exact right moment so it kills the intended target. The problem is how to manipulate a specific icicle to fall on the premier's head when he's sitting outside, right? As Andrew said, it looks so random."

Cindy butts in. "Andrew's an asshole."

Ralph laughs, "That's for sure."

"Anyway," I continue. "I think it *looks* random, but it wasn't. It was deliberate. If someone chipped away at the base of the icicle and then turned the roof heating coils on, one would have a very good chance of making that thinned out icicle fall right when someone was sitting under it."

Ralph tilts his head and considers the possibility. "I can see how that would work. The icicle would melt faster than the rest, so it would fall first. No warning would be given by the others falling. It wouldn't be a hundred percent given, but a good chance."

"The only problem then is the placement of the chair," Cindy says, starting to poke holes in my theory, which I suppose is a good thing, as it keeps us all thinking.

"Ya, right," says Ralph. "How could one determine exactly where the premier would sit?"

I think about this. "Well, Andrew said—"

Cindy interrupts me: "The *asshole* said—"

I laugh. "Ya, ya. *He* said that the switch to the coils was on when he arrived. The cleaner had told him that she'd flipped the switch off. That indicates to me that someone in the rental group had turned the switch back on when they got here. After the cleaner had left. Maybe that same person had put the chair outside for the premier to sit in. Like it was a nice thing to do, to make him comfortable after his hard job. Someone like his *wife*."

Ralph says, "I can't quite see a woman climbing up a ladder and chipping away at the base of an icicle. Not that I'm sexist or anything." He puts his coffee cup down a bit harder than he'd needed to.

"Maybe the wife does wall climbing and isn't afraid of heights."

"Unlike you," says Cindy, who could scale trees no problem.

I shrug. "So, I'm afraid of heights. So what?"

Ralph interjects, "I doubt his wife would be into that, but you never know. Have you ever seen her?"

"No, have you?"

"She wears high heels in the middle of the day."

"Ralph."

"I'm just saying."

Cindy starts tapping away on her phone. "I'm asking Alison Trent in the research department to send me a photo of the premier's wife."

"Huh," I mutter. "Come to think of it I've never seen her. Not even when he was elected. He sure protects his privacy. But even if she's a skinny little thing, looks can be deceiving. She might be able to scale a ladder and chisel away."

Cindy's phone pings. "Alison says this is a picture of her from a year ago."

We crowd around Cindy's phone and look at the white teeth of Mrs. Kahn. Cindy holds the phone at arm's length and wiggles it back and forth. "Does this woman look like a murderer?"

Clearly, we're looking at the face of someone who was from the rich 1% club. Bleached-blond hair, deliberately mussed, deliberate dark roots, sparkling blue eyes, probably under tinted contacts, gold filigree roses in tiny ear lobes, a perky little nose.

Ralph says, "One never knows what a murderer looks like. It could be anyone. But as Robin pointed out, this woman may lift weights and climb rock walls. But I think she's pretty into her looks, wearing high heels in the middle of the day, and likely doesn't climb ladders in them."

"Nonetheless," Cindy says. "I think she should be talked to."

Ralph says, "Let's wait at least day. She just lost her husband. I mean, she could be crowing, but maybe she's devastated."

That's true, I agree with him there. "It'll take that long for us to pack up, shut the place down, and get back to Toronto anyway. Why don't Cindy and I drop in on her tomorrow morning, unannounced?"

Ralph frowns. "That might be a job for the police." He sips at his coffee. "Do you even know where she lives?"

His tone is so snarky. It's really starting to bug me. Where has my gentle, kind, supportive, considerate Ralphie gone? What is up with him?

"I think Cindy and I might be able to glean more information from her than the police," I tell him. "She might like to talk to female reporters. She might finally enjoy being in the limelight. And Ralph, of course we know where she lives. People protested outside the premier's house during the pandemic. Cindy covered the protest when it got violent. Right, Cindy?"

"Yup," Cindy confirms. "He lives in the west end, over by the Humber River. I know the place well. In fact, I even saw her. She was screaming at the protesters to get off her lawn. I herded them across the road."

Ralph says, "Well, they should have stayed off her property. No wonder she was furious."

His mood is pinging all over the place. Why is he being so confrontational? The air in the kitchen vibrates with his tension, spreading out long tendrils of electricity. Even Lucky can feel it.

He's left the room and is now sitting on the couch in the living room, looking out the window, then looking at us, then looking out the window.

"Let's have breakfast," I say. "There's some eggs and toast, and I'm happy to make it."

"No cereal?" Ralph says. "You didn't bring cereal? You know I have granola every morning."

Fuck, my patience was being tried. "First of all, I didn't pack the food, you did. So don't blame me. Secondly, it's always good to shake it up a bit, Ralph."

"Oh, okay." He walks into the living room, sulking, and sits on the couch next to Lucky. He scrolls on his phone and shouts to me in the kitchen, "Hey Robin, your article is in the *Express*. First up. Looks great."

Really? "Looks great?" I can't figure this guy out this morning.

After breakfast, we all go upstairs to pack up. Ralph had been fine at breakfast, maybe a little quieter than usual, but not ornery. He'd almost seemed back to his old self. As we strip the bed I say to him, "So, you want to tell me what's going on?"

He looks surprised and then averts his eyes. "What do you mean, 'going on'?"

"I don't know, Ralph, you seem off to me. A little crabby? Cranky? Are you worried about something?"

He gives the far corner of the fitted sheet a hard tug, trying to get it off the mattress by force instead of reaching underneath and lifting the elasticized end off.

"I mean," I say, "look at you. You're so impatient. Usually you're so easygoing. Here." I say, as I walk toward him, watching him struggle. "Let me get that for you."

He steps back, giving me room to slide the sheet off the mattress. "I've got a few issues to deal with," he grumbles.

I can barely hear him, but Ralph isn't one to talk about his emotions at all, so at least this is a first step. But I have to tread carefully. I don't want to scare him off. Should I laugh lightly, totally nonchalantly, or should I just say, "Hmmmmm"? Before I can decide on my approach, he speaks.

"It's my wife," he blurts out.

His wife? I thought they were divorced. "Don't you mean your ex-wife?"

"The divorce isn't finalized yet, so yes, my *wife*." He spits out the word. "She wants my whole pension, and all the proceeds from the house."

"Well, that's not the law. She can't do that."

"She's claiming emotional cruelty from being married to a cop. Says it was traumatic. Says she'll never be able to work."

"Oh, Ralph, that's just bullshit. I've lived with you for over a year and you've never, ever been cruel to me. Plus, you keep your job to yourself. I'm sure you've always been like that. There has to be tight lips in your job. How can be she be traumatized by something she knows nothing about?"

He says nothing and then suddenly explodes. "She's also saying I abused my youngest daughter."

Oh no. I've seen how something like that plays out. "That's ridiculous. How did you allegedly abuse her?"

"Apparently, I hit her a lot. Daily."

"Right. I can totally see you doing that." I scramble through my brain, trying to come up with his daughter's name. Finally, a bingo. "And what does Mara say?"

"Mara doesn't speak about it."

"Why not?" *Why won't he just talk to her about it?*

"Mara doesn't speak."

"What do you mean?" I'm clearly not following this very well.

"She's severely autistic. Non-verbal." Ralph takes the fitted sheet from me and bundles it into a tight knot. He pitches it into a corner with the used towels, all waiting for the washing machine.

Ralph had never talked much about his children to me. I know he has three—two girls and a boy—but that's all the detail I know. Whenever I bring up his family, his lips clamp shut so hard they turn white and pain etches deep lines around his eyes. I had learned years ago to not bring the subject up. But here we are now, stripping a bed that we had made love in, talking about his past.

"What about your other daughter? What does she say about this?"

"She won't talk to me."

"Did you fight about something?"

"No, her mother has turned the kids against me. My son won't answer my emails, texts, or calls either."

I can't imagine my children shutting me out like that. No wonder he doesn't like talking about his family. So much pain.

I take a step toward Ralph. I'm not sure about what to say about all this, but I know what I have to do. I have to meet him in a way that he understands and isn't threatened by. I wrap my arms around him, tilt my head and kiss his chin. We stand in each other's arms for a few minutes in the morning sunshine streaming through the window. I stroke his back, much as I would a feral cat, carefully and gently, slowly so as not to startle. I whisper, "I'm here, Ralph."

He leans on me and whispers back, "Thank you, Robin."

Then, he straightens his spine to his full height and says, "Right. Let's finish packing the house up and figure out what happened to the premier. I like your theory, Robin. But it has a few problems. Before we leave here, let's look for a chisel and if we find one, let's put it in a plastic zip-lock bag and have it checked for fingerprints. DNA might show up as well, if the person took their gloves off to chip away."

"What if they didn't cut themselves? No blood?"

"Doesn't matter. They can get DNA from sweat these days."

The idea doesn't make me very hopeful. It's still pretty cold out for sweating. And taking gloves off. "We should also check out the ladder," I say. "Maybe there'll be mud on it that will match someone's boots."

Ralph thinks about this as he folds his clothes and puts them into his suitcase. I fold my stuff as well, shoving it into my green garbage bag. Ralph never comments on this, my strange way of packing and travelling.

He says, "I don't think matching the mud will be definitive.

Everyone will have mud on their shoes. That won't signal out a specific person."

I smile. "Actually, I think it might. Andrew had the outer walls of the basement waterproofed in the fall and the workers filled in the space, the trough, between the basement wall and the yard with gravel from a nearby pit. No one else, I'm pretty sure, would have this specific dirt on their boots except for the person who was positioning a ladder by the wall and then climbing up it. I guess the premier might have.this gravel on his boots, and we would as well, now that we've been near the edge of the house, but when the rental group arrived, no one would have reason at all to go there. Or at least I don't think they would. Except the person who put the chair by the wall. And logically, this would be the same person who climbed up the ladder."

Ralph looks at me, his dark brown eyes assessing what I'd just said. "I think the best way to do this then is to take samples from the earth by the house, from everyone's boots, and from scrapings on the ladder. There just might be a match. That should be definitive. Where is the ladder anyway?"

"I imagine it'll be in the shed. And the chisel will be there as well."

Ralph zips his suitcase shut. I tie a knot in my green garbage bag, and we trundle down the stairs.

Cindy is on the couch, patting Lucky. She can sense right away that the air between us has cleared. "Looks like you two are playing nicely again so I won't have to take my toys and go home. Although I'm all packed and ready to go. Even the spotlights are in my car."

I laugh. "Wow, you've been busy. And ya, we're good. We're going to look for a chisel in the shed and take scrapings from the ladder and beside the house. Cop tests." I add to make my point. Remembering how she can sometimes feel left out, I say, "Want to come?"

She jumps off the couch, smiling brightly. "You betcha."

CHAPTER 22

RALPH PULLS ON HIS BOOTS and says to me, "I think we're going to need a few zip-lock bags. Do you know where they are?"

Of course I do. He knows that I do. This is just his way of suggesting that I grab some. "Sure. Bottom left-hand drawer." I point into the kitchen. And this is just my way of telling him to get them himself.

Ralph smiles and opens the drawer. After a year together, he knows this game well.

"And a marker?"

I'm one step ahead of him on this and have already grabbed one.

As the three of us traipse across the yard to the shed, Cindy says, "The Huntsville cops won't like it at all if this is a murder."

"Well, that's just too bad. They'll have to deal with it. Of course it's a murder." My belief in this had grown firm overnight. "We just have to figure out who did it."

"Probably the mayor," Cindy says.

"Why would you say that? McCormick is a good enough guy. I think it was someone else in the rental party."

"Like who?"

"Whom. Not who. Dative case."

"Shut up, Robin. Like whom-m-m."

"Hmmm. That sounds funny. Maybe you were right."

"Like who, then."

"Like maybe his wife. If it was a sexual reason. Or the head of

Ontario Hydro if it was a money reason. It could even have been the son of Emily Eagle. Although I doubt that."

"I agree," Cindy says. "It's usually sex or greed. The two big motivators of murder."

Ralph drags open the shed door. "At least someone shovelled in front of the door so it'll open."

Cindy says, "I wonder who?"

I pull out my phone. "I'll text Andrew and ask."

My phone pings two seconds later. "He did." A chill envelops my body. *He did?* Does that mean he had something to do with the murder? Did he shovel out the shed so he could get to the chisel and ladder? Cindy and Ralph both look at me, their eyes full of the same horrible thought.

My phone pings again. I laugh with relief as I read it. "He said he shovelled it to get the pickaxe to show Ralph." I feel almost giddy with relief, although the dark thought circles around my heart like a noose. Could this just be an excuse? Had he shovelled it out previously? When we asked him to get the pickaxe, had he been gone long enough to shovel out the front of the shed?

Ralph says, "Right." He must sense my suspicion. Did he have a few suspicions of his own?

He ducks his head and enters the shed. "There's not much room in here. You'd be better off being outside while I hunt around." Cindy and I wait impatiently outside the shed, listening to Ralph move things around inside.

"I found a chisel," he calls from inside the wooden structure.

I hear rustling and then his arm appears as he hands out the chisel in a medium-sized freezer bag. "Here, take this."

I hold the bag up in front of my face, inspecting the chisel through the plastic. No way could I see fingerprints. Cindy draws closer and squints at it. I hear some scraping from behind the shed's door. Ralph's arm reappears with another bag.

"And here, take this. Label it 'Dirt from ladder. Bottom rung.'"

His arm disappears and I hear yet-more scraping. And then Ralph himself steps out holding a third bag. "Robin, can I please have the marker?" I peer over his shoulder as he writes on the bag. "Dirt from feet of ladder."

"Why are you collecting dirt?" Cindy asks. She hadn't been part of the explanation of the new gravel and fill shovelled around the edge of the house when the foundation had been waterproofed.

"We, meaning Andrew, arranged to have the basement waterproofed last fall, which involved digging a deep trench around all the sides of the building. After lining the basement wall with waterproofing, the construction crew filled the excavation with new fill from the local gravel pit."

Cindy cottons on right away. "So, whoever climbed up the ladder would have stepped on this fill, which is now pretty muddy, and it will be on his or her shoes."

I'm always impressed with the speed with which she puts things together. "Right," I say, smiling. "So now all we have to do is check the bottoms of all the renters' shoes and we will see who climbed the ladder. The evidence will be pretty strong."

Ralph puts in his two cents: "Plus, we have the chisel. It probably has some fibres of gloves or DNA or fingerprints on it that will provide another link to the killer."

Cindy rubs her hands together. "Now we're making progress. Let's get to the city and start checking people out."

Ralph gives her a look. "That's a job for the police. We're dealing with a murderer here, Cindy. A killer. It could be very dangerous. So, let the police do our job."

She says, "Oh, Ralphie."

"Don't call me that. And listen to me." He pulls himself up to his full height and puffs out his chest. "I'm not joking. It could be very dangerous. Murderers *kill* people."

Cindy laughs, turns on her heel, and walks as smartly as she can back into the cottage, her shoes sucking up mud as she goes. A minute later, we hear her car take off.

I say to Ralph, "Let's do it like this. You interview Emily Eagle's son, the mayor, and the hydro guy. Cindy and I will do the wives. It isn't likely to be one of the wives, right? So that should be pretty safe."

"I don't know, Robin. One never knows what lurks in a person's mind. I'd feel happier if you just left this alone."

"No, it'll be fine. Besides, you know Cindy, she'll do what she wants regardless of your instructions."

"I could have her charged with blocking an investigation." He doesn't really mean it.

"Oh, c'mon Ralph. You'd never do that. Plus, you know that won't frighten her off. What do you say, Ralph? It's just the wives. And believe me, if we don't set some parameters, she'll go after *all* the suspects. This way we can say, for the sake of speed, you'll do half and we'll do half."

He looks at me, thinking, adding it up. I know what I had said makes sense. "Okay, Robin, it's a deal. But you rein her in, don't let her get near the main suspects."

"Okay. I'll talk to her. Thanks, Ralph. It's been a pleasure doing business with you."

He laughs and winks at me. "I hope we have some more business later on."

"Oh, Ralph."

I tuck my hand into his big paw as we walk companionably back to the cottage. Moving in high gear, we pack up the food, grab the pup, and take off back to Toronto.

"Listen," Ralph says in the car, "I have to talk to the cleaners before we leave. I've got their address here from the database. Neither of them have any priors, and I doubt they had anything to do with this, but I really should cover all the bases, and we're here now."

He drives through town and pulls up in front of a house on Mary Street.

"I'm guessing you'd like me to wait in the car."

"Thanks for understanding, Robin."

He isn't in there very long. When he comes out of the house, he gives his head a little shake. It hadn't been them.

"Good alibis?" I ask once he's stuffed his long body into the seat.

"Not just that, they were believably honest. Even the kid admitted he'd hidden in the woods, smoking weed. He got frightened when we arrived and ran, dropping his knapsack. Did you know anything about that?"

"Yes, Kim has it now. We found it when we'd gone into the woods, following Lucky."

Lucky gives a snuffle when he hears his name.

"I also asked them if Andrew had directed them to leave the heating cables on or off. They both said 'on' simultaneously. I have no reason to disbelieve them. They had no reason to lie."

"That means Andrew lied. He said they were off when he arrived. But they were on when he arrived, meaning he turned them off after Kahn had been killed."

"We're not sure it was him. But maybe there'll be some forensic evidence on the switch. DNA. A partial fingerprint. This will help prove who it was that turned the switch off."

Ralph puts his key in the ignition and we're off. As the miles zip by, I ask Ralph, "Don't you think we should be talking to the Huntsville cops? Let them know what you're up to?"

He guffaws. "Nope. They want this to be an accident and an accident it will be. They won't investigate. So far, that's obvious. They didn't even protect the scene. Nope. They're protecting the revenue they get from tourism. But me? I don't like murderers running free."

When we get back to Toronto, Ralph goes into work, his bags of goodies held tight in his hand. As soon as the front door slams shut, I sink into a living room chair and call Cindy. "So, who do you want to do first? Which wife?"

"Wives? I want to get my hands on that CEO."

"It's better if we split the people up, Cindy. Ralph can take some and we'll take the rest. It'll be faster. He's downtown already, so he can get to the business-type people faster than we can." I know that sounds lame but since Cindy lives in North Toronto, I thought she'd buy it. To my amazement, she does.

"Let's meet at the premier's house in half an hour."

"Make it forty-five minutes and I'll be there. I have to give Lucky a small walk and eat some lunch."

"Oh, you're right. I lost track of the time. Oh, my God. It's one-thirty. No wonder I'm starving. Okay, I'll see you there at…let's say two-thirty. An hour should be ample time."

I tug Lucky around the block, scarf down a peanut butter and jam sandwich, hop in the car, race across town, and beat Cindy to the premier's raised bungalow in the west end by five minutes. While waiting for her, I call my daughter. After five rings, she answers the phone, her voice dragging with exhaustion. I must have woken her up.

"Oh, hey Mom," Maggie says.

I don't like the sound of her voice. "You doing okay, sweetie?"

"We're all fine. Just really, really tired."

"I'm sorry, honey. Babies are such hard work." I do some mental math and count the minutes it would take to interview three wives. Probably not too long. They all lived in the west end. "Why don't I come over after work today and hold the baby while you and Winchester get some shuteye? I could be there around six. Does that work?"

"Oh, Mom, that would be wonderful. Thank you so much."

Cindy squeals around the corner and screeches to a stop behind me.

"Gotta go, darling. See you in a few hours."

"Yup. I'm guessing Cindy has arrived." She laughs and hangs up just as Cindy taps on my window and gestures at the house. "Hurry up," she mouths.

Before my eyes, a Land Rover turns into the driveway. Three doors open simultaneously. A thin leg appears from the passenger side and Mrs. Kahn steps out, followed by two other women, all blond, all thin, all dressed in Eddie Bauer meets Holt Renfrew. All three are wearing Blundstone boots. Oh, how I love individuality.

Cindy leaves me in the car as she beelines up the driveway, smiling and extending her hand. "I'm so sorry, Mrs. Kahn, for your loss. I'm Cynthia Dale from the *Express*. You'll remember me from last year when I forced reporters off your lawn onto the opposite sidewalk."

Great introduction. I hoof up the paving stones to the group.

Mrs. Kahn, the well-bred politician's wife that she is, holds out her hand to shake Cindy's. But in that moment, I can see that there's no way she had killed her husband. Her eyes are swollen from crying. Her shoulders are drooped, as if the weight of the world was too much to bear. A tremor shakes her fingers. Her beautifully cut hair is lank and hanging in greasy strands. She hasn't showered. This woman is clearly in acute grief.

"Hello," she says. Her voice is low and throaty, thrumming like a diesel engine on a Ford 150 truck. "This isn't a good time."

"Yes," says the ever-agreeable Cindy. "But your husband was a very important man in Ontario and had a wide support base. I would like to do an article about the wonderful family man he was."

God, could she ever spin it.

Mrs. Kahn's eyes drift over to me. "Please call me Carol. And you are?" she asks.

I step forward and offer my hand, first rubbing it on my pants to make sure it isn't grimy. "I'm Robin MacFarland, also from the *Express*."

"So, two reporters. My, aren't I in demand."

I can't decide what she must mean by that. Is she being sarcastic? Snide? Rude? Flummoxed, I decide it's probably best not to respond. Bizarrely, I can't keep myself from focusing on her neatly pressed, plaid flannel shirt.

Cindy takes over, as I'd been hoping she would. I'm not good in social situations. Not that this is that social of a situation, hounding someone whose husband has just died. I avert my eyes from the woman's shirt and look down. All three pairs of Blundstones are pristine. No mud seeping around the edges.

"Again, I'm so sorry for what happened yesterday. You must feel awful," Cindy continues.

That's my gal, tossing out the sympathy card.

"You have no idea, no idea, what it's like to lose your partner suddenly to a stupid accident. He was so tired, he just wanted to sit in the sun for a bit to get ready for the meeting after dinner. And then crash, he fell backwards and hit his head." She spreads her hands beseechingly. "And then gone. Just like that." She snaps her fingers and shakes her head in disbelief. "What am I going to tell the children? That the Lord works in mysterious ways?"

I wonder what she would say to them if he had been murdered. I pipe up, "I do understand. *My* husband went out one night to get coffee filters and he was hit by a drunk driver. Killed instantly. It was shocking. I'm so sorry this happened to you."

Mrs. Kahn looks at me with her very sad eyes and I watch as a tear rolls slowly down her cheek. Her two friends gather protectively around her. I feel I have an in, having established a common bond, and turn to the other two women. "Hi, it's so kind of you to be here for your friend. Nice to meet you. I'm Robin MacFarland."

Prodded into social norms, the two women introduce themselves. One was Melissa McCormick and the other, Rebecca Rowland. *Bingo.* All the wives in one spot. And none of them have mud on their boots. I meet Cindy's eyes. We're on the same wavelength: talking to these women is a waste of time. But I did have one question I want them to answer. Cindy charges into the conversation before I have a chance to ask it.

"Why don't Robin and I come back later, when things aren't quite so raw? There's no rush. We can do the article anytime."

Mrs. Kahn says, "I appreciate that. This really isn't a good time."

I don't want to leave, not without getting my question answered, but now that we are on our goodbyes, I feel obliged to leave. Just shit. "Thank you for your time. Again, I'm sorry for your loss."

I turn to walk away, frustrated. But if Columbo can do it, so can I. I toss my question over my shoulder, as if it doesn't matter.

"Who put the kitchen chair beside the cottage?"

The three women look at me and then each other, heads tilted, thinking, puzzled. Melissa McCormick answers. "Nobody," she says. "It was already there when we arrived."

The other two women nod in agreement.

CHAPTER 23

CINDY AND I STOP DEAD in our tracks. If the chair had already been there when the renters arrived, who had put it there? Cindy spreads her hands wide and lifts her shoulders in a how-can-this-be gesture. She says, "Nobody? Well, someone put it there."

Mrs. Rowland shakes her head. "No, I'm quite sure it was there when we pulled up." She turns to her friend. "Wasn't it, Carol?"

Mrs. Kahn replies, "I'm absolutely positive it was. My car was the first to arrive and it was certainly there, sitting in the sunshine. It looked so inviting. That's probably why Philip wanted to sit in it," she adds with a catch in her throat.

Melissa McCormick looks startled, as if a terrible thought has crossed her mind, ruffling the dyed and plucked hairs of her well-tended eyebrows. "Why? Is this important? Was there something wrong with the chair? Is that why Philip fell backwards?"

In the lightest tone I can muster, I say, "No, no, there was nothing at all wrong with the chair. The chair was fine. No cracks or broken cross or side stretchers."

"Stretchers?" Carol Kahn looks mystified.

I say, "You know, the bars holding the legs in place."

By way of explanation, Cindy adds, "Robin works in the Home and Garden section of the paper. She knows all kinds of stuff."

"Oh."

"And again," I say, "I'm sorry for your loss. Cindy and I have to get back to the office."

We say our goodbyes again and take off in our separate cars, trying to look sedate and not as if we've just acquired a very key piece of information. When Cindy rounds the corner, she puts on her indicator and pulls over. I stop as well, fling my car door open and slide into the passenger seat beside her.

Breathless, I ask, "You know what this means, don't you?"

"Oh, ya. It means either Emily Eagle murdered the premier, or her son did. Let's get back to Huntsville and interview them."

I shake my head. "No, Ralph has already talked to the cleaners. He didn't like Emily or her son for this. He said they were too honest. The boy even admitted he'd been smoking in the woods and dropped his knapsack. That he felt guilty for being on our land and that's why he ran."

"Really? That *is* honest. Despite what I think about Ralph, he is a good judge of people."

I laugh. "Well, he's certainly got you pegged."

Cindy buffs her nails on her lapel. She's always taken pride in her reputation as a hard-nosed reporter. And then, she sits so still I can almost hear the wheels turning in her brain. Finally, she turns her head and looks at me, eyes blazing. "Somebody's lying."

"Maybe."

"There's no 'maybe' about it, Robin. Either somebody's lying or there's a killer out there that we don't know about."

She's right about that. "Okay," I say, opening her car door. "I'm going home. I'll talk to Ralph."

When I open the front door, Lucky charges across the living room floor and nearly bowls me over. Must be his dinner time.

I walk into the kitchen, calling out Ralph's name. I don't know if he's made it home from the police department yet. The house has that air of emptiness and my voice echoes loudly through the vacuum. So, not home yet. Lucky dances at my feet as I go to the cupboard to get out his kibble, talking away to him. "You want your din-din? Is it dinner time? You're such a good boy. Here you go." I place the dish of hard chunks on the floor.

He gobbles up his food while I scrabble in the fridge for dinner fixings, tossing ingredients for a stir fry onto the counter. While I chop it up and throw it all into a pan, I hear Ralph's key in the lock.

"Honey, I'm home," he shouts in a parody of some TV show from his childhood.

"Hi, sweetie, I'm in the kitchen."

He walks through the door and my heart does that little skip it always does when I see him. "So, how did it go with your interviews with the mayor and the hydro guy?" I kiss him on the lips.

Ralph extricates himself from my hug and opens the fridge door, plucking out a bottle of white wine. He holds it up for me to see. "Let's have a drink before dinner. It's been a very long day. I have news."

"So do I," I say. "And the rice has to cook anyway."

I turn the heat off under the vegetables, turn down the heat on the rice, and we settle into the comfortable chairs in the living room. "You go first," I say, holding my glass up in a toast. I wonder what his news is and if it matches mine.

"Well, first of all, I called my lawyer for the divorce proceedings and she said she'd heard from my wife's lawyer about the new allegations of child abuse. The two lawyers know each other well because they went to school together and have what I'd say is a pretty good relationship. Anyway, it was agreed between the two of them that the accusations are baseless and that my wife's lawyer will do what she can to move the case forward and talk about a final settlement."

"Really? That's fantastic, Ralph." I take a sip. "I never for one second believed that you would hit a child."

He looks disgusted at the thought. "And the news gets a bit better. My son called me. I was astonished. He said he's moving out and that he'd like to meet up with me. Dinner." Ralph tips his glass toward me with a smile on his face. Another toast.

"Oh, that is so good. I'm so happy for you. Maybe this is the beginning of healing your relationship with at least one of your children."

"I really hope so, and I hope the other kids will follow suit, once all this divorce mess is cleared up."

"I hope so too, Ralph. We can get a bigger dining room table."

Ralph stares off into the distance, almost as if this was too much to hope for, my family blended with his. He comes back to earth and asks me, "How did your interviews go with the three wives?"

I don't really know where to begin, the information is so astounding. "No, you tell me. How were your interviews with the mayor and Rowland?"

Ralph crosses one leg over the other and settles back into the cushions. One arm stretched out over the back of the couch. But I'm not fooled. This is Ralph trying to look relaxed.

"What?" I ask.

"Frankly, Robin, I don't think they did it. Both of them were very cooperative. They let me take DNA swabs from their cheeks, no problem. They both gave me the shoes they'd been wearing. In fact, one guy, McCormick, showed me a group photograph that he'd taken with his cell phone timer of them all so I could see that the shoes he offered me were the ones he was wearing. And when I checked Rowland's shoes, they were the same ones in the photo. But I'm suspicious, Robin. It's easy enough to wear different shoes. I'd like to go back to the wives and ask them if either of their husbands changed shoes.

"And I talked to McCormick specifically about his relationship with the premier. He was very candid. Admitted outright that he hated him. Hated his policies about withdrawing Ontario funding from injection sites, hated his policies about very low provincial funding for shelters. The mayor loves Toronto and I think he takes it personally that his city has a homelessness problem. But no, I don't think he killed Kahn.

"I was a little more focused on Rowland, despite his cooperation. He told me they were at your cottage to talk about and negotiate some sort of big energy deal that had to do with purchasing wind and solar power from Quebec. It involved financing the solar fields and turbines, with money coming from Ontario investors. Apparently, the new power grid was going to replace the huge dam in James Bay that was constructed in the seventies."

"Yes, I know all about that, Ralph." I tell him. "It caused a generational surge of homelessness in Toronto. I was writing an article on it when the premier got murdered. The decommission of the dam has raised a fury in the hearts of those families who had been displaced by the flooding of the land to create the dam that generated the power. There's even a group of Indigenous youth who are rising up against it all. Plus, I had heard from the director of a homeless shelter on Queen Street that the mayor hated the premier because of his policies. Anyway, she called the dam environmental displacement or something. I'd have to look the term up my notes."

Ralph raises his eyebrows, taking this in. "Well, that kind of makes the mayor a prime suspect, but I just didn't get that vibe off him. Anyway, this Rowland fellow wanted the deal to go through and was prepared to throw financing at it from his private investors. Nonetheless, I didn't like Rowland as a person, he's pretty arrogant, but I'm confident he didn't murder the premier. Both of them seemed supportive of the energy deal, which seems to be the kingpin in this whole mess."

My phone pings. A text. "Oh, my God. It's Maggie. I forgot that I had promised to pop by her place to help her out. She is exhausted, Ralph. Good thing she texted." I type madly and reassure her that I was coming over after dinner.

Our wine finished, I realize that I'm starving. I dish up the stir fry and rice and Ralph and I eat at the kitchen table. We're both famished. Once the crisis of hunger is abated, Ralph asks, "So, what did you and Cindy find out from the wives?"

I say, "They didn't do it."

"You sound pretty sure about that."

"I am."

"Does Cindy think the same thing?" He puts his fork down, waiting for the answer.

"Yup."

"Come on, Robin, don't make me beg for details."

"Well, I figure the person who murdered the premier was the

one who put the chair beside the cottage. You have to admit, the location of the chair is very important. Right?"

"Well, yes, I guess so. The chair had to go directly under the chiselled icicle. Ya, so you're right."

I splatter more soy sauce on my rice. "So, I asked the question, 'Who put the chair beside the cottage?'"

Ralph looks up from his almost-finished plate of food. "What did they say?"

"They said, 'Nobody.'"

"Nobody?"

"They said the chair was there when they arrived. That it was sitting in the sunshine, looking inviting."

"Really?" He looks gobsmacked. "Were they lying?"

"I don't think so. I forgot to mention that the three of them were together. Who knows where they'd been. And they all agreed that the chair was already there when they arrived and I didn't catch even a whiff of guilt."

"Well, that implies the cleaners put it there. They're the only people who were there before the group arrived."

"But you said to me after talking to them that you didn't think they'd done it. They were too honest."

"Well, someone is lying."

"Not me."

He gives me an old-fashioned look, some humour mixed with acknowledgement.

I say, "God knows they have motive enough to kill the premier, Ralph. They've no doubt lost family members to drug addiction and preventable death because of the premier's policies. Their families have lost their homes. The fury born of helplessness can be blinding."

"Nice sentence, Robin, and very true, but I really don't think they did it. Someone else did. Someone who's completely off our radar. But I'd better be thorough. I'm going to call the police up there and ask them to reinterview the Eagle family."

I clear away the plates and say, "And I'm going to visit my brand-new grandbaby."

As I put on my spring jacket, Ralph says, "I'll walk Lucky and do up these dishes."

I blow him a kiss and head out into the night. As I head over to Maggie and Winchester's place, I go over and over the facts we have. Only one fact is really important. The chair. Who put the chair there? When I arrive at their apartment at Richmond and Portland, I am surprised to see Andrew's car, parked neatly at the curb. So, the uncle is *actually* doing his duty, welcoming his first niece into the family. *Ugh.* The door is unlocked so I walk in to what should have been a happy domestic scene if I was anywhere else. Andrew greets me with fake bonhomie and Jocelyn holds the baby over her shoulder, a receiving blanket protecting her white suit from baby barf.

Maggie looks at me beseechingly. She doesn't want these people here. Although I have never said a bad word about Andrew and his wife to my children, they had figured it out. Years ago, Maggie had whispered to me in the kitchen, "You know Mom, Andrew is an asshole."

I'd replied back, "Oh, I know."

"Andrew and Jocelyn, how nice to see you. Have you been here long?"

Jocelyn replies, "Oh, just minutes, it seems. She is such a darling little girl."

Andrew leans over the baby, whispers in his wife's ear, "You know what I think about mixed-race marriages."

He said that loudly enough for all to hear. God, he is such a racist.

"Put it away, Andrew. Not here, not now."

He looks at me, feigning wide-eyed innocence. Maggie's eyes fill with tears. Winchester goes on the attack.

"Look man, when you come into my house, you take your shoes off at the door. You treat my place and everyone in it with kindness and respect."

Andrew looks down at his shoes. They're the same ones he'd had on at the cottage, the stupid tasselled loafers, and sure enough, he'd tracked in dirt. There is a trail of mud to the front door.

"Andrew," I admonish. "Don't bring your dirt in here."

He is winding up for a barbed retort when my phone pings. A text from Ralph. "Excuse me," I say and read the text with my back turned.

Is Andrew there?

That's surprising. How on earth did Ralph know that he's here? My fingers flew over the letters.

Yes. Why? Do you want to talk to him?

Don't let him leave. I'm coming.

What's this about?

I had his phone tracked for the last twenty-four hours to see where he'd been. I really didn't think the Eagles had murdered anyone so before I called the Huntsville police, I asked the department to locate Andrew's whereabouts. Someone put the chair beside the cottage before the renters arrived and he was the last option.

And then, Ralph types in the real bombshell: **He was at the cottage when the premier was killed.**

I text back: **No, I think you're mistaken. I'd talked to him when he was driving up from Toronto. He was heading north. Even Jocelyn said so. And this was after the death. I heard his wheels on the pavement. He was on the highway.**

He was driving into town from the cottage, Robin. That's the road he was on.

I look over my shoulder at Andrew who was still trying to make nice with Winchester, chatting away. He'd kicked his shoes off by the front door and was now in his stockinged feet. One shoe had turned over in the jumble of footwear. *Gravel.* Muddy, dried gravel in the arch by the heel. I feel the blood drain from my body. Andrew? A killer? No, it can't be true.

Ralph texts, **Keep it light. I'll be there in less than five minutes. Keep him there.** And then a heart emoji.

I turn back to the group that was crowded around the little baby. "Anyone want tea or coffee?"

Jocelyn pipes up, "A cup of tea would be nice."

Andrew frowns at her. "No, we'd better get going. I have a lot of money to raise."

"Oh, Andrew," she says, "It's the weekend. Relax for a bit. Enjoy your new niece."

He shoves his hands in his pockets and his chin forward. "You know, Jocelyn, I'm on a deadline to raise money for Ontario's SMRs." He looks like he wants to swallow his words.

SMRs? What on earth are SMRs? "What's that, Andrew?" I ask.

He looks at me as if he'd let a secret slip. Guilt flies across his face so fast I can't tell if I'd actually seen it.

"Small Module Reactors," Jocelyn answers for him. "Some provinces have agreements in place to build small nuclear reactors to generate power for remote communities. One can power up homes and businesses for about 300,000 people."

"And Andrew is raising money for them?" I look pointedly at Andrew but direct my question to Jocelyn. Maggie and Winchester watch this interchange with great interest.

"Oh, yes. He's so good at that. He'd do anything for his clients." *Including murder?*

I direct my next question to Andrew. "But what about the solar fields and wind turbines to replace the hydroelectric dam at James Bay? I thought you were raising money for that project?"

Andrew starts edging toward the door and bending over to put on his shoes. "Come on, Jocelyn. Let's go."

"Andrew?"

"Well, Gobin, obviously that project died with the premier of Ontario. He was the one pushing for it. The SMRs were another project I was working on."

So, he'd killed the premier to get rid of the competition for the SMRs? Just as we'd suspected: money and greed were at the root of the premier's murder.

Andrew stops putting on his shoes and looks at me intently. He knows that I know. A shiver vibrates up my spine.

Where the hell was Ralph?

Jocelyn says, "Oh, Andrew, relax. Just enjoy your family for a change."

Ralph bursts through the door, handcuffs in hand, and knocks the bent-over Andrew off balance. "Andrew MacFarland, I'm arresting you for the murder of Philip Kahn."

Andrew dusts himself off and says, "You'll never prove that." He's acting all nonchalant, one shoe in hand, pulling away from Ralph.

"I'll take that shoe," Ralph declares and he reaches for it. "The forensic team in Huntsvillle are examining that cable switch as we speak. Maybe they'll find your DNA, or a print."

Andrew says, "I want to call my lawyer," and clamps his mouth shut.

Ralph frog-marches Andrew out of the room, his hands cuffed behind his back. Through the open front door, I can see two uniforms waiting to take him from Ralph.

Ralph turns and mouths to me, "Sorry." He knows how serious this is.

The baby starts to wail and so does Jocelyn.

Maggie whispers, "Holy fuck."

I look into the darkness and see Andrew's back, ramrod straight, as he is passed over to the uniforms. Then, for a fleeting second his face is illuminated by the streetlight as they turn him around to push him into the cruiser. The fury in his eyes sparks as he sees me in the doorway. A fission of fear zings up my spine. Does he know he's been caught because of me? An officer puts his hand on Andrew's head, pushes it forward, and shoves him into the back seat. The other officer is crowding in, offering no hope to Andrew if he is entertaining thoughts of escape.

Jocelyn is now standing behind me. Her body presses against my back and I bizarrely register the sweet smell of her perfume as it wafts into the night air around me. My brother is being arrested and I am dwelling on cologne. She is mumbling something that I can't quite hear. Is she saying, "He didn't do it," over and over?

Yes, he did, Jocelyn.

My brother is a murderer. The awful truth jangles in all the corners of my brain. What does this mean to my family? Oh God, how will my parents react to this horrible twist to their peaceful lives? What does it mean to my children? They never liked him, but still, he is their uncle. He is *family*.

Will the stench of his guilt blanket us all?

The ghostly gloom of the night swirls around me. Specks of black float in front of my eyes. My heart is booming in my ears. This is too much for me. I'm going to faint. No, I refuse to. I lean against the doorframe as the cruiser pulls away from the curb. Ralph rubs his hands on his pants as he walks back toward me. He envelops me in his arms and then strokes my head, murmuring gently. My heart settles down and I look up into his worried eyes.

"This is horrible. Just horrible."

"Yes, Robin, it is."

He keeps stroking my head.

"I don't know what it means to my family. I don't know what it's going to do."

"I understand."

"I guess you have to go to the station."

"Yes."

"To put my brother in jail. Because of me."

"He's putting himself there. It has nothing to do with you. You just found out the truth, Robin. That's what you're good at."

His words slowly sink in. It's the truth. My brother is a murderer. "You better go."

He puts his hands on my shoulders and holds me away so

he can look directly into my eyes. "This is a very difficult time. Your family needs you, Robin. Go back inside and hold everyone tightly. I'll see you at home later. I love you. Always."

With that Ralph turns and walks briskly to his car. As I watch him go, I know I have to rally support around me. From out on the porch I call Cindy.

When I hear her voice I say, "It was Andrew. My brother. He killed Kahn." And then I start sobbing uncontrollably.

"It's okay Robin. I'm coming. Where are you?"

I give her Maggie's address and say thanks before I take a deep breath and head back into the house.

ACKNOWLEDGEMENTS

I would like to thank the hard-working people at Inanna who are guiding their lovely feminist press into future decades with care and compassion. I am also grateful to the people in my life who are so supportive of my efforts to reveal terrible social and environmental issues in an accessible and light-hearted way.

Sky Curtis divides her time between Northern Ontario, Nova Scotia, and Toronto. She has worked as an editor, author, software designer, magazine writer, scriptwriter, poet, teacher, and children's writer. Sky has published over a dozen books and is passionate about social justice issues and the environmment.

Her poetry has appeared in several literary journals, including *The Antigonish Review*, *Canadian Forum*, and *This Magazine*. Her debut novel, and the first in the Robin MacFarland series, *Flush: A Robin MacFarland Mystery*, was published in 2017 and was shortlisted for the 2018 Arthur Ellis Award for Debut Crime Fiction. The second in the series, *Plots: A Robin MacFarland Mystery*, was published in 2018. The third book, *Traps*, was published in 2019. *Power* is the fourth book in the series.